Maggie's tre[illegible] she felt Shanaco's sl[illegible]en them to spread in[illegible]hed and toyed with h[illegible] beyond her mouth.

At once Maggie became aware of the strong arms wrapped tightly around her, pressing her close against his tall, lean body. Her soft breasts were flattened against the hard planes of his broad chest, her nipples tightening and tingling from the intimate contact.

She couldn't help herself—she lifted a hand and tangled her fingers in his silky blue-black hair and sighed. Shanaco drew her closer, deepened the kiss and urged her arm up around his neck.

For a long, thrilling minute they stood there in the dying sunlight kissing as if they were lovers too long parted. Until finally Maggie gathered her wits, realized what they were doing and anxiously pulled away. And then she smacked Shanaco hard across his arrogant face.

"I will do all the deciding when I wish to be kissed!" she told him heatedly.

"Then you had better stay away from my cottage," Shanaco calmly replied.

Also by NAN RYAN

NAUGHTY MARIETTA
THE SCANDALOUS MISS HOWARD
THE SEDUCTION OF ELLEN
THE COUNTESS MISBEHAVES
WANTING YOU

And watch for

DUCHESS FOR A DAY

Coming February 2005

CHIEFTAIN

ISBN 0-7783-2013-8

CHIEFTAIN

Visit us at www.mirabooks.com

Printed in U.S.A.

CHIEFTAIN

One

On a chilly October evening in 1875, Shanaco, a mixed-blood Kwahadi Comanche, was playing poker in a private upstairs room of a plush Santa Fe, New Mexico, saloon. Shanaco was dressed in dark evening attire, as were the other four well-heeled white gentlemen seated at the table.

On either side of the handsome half-breed, perched on velvet stools, was an eager female. A beautiful blonde sat on Shanaco's right, a voluptuous brunette on his left. The blonde's slender arm was draped on the Kwahadi Comanche's shoulder. The brunette's red-nailed fingertips rested lightly on his trousered thigh.

Shanaco took no notice of either woman. His focus was fixed on the five cards he held closely in the palm of his right hand. He liked what he saw, but he gave no indication of his satisfaction. No one was better at presenting the classic 'poker face' than the steely-eyed Shanaco.

He was a skilled player who knew the odds and wasn't timid about betting. He easily read his opponents and was a master at bluffing. Shanaco consistently did well at cards. Some called him lucky.

Over the years Shanaco had won enough to buy a small tract of unclaimed federal land in a lush valley south of Glorieta Pass. There—doggedly working alone—he had built a modest cabin and split-rail corral on the New Mexico property. Within the next year he planned to stock his ranch and make a real home of it.

He had, from the minute he took possession of the land, ignored the angry stares and veiled threats of the nearest white settlers. He kept a loaded rifle at the ready to defend his homestead.

The isolation and solitude of the place suited him, soothed his soul. When he needed company, he'd ride down into Santa Fe for a couple of nights. Whiskey and cards and women, his three major weaknesses, were here to be had. Separately or all together. On this brisk autumn evening, Shanaco preferred to have all three at once.

Cupped in his hand were five cards that every seasoned poker player dreamed of drawing. Before him sat a shot glass and a bottle of bonded Kentucky bourbon. On either side of him was a pretty woman, each one eager to become more intimate.

Respectable white men were less than gracious and cordial to Shanaco. They allowed the mixed-blood Comanche to play cards with them, but away from the poker table they avoided him. Wanted nothing to do with him. It was the opposite with respectable white women. He had no trouble attracting the fairer sex.

At twenty-six years old Shanaco stood six foot two and weighed one hundred and eighty pounds—all lean, hard muscle. His thick shoulder-length hair, tied back with a slender ebony leather cord, was as black as the darkest night. His heavily lashed eyes were a striking silver-gray. Those arresting eyes could be as cold as pale frozen ice—or flash white hot with unmasked hatred. Or smoulder with sexual fire.

Shanaco was a highly intelligent man. He was well aware that it was more than his good looks that made him so appealing to women. His mixed-blood was, perversely, a strong magnet for females. Long ago, when he was little more than a boy, he had become accustomed to having beautiful white women make overtures to him. They were drawn to the danger he represented, thrilled by the prospect of making love to a renegade Comanche chieftain—to a warrior credited with leading murderous raids against the whites since he'd turned sixteen.

Shanaco was both mildly amused and quietly insulted by their desire to be sexually defiled by him. Each time he took a willing white beauty in his arms, he saw—written clearly in their flashing eyes—an unmistakable fear mixed with burning lust. They were afraid of him and that excited them to a fever pitch. They did not expect, nor did they want, a gentle, caring lover.

Shanaco gave them what they wanted: a hot, fierce,

crude coupling that pleased them and meant nothing to him, other than meaningless physical release. The tempestuous loving involved only his lean, powerful body, never his heart or mind.

The game of cards did engage his keen mind and was, quite often, every bit as satisfying as giving a naked white woman what she desired.

Now, as he quietly studied his cards, Shanaco glanced up.

The sixty-two-year-old president of the Santa Fe State Bank shook his silver head and said with a loud sigh, "I'm out."

"Same here," said a wealthy young rancher, frowning as he tossed his cards onto the green baize.

"Too steep for me," echoed a third, dropping his cards, facedown, and pushing his chair back to rise, stretch and roll his tired shoulders.

"Well, well," said a middle-aged man who had recently inherited a sizable mining fortune from his late father. "Looks like it's just you and me, Chief." He looked pointedly at Shanaco as he shoved five glittering gold jettons toward the table's green baize center. "Going to cost you this time around, Comanche. I see your five hundred—" he licked his loose, fleshy lips "—and raise you five." He dropped five additional jettons atop the sizable stack at the table's center and goaded, "Want to hold a little powwow with them there two white squaws before you decide?" He laughed raucously then. The others politely chuckled.

The man's needling did not cause so much as the flicker of a dark eyelash from the motionless, silent Shanaco. His expression never changed. He continued to quietly study his cards without emotion, revealing nothing. When at last he spoke, his voice was low and well modulated.

"Guess I should drop out," he said, as if seriously considering such a move. His grinning opponent was already nodding happily and starting to reach for the stack of chips. "However," Shanaco spoke again, gathering up several of his own jettons and tossing them onto the stack, "I believe I'll just have a look at what you've got, sir. See your five hundred and raise you a thousand." He looked up then and smiled ever so slightly.

The other man scowled. He rubbed his chin. "You're bluffing again, aren't you, Chief?" Shanaco said nothing. The man cleared his throat nervously. He looked around at the others, as if expecting advice or assistance. No one said a word. He took a deep breath and stated, "I won't let you get away with bluffing me this time! I'm on to you, half-breed. Yes, I am. I call!" He tossed in ten golden jettons.

Without fanfare, Shanaco spread out his cards, faceup on the table. "Four queens," he said as he leaned back in his chair and placed a bronzed hand on the blonde's silk-gowned knee. She laughed gaily, as did the brunette.

The loser made a face, cursed under his breath and slammed his cards down.

"It's getting late," said the bank president, "time for me to call it a night."

Another quickly agreed. Shanaco remained seated, respecting the poker players' code. A participant did not break up the game when he was winning. Indeed, he remained at the table until everyone else expressed a desire to quit.

Within five minutes all the other players, including the unhappy mine owner who had lost the last big pot, had donned their jackets and departed.

Shanaco called over the white-coated waiter who had been hired for the evening. As the game's winner, Shanaco took care of the man. He paid him well for his services and requested that he gather up all the jettons and lock them up in the safe downstairs.

"Yes, sir," said the smiling waiter. "Shall I count them out and give you a receipt while you...?"

"I trust you," said Shanaco, who then turned and smiled at the gorgeous brunette.

She smiled back and stood up. The blonde rose as well. Both were tingling with growing excitement. Shanaco pushed back his chair and unhurriedly got to his feet.

He looked from one beauty to the other. Both were lovely. Both were willing. He couldn't decide which one he most wanted. He took a twenty-dollar gold piece from his pocket and handed it to the brunette.

She read his meaning. She nodded and said to the blonde, "You call it, Dana."

"Heads," said the blonde, hoping to get lucky.

The brunette tossed the gold piece in the air, caught it and slapped it down on the green baize.

"Thunderation!" she exclaimed, "heads. You win, Dana."

"Better luck next time, Shari," said the blonde, who laughed musically and slipped a possessive hand around Shanaco's arm and declared, "I'm all yours, Chief. Where would you like to go?"

Shanaco gave no reply. He leaned down, kissed the brunette's cheek and said, "I'll be in town for a couple of days."

Shari nodded, then watched with a protruding lower lip as Shanaco draped his black suit jacket around the smiling Dana's bare shoulders and ushered her out of the smoky room.

"I've a suite at the La Fonda," Shanaco said as the pair exited the noisy saloon and stepped out into the cold night air.

"Take me there," said Dana. "Now."

Once inside the darkened hotel suite, Dana thrilled to the strong arms that came around her the minute the door was closed. His kiss was burning hot, his tongue boldly probing. While his lips moved aggressively on hers, Dana shivered with pleasure. His hand cupped the softness of her breast and a callused thumb stroked her nipple through the silk fabric of her dress.

Shanaco wasted no time. Without taking his lips from Dana's, he reached inside the jacket and yanked the silk bodice of her gown down her arms and to her waist.

Dana shivered.

Shanaco's lips left hers, came around to her ear. "Cold?"

"I...a little," she whispered, though she was not.

"Raise your hands and grip the satin lapels of the jacket."

Dana didn't question him. She complied, lifting both hands and firmly clutching the slippery lapels of the dark evening jacket he had gallantly draped around her shoulders.

His mouth was back on hers then, his teeth toying with her bottom lip, playfully biting her. His tongue tasted, teased, then took total possession. While he kissed her, his hands deftly finished relieving her of the ball gown.

Dana anxiously gripped the jacket lapels and trembled deliciously. Shanaco's lips left hers. He raised his head. His silver eyes flashed in the shadows when he eased the dress over her hips and down her pale thighs. The dress was caught between their pressing bodies. He moved back a step. The gown slithered to the floor, pooling at Dana's feet.

Dana wore no underclothes.

Shanaco was not surprised.

"Step free of the dress," he commanded, and she obeyed, kicking the discarded garment aside with the toe of her kid slipper.

She watched in tense anticipation as Shanaco's

hands went to the buttons of his white shirt. When it was open down his bronzed chest, he yanked the long tails free of his trousers, shrugged his long arms out of the sleeves and dropped it to the floor.

Dana winced when he moved back against her, his pelvis firmly pressing hers. She started to release her hold on the jacket lapels, but he stopped her.

"Don't do it," he warned. "Keep the jacket on and don't move your hands. No matter what I do to you, don't let go of the lapels."

Breathless, slightly apprehensive, Dana wondered at the strange command. She no longer needed the jacket for warmth. She was not cold. She was furnace hot. But she didn't dare cross Shanaco. She couldn't forget for a second that this darkly handsome man was a half-breed Kwahadi Comanche, a fierce warrior who might do God-knew-what to her if she did not obey him. He was, underneath the impeccable grooming and smooth manners, a barely civilized savage who took what he wanted, when he wanted. And tonight he wanted her. What would he do to her? Tie her up? Torture her? Take her repeatedly until she cried for him to stop?

Shanaco easily read the foolish woman's thoughts. It made him angry. *She* made him angry. He was a man, not an animal. But she expected him to behave like one. Damn her and all the others like her.

His teeth grinding, Shanaco slipped a hand inside the open jacket, toyed for a second with a pale, heavy breast, plucking at the distended nipple with his fingertips, before sweeping his hand down her quivering belly. His long fingers were not overly gentle when they went between her legs.

Dana panted her approval.

Shanaco expertly stroked her until she was wet and squirming and pressing against his tormenting hand. Then he took his hand away, opened his trousers and freed his pulsing erection. Dana felt it throb against her belly and wanted more than anything to throw off the suit jacket and grab hold of that awesome male power and take it all—every throbbing inch of it—inside her.

She didn't do it.

She was afraid to disobey him.

So she stood there holding tightly to the lapels of the jacket and waited, suspended in expectation and apprehension. Soon she was thrilling to the forbidden things he was doing to her. His warm hands were everywhere on her, his lean fingers in her. His hot mouth spread fire all over, his lips and tongue adroitly painting and stroking her body as if it were a waiting canvas and he an eager artist.

Dana winced when Shanaco abruptly lifted her right leg up and pressed her bent knee against her chest. Then she gasped with shocked pleasure when he bent his knees slightly, reached between them and shoved his huge, hard erection up inside her.

It was all she had hoped it would be.

Sighing and panting and managing to balance on one weak leg as she clung obediently to the jacket lapels, the blonde felt as if she were being torn apart by this handsome savage. She loved every punishing moment of it. She never let go of the satin lapels. Idly, she wondered if the strange order had been issued so that she would be helpless against him and he could do anything he pleased to her.

If so, it pleased her, too.

Her eyes closing, she pretended that they were in the wilds and that he, in breech cloth astride a mighty stallion, had come upon her coach, dragged her out, shoved her dress up and taken her there against the carriage while the stunned driver choked with fear and outrage.

The fantasy became real and Dana fairly vibrated with ecstasy. Within minutes she was climaxing, screaming out in her bliss. Whimpering when finally it ended, she felt the jacket being pushed off her trembling shoulders. She sagged gratefully against the broad, coppery chest before her and inhaled deeply of Shanaco's unique male scent.

Shanaco picked up the limp Dana and carried her to the bed. He sat her on the edge of the mattress, knelt before her and slipped off her shoes and silk stockings. He rose to his feet and Dana was delighted to see that his impressive erection, all shiny wet from being buried inside her, was still very much in evidence. She was glad and grateful. Already she was wanting more of this man's thrilling mastery.

In seconds they were stretched out naked on the bed and making love again. Now Shanaco really gave her what she wanted. He tormented her with his sexual prowess. He plunged deeply, rhythmically into her until he had her so hot she was on the verge of another stunning release.

So he stopped in midstroke and pulled out of her. Frantic, she begged him and kissed him and stroked him until finally he rose up over her, pushed her legs wide apart and gave it to her again.

And yet again.

The lusty pair continued to dally until—much later—the sated, exhausted Dana was finally pleading with Shanaco to stop. When at last she fell asleep with him still moving deep inside her, Shanaco let himself come, spilling himself into the sleeping blonde beauty.

With a groan he tumbled over, stretched out on his back beside Dana and fell instantly into deep slumber.

Two

Fort Sill, Oklahoma Territory

A full harvest moon shone down upon the sprawling Indian reservation located on the west bank of Cache Creek in western Oklahoma. Hundreds of tepees dotted the rolling hills and windswept prairie that bordered the Wichita Mountains.

At the center of the reservation, stone buildings surrounded the large post quadrangle. The Indians called the post "the soldier house at Medicine Bluffs." The garrison called it Fort Sill.

Maggie Bankhead called it home.

The twenty-two-year-old red-haired, blue-eyed Maggie Bankhead had been born and raised in Tidewater, Virginia, the youngest of four girls and a child of privilege. Hers had been a life of luxury and ease with a loving family and a houseful of dutiful servants.

Maggie's father was a prominent banker from an old southern family of prerevolutionary Irish stock. Her mother, the refined Abigail, boasted an equally impeccable lineage. Many of the foremost Confederate heroes, including Robert E. Lee, were part of Abigail's extended family.

Doting parents, the Bankheads' wish for all their beautiful daughters was successful marriages to suitable gentlemen. It was not a wish shared by the spirited Maggie. Rebellious by nature, inquisitive to a fault, determined to think for herself and do as she saw fit, Maggie, unlike her sisters, had gone against her parents' wishes.

Maggie had, six months ago, left her childhood home and traveled west to teach English to the reservation Indians. Her parents had been horrified but not surprised. Maggie had consistently turned a deaf ear to her mother's cajoling to allow suitable young men to call on her. Maggie had blithely ignored her older sisters' warning that she was going to wind up a lonely old maid. Maggie's father had long ago given up on expecting his youngest, and secretly favorite, child to fit into a specific mold and behave like his other children. Maggie had—from the cradle—been a handful. Lively. Stubborn. Opinionated. Fearless.

An enthusiastic Maggie had moved to the Oklahoma Territory and hadn't looked back, had not regretted her decision for a minute. From the day she had arrived—a beautiful spring day in late April—she had known she was where she belonged.

While she missed her parents, her sisters and her many friends back in Virginia, she found her simple life at the fort to be, for the most part, fulfilling. She liked being independent, liked living alone in the little one-room cottage assigned her, liked taking care of herself.

Blessed with a self-deprecating sense of humor, she often laughed at herself as she tackled elemental tasks like making the bed or brewing hot tea or sweeping the rough plank floors. She had never once—in her twenty-two years—lifted a hand to help with such menial chores. She was having to learn to be self-reliant as surely as the reservation Indians were having to learn the English she taught.

Maggie found it rather rewarding to polish the battered furniture or pick wildflowers for the table or to tuck freshly laundered sheets over the edges of the bed's feather mattress.

Only occasionally, at day's end when she was alone and sitting on the porch gazing at the sun setting over the low Oklahoma hills, did her heart ache dully for something she could not name.

She didn't know what she yearned for. She was not overly homesick, nor was she particularly lonely. She was, in fact, happier in Oklahoma than anywhere ever before and she felt that her life had real meaning. She was convinced that if the displaced Indians were to have any chance in the white man's world, they had to learn to read, write and speak English.

She was eager to teach them, and to her delight, many were eager to learn. They crowded into her classroom each morning, their dark eyes shining, copper faces well scrubbed. Respectful and ready to be taught.

The little ones in class had come to love Maggie.

Maggie, in turn, loved them.

She had grown fond of all her students but couldn't keep from having favorites. One was the tiny Bright Feather, an adorable orphaned Kiowa boy who, sadly, had been lame since birth. The other was an aged Kiowa chief, Old Coyote. Both Bright Feather and Old Coyote held a special place in Maggie's heart.

Outside the classroom, Maggie had easily made friends with the officers' wives as well as with many of the soldiers garrisoned at the fort. And, of course, there was James W. James, the fort's Indian agent and the man responsible for her being at Fort Sill.

Called Double Jimmy by everyone, the fifty-seven-year-old agent was honest, hardworking and truly cared about the Indians' welfare. Maggie's closest ally and fervent protector, Double Jimmy was an old and dear family friend. He had served with Maggie's father, Major Edgar Bankhead, in the Grand Army of the Potomac. The two men had become like brothers and the widowed Double Jimmy had visited often—staying weeks at a time—in the Bankheads' stately Virginia home.

A natural-born storyteller who spoke English, Spanish and Comanche, Double Jimmy had painted such vivid pictures of the frontier that young Maggie's interest had been piqued. His stories of life in the West and of the bitter conflict between the whites and the Indians had made her decide what she wanted to do with her life.

From the minute Maggie had arrived at the fort, her flaming red hair and fair good looks had captured the attention of several young officers eager to court her. She was flattered, but her head was not turned. Maggie was used to having handsome young men buzz around her.

Maggie enjoyed the company of males and was totally comfortable in their presence. She found men were generally much better company than women and she could hold her own in their lively conversations.

But she was not interested in finding a sweetheart. The only officer she had allowed to escort her to the rare fort picnic or party was the mannerly Lieutenant Dave Finley.

A quiet trustworthy young man from Jackson, Mississippi, the tall, slender, sandy-haired Lieutenant Finley was boyishly handsome and a dedicated soldier. A proud West Pointer, he had a sterling reputation, was well liked by his fellow officers and considered to be a "good catch" by the officers' wives.

Maggie was not looking for a good catch. She did not, she would tell anyone who asked, intend to get married. Ever. She had no desire to be a wife and mother. Furthermore, she had no need of a man to take care of her. She could take care of herself, thank you very much!

Maggie had, right from the beginning, made it clear to Lieutenant Dave Finley that while she thoroughly enjoyed his company, they would never be anything more than friends. The infatuated lieutenant took what he could get and hoped that one day Maggie might change her mind. Until then he was determined not to upset the applecart and be banished from her sight. She could be, he had quickly learned, quite volatile and unpredictable, traits that tended to make her all the more exciting and appealing.

Now as the full moon climbed higher in the Oklahoma sky, Maggie and Lieutenant Finley sat on her porch steps and talked as the hour grew late. Her arms locked around her knees, Maggie gazed dreamily at the stars twinkling overhead while the lieutenant gazed dreamily at her.

"I should go in," Maggie finally said, not moving.

"Stay awhile longer," coaxed Dave Finley. "It's so nice and peaceful out here."

"Yes, it is," she agreed. Maggie inhaled deeply, unlocked her arms from her knees, lifted her hands and swept her untamed red hair back off her face. She smiled with pleasure when a cooling breeze stroked her cheeks. "Finally the weather is beginning to change. There's almost a nip to the night air. Lord, let's hope the searing heat of the summer is behind us." Her head swung around. "I arrived at the fort in late April and it was already quite warm. You've been here in the winter, Dave. What's it like?"

Lieutenant Finley grinned. "Cold. As cold in the winter as it is hot in the summer. The wind comes sweeping across the prairie and goes right through you. I've drilled on early mornings when I honestly feared I'd get frostbite and lose my toes."

Maggie made a cluck of sympathy. "Poor Dave," she said, turning to look squarely at him, the moonlight striking her full in the face.

Dave Finley stared at Maggie, enchanted. Maggie saw him swallow hard and noted the little shudder that swept through his slim frame.

"Now, Dave..." she began.

"Oh, Maggie, girl," Dave interrupted, his tone soft, his eyes softer.

He lifted a hand and gently placed it in her bright red hair at the side of her head. Maggie sighed. He wanted to kiss her. She knew he did. She would have let him, but she knew she shouldn't encourage him. It wouldn't be fair to let him think that she shared his feelings.

"Dave," she said again, placing her hand atop his where it lay against her hair. "You know that your friendship means a great deal to me and—"

"One kiss, Maggie," he said. "That's all. I'd never ask for anything more."

"Oh, for heaven's sake," Maggie exclaimed, growing exasperated. "Kiss me and get it over with then!" She closed her eyes, puckered her lips and looked as if she were about to take a bitter dose of medicine.

Dave Finley shook his head sadly. Then he laughed. "Open your eyes, Maggie, I'm not going to kiss you."

Her eyes opened in surprise. "Why not? I said you could."

Smiling indulgently, he took her hand and, rising, drew her to her feet with him. "I don't want to kiss a woman who acts as if she's about to be horse-whipped."

"I was not, I—"

"Good night, Maggie." The lieutenant leaned down, brushed his lips against her cheek.

Maggie smiled at him. "You're not angry, are you, Dave?"

"Perhaps a little hurt, but I'll get over it."

Maggie patted his shoulder affectionately. "I wouldn't want to lose a friend like you."

"You won't." And then he was gone.

Maggie watched him walk away. When he disappeared around the corner of a stone building, she stood for a few moments longer in the moonlight, then turned and went inside.

"It's me," she said softly in the darkness.

Pistol, her beloved silver-furred wolfhound, raised his head, barked a lazy greeting, then went back to dozing before the cold fireplace.

Maggie didn't light a lamp. She undressed in the darkness. She drew her nightgown down over her head, yawned and got into bed. She stretched out on her back and folded her hands beneath her head. A gentle night breeze lifted the window curtains directly beside her bed.

Maggie sighed with pleasure. Fall had finally come.

She so looked forward to the brisk autumn days and the cold clear nights. And she wondered what exciting new changes would the new season bring?

Maggie's blue eyes flashed with anticipation. Smiling, she turned onto her stomach, yanked her gown high up on her thighs and punched her pillow.

In minutes she was sound asleep.

Three

In the middle of the night Shanaco awakened abruptly from a deep, dreamless slumber.

His hundred-year-old Comanche grandfather was calling to him as clearly as if the ancient chief were here in the room.

Shanaco lunged up in bed.

Heart hammering, he swept his long, loose hair back off his face and swung his legs over the mattress's edge. He reached for the thin leather cord lying on the night table and hurriedly tied back his hair. The movement awakened the blonde.

"What is it?" she asked sleepily. "What's wrong?"

"I have to go," Shanaco said, and stood up.

"Go? Now? It's the middle of the night, still dark outside," said Dana, sitting up, clutching the sheet to her breasts. "Get back in this bed, lover."

Shanaco did not reply. He crossed the room, pulled open a bureau drawer and removed a pair of soft buckskin trousers and matching shirt. He drew on the pants, laced up the front fly and grabbed the buckskin shirt. He slipped the shirt over his head, shoved his arms through the long sleeves and didn't bother with the laces going down the center yoke to mid chest.

He bent from the waist, lifted a pair of well-polished boots from the carpeted floor and went back to the bed. He sat down on the bed's edge to pull on his stockings and boots.

"I won't let you leave," murmured Dana as she tossed off the covering sheet and came up on her knees behind him. She threw her arms around his neck, leaned against him, placed her lips against his left ear and murmured, "I'm sorry I went to sleep on you last night. I'm wide-awake now and I'll stay awake for as long as you want."

No response.

She tried again. "Shanaco, please, please...put it in again and leave it in. Give to me, Shanaco. Come on, take off your clothes and make love to me."

Bored with her and annoyed by her whining, Shanaco was even more annoyed that his grandfather was summoning him home. He didn't want to go. He had no choice. He had to.

"Maybe I'll see you next time I'm in Santa Fe," he said. He threw off her clinging arms and again stood up.

"Where on earth are you going at this hour?" she asked, pouting, sinking back on her heels in the bed.

"Texas," Shanaco said, and left.

He hurried downstairs, woke up the night clerk, collected his poker winnings and went to the livery stable for his horse. He swung up into the saddle and set out for the Palo Duro Canyon, where the once mighty Comanche had their last stronghold.

Five days later, as the warm October sun was setting, an exhausted Shanaco urged his winded black stallion down a narrow, serpentine trail into the yawning chasm where he had spent most of his life.

His aged grandfather was patiently waiting.

Gray Wolf's eyes lighted when his tall grandson ducked into the tepee. He stirred himself with a series of movements, slowly, his brittle bones creaking as he attempted to straighten his frail back to appear more imperial.

"I calculated it would take you four-five sleeps to get here," said the old chief in their native tongue. "I expected you before the setting of today's sun."

"The sun's been down for only a few moments, Grandfather," Shanaco replied as he dropped down and seated himself cross-legged before the old man.

The chief nodded and his eyes twinkled slightly as they examined Shanaco, pleased by the sight of the imposing young man that his own noble blood had helped to create.

"So it has," he conceded. The hint of a smile immediately disappeared and without preamble, he stated, "I have done much thinking, Grandson. I have called on the Great Spirit, asked that he speak to my heart. He did and I have come to a hard decision." He paused and blinked back unshed tears that suddenly sprang to his dark eyes.

"Tell me, Grandfather," said Shanaco, leaning forward.

"The People cannot last another winter," the chief said sadly. "We cannot graze our livestock and the great buffalo herds have all but disappeared. The People will starve if they stay here in the canyon." Shanaco nodded his agreement. The chief continued, his tone somber, "They must go away from the Llano Estacado and Palo Duro, away from this land that was once all ours. It makes my heart weep."

Shanaco drew a slow deep breath and shook his head in sympathy and understanding.

"I have met with the white leaders," Gray Wolf stated. "I have agreed to no longer make war." He sighed wearily and said, "It is over, Grandson."

"Yes, Grandfather," said Shanaco respectfully, knowing it was a sad day for the old Comanche chieftain. Gray Wolf was the last, and most powerful, of all the signatory chiefs to finally concede defeat.

"At my knee," said Gray Wolf, "you learned that a warrior's duties are to protect the women and children and to face danger and death without complaint or fear." Shanaco started to speak, but the chief raised a hand to silence him. "You were always brave, but you chose the white man's road, learned the white man's ways. Now you must help our People learn to travel the white man's road. You must lead them onto the reservation at Fort Sill in the Indian Nations."

Shanaco immediately began protesting. He conceded that the tribe should give up and move onto the reservation, but he strongly objected to being the one to lead them there. His arguments were sound. He had drifted back and forth between the two worlds since his father's death. He had not lived in the Palo Duro village for several years.

He had taken a different path.

He reminded his grandfather that he was resented, even hated, by some of the young Comanche warriors for his white blood. And, he would *never* live on the reservation himself.

Concluding, he said, "I cannot do it. I will not—"

Angrily interrupting, Chief Gray Wolf said sternly, "You will obey me! I am the father of your father and you will do as I say."

Shanaco looked at the badly wrinkled face before him, fierce even now after all his power was gone and the long years of a hard life had taken their toll. Those dearest to the chief were all dead: his two wives, his four daughters, five grandchildren. And, his only son—Shanaco's father—the fearless Chief Naco. Shanaco was the old chief's only blood relative left alive.

"I will obey you, Grandfather," Shanaco said meekly.

The chief's eyes lighted again as they had when Shanaco first ducked into the tepee. "My little cub," he said with affection, and reached for Shanaco's hand. Shanaco wrapped his strong fingers around his grandfather's thin, clawlike hand and felt his heart squeeze in his chest.

"I will not go with you, Grandson," said the chief. "I have lived long enough. Bury me here in the canyon." He withdrew his hand, reached for his pipe.

Shanaco shook his head. Then he laughed. "Grandfather, you cannot decide when you will die."

But when dawn broke the next morning, Shanaco went to the tepee of his grandfather and found the old man dead.

Shanaco now had no choice.

He would have to lead the dwindling band onto the Oklahoma reservation.

At Fort Sill news quickly spread that the last major warring band of Comanches had finally given up and were now heading for the reservation. A flurry of activity ensued as the post prepared for the tribe's arrival.

No one knew the exact hour or day when the Comanches would reach the reservation, but the entire fort community, whites and Indians alike, wanted to be there to watch their arrival. It was said that the half-white young chief known as The Eagle would be leading the Comanches into Fort Sill.

Excitement mounted as the days went by.

And then on a crisp morning in late October a lone sentry galloped into the fort to announce that the Comanches were approaching the gates. Mounted soldiers of the Fourth Cavalry rode out to meet the advancing cavalcade.

Everyone at the fort was quickly alerted. People

dropped what they were doing and hurried toward the parade ground. Maggie was informed and immediately dismissed her morning classes.

A crowd swiftly gathered near the fort's front gates. In that growing throng was the curious Maggie. As the band of Comanches rode through the fort's tall gates, Maggie experienced a tingling excitement. Eager to get a close look at this warring band, she anxiously made her way forward through the crowd to the perimeter of the parade ground. She wasn't satisfied until she had maneuvered into a position where no one was in front of her.

Maggie felt the buzz of anticipation that swept through the onlookers. Since learning that the Comanches were coming, Maggie had heard many tales of the hell-raiser, mixed-blood warrior who, despite his many escapades, was still so respected by the majority of his People that he would be the one bringing in the band.

His name was Shanaco.

The Eagle.

Some called him a half-breed. Some called him a devil. But no one, it was said, questioned his intelligence, iron will or brute strength. The only son of the great Comanche war chief, Naco, and his blond captive wife, Shanaco had, from the time he turned sixteen, drifted back and forth between the white and Indian worlds. Riding and raiding with the Comanches one night, dressing and living like a white man the next.

It was whispered that Shanaco was not content in either world. Restless, brooding, menacing—an air of extreme boredom masked a volatile nature.

Maggie lamented the fact that Double Jimmy was not present to share this momentous occasion. He would be disappointed that he had missed it. And, if anyone could have made the Comanches' painful transition easier, it was the dedicated Indian agent.

Double Jimmy was, this very minute, en route from Washington where he had gone to plead for more beef and clothing for the reservation Indians. Had he known that the last of the Comanches were coming in, he would surely have postponed his trip.

The regimental band struck up "Gary Owen" and Maggie's heartbeat quickened. From his place on the reviewing stand, the portly commandant of the fort, fifty-one-year-old Colonel Norman S. Harkins, came to his feet.

Colonel Harkins had served under Double Jimmy in the war. The two men had a great deal of respect for each other. Double Jimmy was aware of Harkins's bitter disappointment at being sent out to this frontier fort. But he knew Harkins to be an honorable man who discharged his duties without complaint.

Maggie glanced in the colonel's direction and suddenly frowned.

At the colonel's side on this fine October morning was his only daughter, Lois. The spoiled twenty-one-year-old Lois was spending several months at the fort with her father while her eastern-based mother traveled Europe.

Lois was blond and lovely, and when she walked down the fort's wooden sidewalks she caused quite a stir among the predominantly male population. Lois Harkins was the opposite of Maggie. While Maggie couldn't have cared less about male attention, the self-centered Lois thrived on it. Couldn't live without it.

Lois was so adept at flirting and teasing that few really realized what she was up to. Maggie did. Lois didn't fool the perceptive Maggie for a minute. Maggie strongly suspected that Lois did a great deal more than just flirt with some of the soldiers.

Now, as the Comanche rode forward, Lois Harkins leapt to her feet. Maggie watched as Lois spotted—at the head of the procession—the most magnificent specimen of manhood Maggie had ever laid eyes on.

The Eagle.

Shanaco.

Dressed as a Comanche, naked save for a scarlet bandanna knotted at his throat and a low-riding breechcloth, Shanaco was astride a nervously dancing black stallion. A fine-looking man, Shanaco had a lean coppery body of perfect symmetry coupled with a muscular, athletic frame. His face was undeniably arresting with high cheekbones, proud nose, strong chin and wide mouth.

Some of those standing at very close range got a glimpse of intense silver eyes shining out the harshly handsome face. His very countenance denoted a high intelligence and innate leadership.

His long raven hair was worn loose, defiantly, and blowing in the wind, a feather tucked into his scalp lock. His broad chest and bare legs gleamed in the morning sunshine. Around his right biceps was a wide copper band, and in his right hand, a war lance. Bells tinkled on his moccasins and on the decorative red trappings on his stallion.

The Eagle rode without effort, handling the nervous black with his knees. He seemed not to be real, not of this world, but a divine image of masculine beauty. A bronzed pagan god in the strength of his prime.

Every eye was upon him, and a great hush had fallen over the crowd. Like the fluttery Lois, Maggie found it impossible to take her eyes off the sullen, majestic half-breed. She found herself hoping he would turn and look in her direction. And knowing that he would not.

He didn't.

Shanaco stared straight ahead, looking neither to the left or the right. The insolent attitude of his princely body, the aloof expression on his cruelly handsome face, made Maggie shake her head ruefully.

This notorious half-breed was in for his share of misery at Fort Sill.

And he would dish out plenty as well.

Four

Armed soldiers had ridden out to intercept the arriving Comanches and their young leader who, through courage and initiative, had attained the statue of honored war chief among his People. The soldiers were aware that Shanaco was revered and respected despite his frequent absences from his tribe.

He was a rarity.

While a white captive woman giving birth to a warrior's child was not that uncommon, it was rare that a half-breed would rise to the prominence of respected war chief and recognized leader.

Shanaco had managed such a feat and he had done it by demonstrating unfailing bravery and superior intelligence. He scoffed at the idea—whispered by the whites—that his success as a leader was due to his mixed blood. His *white* blood. It was said that it made him more intelligent than his fellow tribesmen.

It was not so. Other full-blood warriors had wholly proven themselves at an age as young as Shanaco.

Two armed blue-clad troopers quickly moved into position, closely flanking Shanaco, as if afraid he might bolt and run. He said nothing, did not turn his head to look at either of them. Behind Shanaco, the rest of the Comanches remained silent. They said not one word, but looked straight ahead, as did their leader.

The crowd stared at the new arrivals, realizing that this was a momentous occasion. History was surely being made on the rolling plains of the Oklahoma Territory.

The last of the warring Comanches had finally been forced to surrender. Feared through the years by the Spaniards, the Mexicans, the Texans and finally all whites everywhere, these conquered adversaries were riding into the fort to lay down their arms forever.

Maggie frowned, annoyed, when she no longer had an unobstructed view of Shanaco. She strained to get one last fleeting glimpse of the notorious chieftain, then turned and left.

Her thoughts once again returning to her students, Maggie made her way back through the crowd and headed directly to the post's supply depot to pick out needed articles for her classroom.

The long possession of arriving Comanches continued. Shanaco, riding between the two uniformed troopers, appeared to be docile, with only a hint of implied defiance in his silver-gray eyes.

Shanaco had every intention, for his deceased grandfather's sake, to be on his best behavior for as long as he stayed at Fort Sill. Which would not be long.

A month. Six weeks at most. He'd stay only until the tribe was settled.

Directly behind Shanaco rode the young men, the brave, strong warriors of the band. Behind the proud braves came the elder statesmen of the tribe, dressed in their finest for this sad occasion. Many wore black war paint on their faces and clutched shields and tomahawks.

After them came the women and children, mounted on the travois ponies, dragging their meager belongings behind them.

Last came the pony herd, numbering less than two hundred. The tribe's young boys skillfully kept the horses bunched in long columns.

The entire band—men, women and children—numbered no more than a hundred. All were totally silent as they surrendered forever the freedom that had always been theirs.

The crowd watching was just as silent. A pall had quickly fallen over the proceedings. The whites had just cause to hate the Comanches—and most did. But even some of those felt a twinge of compassion for these once-powerful Lords of the Plains who would now be nothing more than dependent children, looking to the government for every morsel of food they put in their mouths.

The somber cavalcade rode across the dusty parade ground, passed completely through the fort and turned north toward the unfinished icehouse. There the receiving troops dismounted and took all the shields and weapons from the Comanches. Shanaco had warned his tribesmen that this would happen. The warriors did not resist, but willingly surrendered their weapons.

Once all the weapons had been collected, the Comanche men were ordered to dismount. Shanaco swung down out of the saddle first and nodded for his tribesmen to do the same. All did so peacefully. Shanaco was relieved. This unpleasant process was going forward more smoothly than he had hoped. He was determined that he would continue to remain totally calm.

But his passionate nature swiftly emerged when he was told that the young warriors, including him, would be locked up for an indefinite period.

Fury instantly leapt into his light eyes and he struggled fiercely against the armed men forcing him into the icehouse, which was to be a temporary jail.

At that moment Maggie stepped out of the post supply store and heard the commotion. Curious, she turned to see what was happening. Shading her eyes against the blinding sun, she was drawn steadily closer, her lips parted, a frown of puzzlement on her face. She watched in shock and horror as an infuriated Shanaco and the young Comanche warriors were thrown into the makeshift prison.

Stunned, Maggie stood for a moment, motionless, unable to believe her eyes. Then her face grew fiery red with anger. Teeth clamped tightly together, her dander up, Maggie dropped her bag of supplies where she stood and hurried headlong toward the icehouse. Her mind was racing. What should she do? How could she help? How could she stop this atrocity?

Then it came to her. Double Jimmy! He would put a stop to this outrage! But a few steps short of the icehouse, Maggie stopped abruptly.

"Oh, no!" she muttered aloud, remembering suddenly that the Indian agent was not at the fort. Double Jimmy was in Washington and wouldn't be back until Saturday morning, more than forty-eight hours from now.

She couldn't wait that long. She had to do something this very minute. There was no other choice. She would go straight to the fort's commander, Colonel Harkins, register a firm protest and demand that he release the Comanches.

Maggie turned and hurried toward the fort's administration offices. Skirts lifted, chin jutting, she crossed the dusty quadrangle, stepped up onto the shaded east sally port and moved quickly to the closed door of Colonel Harkins's office.

"May I be of assistance, Miss Bankhead?" a provost marshal, who was waiting at the door, asked.

"I must speak with Colonel Harkins at once!" Maggie declared, and rushed right past the startled officer.

She rushed inside the sandstone building and was headed for Colonel Harkins's back office when his aide-de-camp, Captain Daniel Wilde, came from behind his desk to block her way.

"I'm very sorry, Miss Bankhead," said Captain Wilde. "You can't go in there. Colonel Harkins is in an important meeting and cannot be disturbed." The captain smiled then, and with a slightly suggestive tone to his voice, said, "Now, if there's anything *I* can do for you. Anything at all."

Maggie glared him. She didn't like Captain Wilde. Married, but with his family down in Texas, he behaved too much like a single man. Anytime he caught her alone, he was openly flirtatious. She didn't approve and had told him so. Now as he took a step closer, Maggie backed away.

"Inform Colonel Harkins that he *must* release the Comanche prisoners at once!" she said. "This is a disgrace! There is absolutely no excuse for incarcerating these men who came onto the reservation peacefully! Promises of fair treatment were made and believed. They have done nothing to warrant such high-handed handling, and if Double Jimmy were here he would never have allowed it to happen!"

Captain Wilde just grinned. "Well now, Miss Bankhead, I'll sure relay your message to the colonel, yes I will. And I certainly appreciate your concern. But you have to understand that these Comanches are dangerous and—"

"Oh, for heaven's sake, they are not!" Maggie snapped. "The army has taken their weapons and horses, how dangerous could they possibly be?"

"Dangerous enough," he said with a sly smile.

"One of those big, naked savages could pose a terrible threat to a pretty young white woman like you."

"Go to blazes, Captain," Maggie said, and turned on her heel to leave.

The captain chuckled. Then called after her, "I'll be sure to give Colonel Harkins your message." But he never intended to do anything of the kind.

Thwarted, Maggie hurried out of the building. Taking a deep breath, she headed back in the direction of the icehouse. Before she could reach her destination, her friend, Lieutenant Dave Finley, intercepted her.

"Maggie, what are you doing here?" he said, surprised.

"Hunting you," she replied. "Dave, we have to do something! Do you know what has happened? The soldiers have locked up the unarmed Comanches! That is unjust and unacceptable. The Indians came in peacefully and surrendered their weapons. Why is the army treating them like criminals?"

"Now, Maggie," said the soft-spoken Lieutenant Finley, taking her arm and turning her about, "you can't go to the icehouse, it's no place for a lady."

As if he hadn't spoken, Maggie said, "Do something, Dave. See to it that these Comanches are released!"

"Their imprisonment is only temporary. Please don't trouble yourself so," he said. "I'm confident that the men will be released within the hour. The troops are only following safety procedures laid out in advance." He ushered her away.

"Laid out in advance?" she repeated. "By whom? Not by Double Jimmy. I know he wouldn't have sanctioned such inhumane treatment." She shook her head, adding, "If only he had gotten back to the fort before the Comanches arrived, this would not have happened."

"I know and—"

"Were the Comanches told they would be imprisoned upon their arrival?"

"I'm not sure, but—"

"I am," she interrupted. "They wouldn't have agreed to come onto the reservation had they been told they would be locked up the minute they arrived! Promise me you'll do everything you can to—"

"I will, I swear it. Trust me, Maggie, in a couple of hours all the men will be freed."

It didn't happen.

An hour passed.

Then two.

Several long hours dragged by while Shanaco and the Comanche braves remained locked up in the hot, roofless makeshift prison. Incensed by their treatment, Maggie again tried to see the fort's commandant but was turned away without being afforded the opportunity to speak with him. She didn't give up. She lay in wait until the portly colonel finally left his office at day's end.

"Give me a moment of your time, Colonel Harkins?'' she said, rushing up the minute he stepped outside, planting herself firmly in front of him.

''Why, anytime, Miss Bankhead,'' he said. ''Anytime at all, you know that.''

Maggie made a face. She knew what had happened. Captain Wilde had never told the fort's commander that she had attempted to see him. Maggie should have known—Daniel Wilde hated all Indians and made no bones about it. If it were up to him, the new arrivals would stay in jail forever.

''Colonel Harkins, you must release the Comanche prisoners at once!'' she said.

The colonel smiled at her as one would smile at an impetuous child. He took her arm and said, ''It's getting dark, Miss Bankhead. You shouldn't be out alone at this hour. Allow me to see you to your cottage.''

''You are not listening to me, Colonel. Those men should be set free. I demand their release, sir!''

Again he smiled and said, ''My dear, you're almost as wilful as my daughter, Lois. She's constantly bossing me about as if...''

Interrupting, Maggie said, ''I am requesting that you do the honorable thing, Colonel. There is no reason why the Comanches should be imprisoned.''

''Well now, child, I will tell you, like I often tell Lois, there are many things you young ladies just don't understand and therefore shouldn't concern yourself with.'' His eyes were kind when he added, ''Teaching English to the Indians is your affair, quelling trouble at the fort before it can start is mine. The prisoners will be freed as soon as I'm certain it is safe to do so. Now, you go on along home and don't be worrying your pretty head about such matters."

When night fell on the fort, the Comanches were still locked up. Morning came and they were not freed. They remained in the icehouse jail throughout the long, hot day and on into another night.

Their incarceration was the main topic of gossip throughout the fort and across the reservation. Unrest spread among the other tribes when they learned what had happened.

Maggie heard disturbing tales of the imprisoned men being fed as if they were feral dogs. Great chunks of raw meat were tossed over the walls to the hungry men.

Word was that the proud Shanaco refused to eat, stating emphatically, "I am not an animal that I will eat meat off the ground."

Five

At five minutes past noon on Monday, the weekly stagecoach rolled to a dust-stirring stop before the reservation's general mercantile store.

The coach's door immediately swung open. Out stepped a strapping middle-aged man with kindly brown eyes, a sun-weathered face accented by a full mustache the color of rock salt, and thick white hair poking out from under a battered brown Stetson.

The big man's booted foot had hardly touched the ground before an eager Maggie Bankhead stepped forward to intercept him. Her giant wolfhound, Pistol, leapt in front of her, barking a loud greeting. Maggie smiled and Pistol wagged his tail as both rushed eagerly forward.

"Double Jimmy, thank heavens you're finally back!" Maggie said without preamble.

Double Jimmy smiled broadly, swept his Stetson off, reached out and wrapped Maggie in a quick bear hug, giving her narrow waist a gentle squeeze. Releasing her at once, he affectionately patted the head of the dog he had given to Maggie when Pistol was just a pup.

"Hey, boy," Double Jimmy said, stroking Pistol's head, and then laughed when the huge dog jumped up on him and attempted to lick his face.

"Pistol, get down!" Maggie intervened, snapping her fingers. "Behave yourself now. Get down, and I mean it."

Pistol obeyed, but he stayed close. He sat on his haunches at Double Jimmy's feet, his pale amber eyes fixed on the big white-bearded man he recognized as a friend.

Pistol was a faithful watchdog to his mistress. If anyone other than Maggie or Double Jimmy came nosing around her little cottage, Pistol bared his sharp canine teeth, growled loudly and prepared to attack. Double Jimmy never worried about Maggie living alone. Pistol would protect her.

"It's mighty good to be home, Maggie dear," he said now, stroking the dog's head again. "Mighty good indeed. I tell you, dealing with all those bureaucrats in Washington is—"

"Tell me about the Washington meetings later," she cut him off, and tugged at his arm. "I need your help and I need it right now."

"You have it, you know that. Has something happened while I was gone?" He put his hat back on, turned and reached into the coach to retrieve his valise.

"Yes, something momentous. The Kwahadi Comanches have surrendered and come onto the reservation. They arrived at the fort Friday morning."

''No!'' said Double Jimmy in disbelief. ''Old Gray Wolf has finally given up and brought his People in?''

''No, not Gray Wolf. I understand that the old chief is dead. His half-breed grandson, Shanaco, brought the band in.''

''Will wonders never cease!'' exclaimed Double Jimmy, shaking his head. ''Shanaco here at the fort? I'd been told that he no longer lived among the Comanches. Leastwise, not full-time. After his father and mother died, they say he drifted away from the tribe. Took up the ways of the whites.''

Maggie interrupted, ''Double Jimmy, the minute the Comanches rode through the gates, Colonel Harkins ordered Shanaco and the rest of the young men thrown into jail. Locked them up as if they were violent criminals.''

''Jesus God,'' Double Jimmy swore, which was rare for him. He was seldom guilty of cursing, especially in front of a female. His sun-tanned face turning red with anger, he muttered, ''Why the hell would Harkins pull a stunt like that? He knows better.'' Heavy valise in hand, he took Maggie's arm and firmly propelled her down the wooden sidewalk, Pistol barking and darting ahead.

''I knew you'd object,'' Maggie said, pleased with Double Jimmy's response. ''So you'll demand that he immediately let them go?''

''I'll lobby for their speedy release,'' he replied, nodding. ''Soon as I see you home and get cleaned up, I'll—''

"I can see myself home and you can clean up later. Time's wasting. Go talk to the colonel now."

Double Jimmy smiled and nodded. "I'm on my way."

Colonel Harkins rose to his feet and greeted Double Jimmy warmly when his old friend walked into the office. He stretched out a hand for the taller man to shake. "Glad to have you back, Double Jimmy."

"Glad to be back, sir."

"Sit down, sit down. Tell me what transpired in Washington."

Double Jimmy took a chair across from the portly colonel, hung his Stetson on his knee and replied, "Apparently not nearly as much as has transpired here. I understand the last of the Comanches came onto the reservation Thursday morning."

"You heard correctly," said Harkins, shaking his head. "The old chief, Gray Wolf, is dead. The mixed-blood grandson, Shanaco, led the People in. The poor starving souls have finally given up."

"Which means they are no longer *warring* Comanches, does it not?"

"That's correct. They've laid down their arms."

"Then why in Sam Hill were Shanaco and the young men tossed into jail?"

"Now, Double Jimmy, I gave this some thought and in my judgment it was the best way to avoid trouble," Harkins quickly defended himself.

"You avoid trouble by locking up the tribe's leader

who has surrendered his arms and led his People onto the reservation? That's a surefire way to *cause* trouble, Colonel."

"I disagree, my friend. It was the right thing to do."

"The right thing? For God's sake, you know full well that by locking up Shanaco, you have successfully angered every single Indian living on this reservation. We've talked about this many times, have we not? You must treat these people with the honor they deserve. You can't look on them as wayward children and then expect them to behave like responsible men."

"I know that, Double Jimmy, but—"

"Colonel, you are lucky your well-intentioned decision hasn't caused half the Indians to flee the reservation. Do you want that to happen?"

"Of course not. But I must consider the safety of the white females that live at the fort. Including my own innocent young daughter, Lois."

Double Jimmy's eyes narrowed slightly. "In all his raids against the whites, Shanaco was even kind to captive men. And he was always merciful to the women and children. He never allowed any women or children to be killed in his battles. He has killed white men, yes, just as you and I have killed Indians. But *never* did he hurt women and children. I'm sure that he never forgot the fate of his own white mother."

Colonel Harkins grudgingly admitted, "I, too, have

heard that the half-breed never harmed women and children.'' He drew a slow breath. ''Perhaps I should reconsider.''

''Yes, absolutely. Please right the wrong. Do it now, this very hour.''

Shanaco moved not a muscle. Only the wind lifted a lock of long raven hair as it lay along his bare bronzed shoulder. He fought hard to hold his temper.

''Get up, you're free to go,'' said the scowling sergeant of the guard, a stocky man with a scar down his left cheek.

Finally Shanaco rose to his feet.

His handsome face showed no emotion as he walked out of the icehouse prison. Apologies were quickly made along with a promise that the fort's commandant, Colonel Harkins, would personally meet with the chief soon to discuss the settlement of his People.

Outside the makeshift jail, Double Jimmy waited. When he saw Shanaco, so tall and imposing and with eyes the color of pewter, he recognized the Comanche leader.

Double Jimmy stepped forward, introduced himself and said, ''Walk with me, Chief. We will talk.''

Shanaco nodded, turned and addressed his men in their native tongue.

Then, leaving them behind, he fell into step beside the older man. As they walked away from the prison, Double Jimmy said, ''I'm the Indian agent.''

Shanaco nodded in silence.

Double Jimmy explained, "I was in Washington when you led your People onto the reservation. Had I been at the fort at that time, I would have intervened on your behalf."

"If you say so," Shanaco finally said.

"I am genuinely sorry for the disrespect shown to you and I assure you nothing like that will happen again. I hope we can put the unpleasantness behind us and go forward." He looked hopefully at Shanaco.

Shanaco shrugged bare shoulders.

Double Jimmy hurried on, "I know you are anxious to get washed up, put on clean clothes, but first there's something I want to show you. Your horse is stabled with the garrison's. So is mine. Let's walk over there, get our mounts and take a short ride."

Moments later the two rode away from the fort with Double Jimmy leading the way. Due south. When he finally drew rein, Shanaco halted his stallion.

Double Jimmy dismounted, dropped the reins to the ground, and said, "As you can see, this is a choice part of the reservation. It has been set aside for your People, Shanaco."

Shanaco, still dressed in breechcloth and red bandanna, pushed his long loose hair back, swung down and unhurriedly walked forward. He examined the thick grass, the tall shade trees, the wide ribbon of water gliding by in the near distance. He was pleased with what he saw. The People had been given a prime spot on the reservation's southwestern edge, bordered by Cache Creek.

"As the recognized chief, you will be assigned your own private quarters just as soon as the dwelling can be readied for you. Shouldn't be more than a few days at the outside." Shanaco glanced around, seeing nothing. Double Jimmy explained, "The cottage is a half mile from here, down around a bend of the creek."

Double Jimmy paused and waited for Shanaco to say something. Shanaco remained quiet.

Double Jimmy cleared his throat needlessly and said, "I understand the old chief passed away."

Shanaco shook his head. "Yes, my grandfather is dead."

Double Jimmy continued, "I had great respect for Chief Gray Wolf. He was a testimony to dignity and bravery. Perhaps it is a blessing that he is gone." He clarified then, "He never had to give up his old, beloved life of roaming the plains and hunting the buffalo that are gone forever."

"My grandfather preferred death to life on the reservation," Shanaco finally said. His head swung around and he looked Double Jimmy in the eye. "I feel the same. I do not intend to stay here."

"I understand how you feel," said Double Jimmy. "But perhaps we can change your mind."

"Never."

Double Jimmy nodded. "Then all I ask is that

while you are here, you work with me as I try to help your People adjust. Will you do that?''

''I will.''

Double Jimmy extended his hand for Shanaco to shake. ''I want to be your friend, Shanaco. Give me a chance to show you that I am on your side and you can trust me.''

Shanaco gripped the older man's hand and shook it firmly. ''Sir, I thank you for your kindness,'' he said politely.

''Call me Double Jimmy. Everybody does.'' He smiled and patted Shanaco's bare shoulder. ''If there's anything I can do for you, let me know.''

Shanaco had no intention of staying one day longer than was absolutely necessary. He appreciated the Indian agent's overture of kindness and believed him to be an honest man. But as soon as he saw to it that the People were settled and were being treated fairly, he would leave.

The prospect of spending the rest of his life on a reservation would be a slow death. He couldn't wait to go back to his remote ranch in New Mexico where he was free to do as he pleased, when he pleased.

Shanaco had been at the fort for little more than a week. Bored and edgy, he took a ride alone. It was a warm, sunny Sunday afternoon. Far away from the fort's scattered buildings and the hundreds of tepees dotting the land, he rode up into the gentle foothills of the Wichita Mountains. At the crest of a hill, he stopped, dismounted and allowed his stallion to contentedly crop the patchy grass.

In minutes the black had roamed away. The stallion went over the top of the hill, down the other side and out of sight. Shanaco wasn't concerned. He had trained the black himself. When he was ready to leave, all he needed to do was whistle and the stallion would come.

Shanaco sat down beneath an elm, stretched his long legs out before him, crossed them at the ankles, leaned back against the tree's rough trunk and lighted one of Double Jimmy's cigars.

For a time there was little sound, save the sigh of the wind and the cawing of birds. Then all at once he heard—faintly—the sound of laughter. A woman's tinkling laughter. He turned his head to listen. The laughter soon grew louder, closer. Squinting, Shanaco looked down and caught sight of the most arresting woman he had ever seen.

She was running barefoot across a meadow that was part dirt and part grass. Close on her bare heels was a huge silver wolfhound, barking his pleasure. The woman's unbound hair and full cotton skirts were billowing out in the wind. Her fair face was flushed with exertion. Continuing to laugh merrily, she impulsively grabbed her long, bothersome skirts and yanked them up to her knees.

The woman didn't see him seated beneath the elm on the hill above. She was unaware of his presence. She believed that she was alone. So she bunched her skirts higher, exposing a pair of the palest, most shapely thighs Shanaco had ever laid eyes on.

He stared, disarmed by her carefree spirit and her natural beauty. And by that blazing red hair unlike any he had ever seen. After a brief moment in which he studied her with undiluted pleasure, she disappeared over a rise. One minute she was there. The next she was gone.

Shanaco blinked.

Had he actually seen her? Had a beautiful young woman with flaming hair and tinkling laughter and ivory thighs actually run past him? Perhaps she was a vision. Surely someone like that could not be real. Shanaco was enchanted. He wanted to leap to his feet and run after her.

He didn't do it.

He sat perfectly still, hoping that she would come back. He waited, tensed, hardly daring to breathe. But she never returned.

After several long minutes, Shanaco gave up. He rose to his feet and whistled for the stallion. In seconds the dutiful black came trotting toward his master. Shanaco climbed up astride the nickering stallion and rode back toward the fort.

How, he wondered, could he find out who the red-haired beauty was? He might never know. He couldn't ask. He'd get thrown back into jail for being too curious about one of the fort's few white women.

His jaw clenched tight, Shanaco cursed the fates that had put this beautiful red-haired woman here on the reservation where he couldn't talk to her, much less hold her in his arms. Another time, another place, it would have been different. He would have seen to that. Had he been home at his New Mexico ranch when he saw her running across a meadow, he wouldn't have hesitated. He'd have gone after her. He would have stopped her, made her tell him her name. Made her...

Shanaco needed a drink.

He headed for the civilian village bordering the fort. He had learned that there was whiskey to be had in the back rooms of some of the businesses. Not that the white proprietors liked serving him, but he didn't give a damn.

His money was as good as the next man's.

The village streets were almost deserted.

Shanaco was dismounting before the general mercantile store when he heard someone say his name.

"Shanaco," Double Jimmy called out.

Shanaco turned and saw the Indian agent hurrying up the wooden sidewalk.

"Double Jimmy," Shanaco acknowledged.

"Been looking for you, Chief," Double Jimmy said, and smiled.

"You have found me."

"So I have. So I have. I wanted to tell you that I've arranged a meeting. You, me, Colonel Harkins and Major Miles Courteen, the second in command. Tomorrow afternoon. Is that satisfactory?"

"It is," Shanaco replied. Then, after only a brief

exchange of pleasantries, he said, ''I took a ride this afternoon, went down to the south part of the res. A young woman with blazing hair ran barefoot across a meadow with a big wolfhound dog racing after her.'' He paused, glanced away, then asked, as casually as possible, ''Any idea who she is?''

Double Jimmy laughed, knowing immediately who Shanaco was talking about. ''Red hair? Barefoot? Silver-furred dog? That could only be Maggie. Pretty Maggie Bankhead and her dog, Pistol.''

Shanaco kept his voice low, level, when he asked, ''She one of the officer's wives?''

''Maggie? Lord, no. Maggie Bankhead is a *miss*. And, she says she fully intends to stay one.'' He laughed again before adding, ''Maggie is a well-bred but fiercely independent Virginia girl who is like a daughter to me. Been good friends with her parents for years. Why, I'm the one responsible for Maggie coming out West. You met her, did you?''

''No. I didn't meet her.'' Shanaco shrugged. Then he said, ''What's she doing here at the fort if she's not married to one of the soldiers?''

''She's the reservation teacher. Maggie teaches English to Indian children. Well, not just the children. Anyone who cares to learn.''

Six

"We won't be seen," he whispered hoarsely, and deftly flipped open the buttons going down her tight bodice.

"But it's a lazy Sunday afternoon," she protested mildly. "Someone might ride out this way." She didn't lift a hand to stop him.

"They'll see nothing but a buggy parked beneath a shade tree," he said.

"Suppose they get curious?" she asked. "Come out here and look inside?"

"Since when are you afraid to take a little chance?" teased Captain Daniel Wilde, lowering his head to Lois Harkins's open bodice and anxiously pressing his hot face against her soft flesh.

Lois giggled then. She stroked the back of Daniel Wilde's blond head while he eagerly pressed wet kisses to the swell of her pale breasts.

"I swear, Danny, you are just too naughty for words." Lois giggled again.

"You don't fool me, Lois Harkins," Wilde gently accused. "You want it as much as I do. You want it here and now and half the pleasure for you is the danger of getting caught. Isn't it?'' Smiling, Lois nodded in agreement. She pushed his face up, reached between them, yanked at her lace-trimmed chemise. When she'd totally freed a full, soft breast from its satin confines, she drew him back to her and reminisced, ''Remember that first time we made love, Danny?''

''How could I forget?'' he mumbled, kissing the exposed nipple as he reached down and lifted her billowing skirts.

''It was my first night at the fort,'' Lois whispered. ''Father invited you and two other officers—Lieutenant Payne and Lieutenant Vane, I believe—to our residence for dinner.''

''I remember,'' Wilde said with a laugh, raising his head to gaze fondly at her.

''He told me that you were his trusted aide-de-camp and that he thought the world of you.''

''And I him,'' said Wilde, and they both laughed.

''Do you recall what happened once dinner was over and father asked you three gentlemen to join him on the porch for cigars and brandy?''

''I declined, because you requested that I stay and keep you company.'' His grin was wicked and his eyes gleamed. ''While the colonel and the others were outside having their after-dinner cigars and brandy, I was inside having you.''

Lois squealed with laughter. ''I'll never forget the look on your face when—midway through the meal—

I reached under the table and casually put my hand on your groin. Aren't I a witch?''

''A beautiful witch,'' he good-naturedly retorted. ''God Almighty, there I was seated at the table with my commanding officer who happens to be your father. Making conversation. Enjoying my dinner. Behaving the polite dinner guest.'' Wilde paused, ran a warm hand up the inside of Lois's stockinged leg, and added, ''While beneath the table you were coaxing me into a full-blown erection.''

''Ah, you were so easy,'' she said with a half-petulant sigh. ''When father introduced us, I knew that I could have you. That I would have you that very evening.''

As if she hadn't spoken, he went on, ''I was forced to sit there for a good half hour pretending that I wasn't in agony.''

''You coward, you wouldn't even look at me.''

''Coward? Hardly. Would a coward have made love to you right there at the dining table?''

''I guess not,'' Lois murmured as Wilde's hand grew bolder, moving higher, stroking a bare thigh. She wore no underwear beneath her full skirts.

Lois would never forget the night they met. It had been such fun, so exciting. She had arrived at the fort that very afternoon. At her father's invitation, the three young officers had come for dinner. She had examined each and quickly decided that the blond, attractive Daniel Wilde was the one.

At least for now.

She had not been in the least deterred when, introducing him, her father had mentioned that Captain Wilde had a lovely wife and two young children down in Texas.

When they went in to dinner, Captain Wilde had pulled out a chair for her, then taken the one to her left. Halfway through the main course, she had lowered her left hand to her lap. Seconds later, she had moved that hand to *his* lap.

Wilde had winced in surprise and everyone—including her—had given him a questioning look. His face flushed, eyes wide, he had quickly raised his napkin to his mouth and pretended to cough.

When he'd calmed a little, she had begun to stroke and mold him through his tight blue uniform trousers. Throughout she had continued to laugh and talk and enjoy the meal. Poor Daniel had hardly touched his food.

When at last her father had invited the young officers outside to smoke their cigars, Wilde was in a fix. He'd no choice but to stay behind.

"Stay and keep me company, Captain Wilde," she had said, and he had, with her father's smiling approval.

The others were hardly out the door before she leaned close and commanded Daniel Wilde to push his chair back from the table. He did and she ordered him to "unbutton your trousers and take it out. I want it and you must give it to me." He had anxiously obeyed. Her heart fluttering with excitement and anticipation, she had tossed her napkin on the table, risen to her feet, stuck her fingers down into her half-full wineglass and spread the port up and down his throbbing length.

Then quick as a wink she had lifted her skirts—underneath which she was bare—climbed astride the highly aroused Captain Wilde, slipped easily down onto him and laughingly demanded that he give her the best he had.

He did.

Oh, it had been so incredibly exciting to make wild, wanton love there in the candlelit dining room with her unsuspecting father and the other young officers right outside on the moonlit porch. She could hear the male voices lifting and lowering and knew that at any moment they might come back in and catch her furiously riding her new blond lover.

That very real possibility had made the fast, frantic coupling all the more exciting. If they had been caught, she would have been packed off to Europe to join the cold, uncaring mother she truly disliked, and poor Captain Wilde's military career would be over.

The danger had been downright delicious.

Lois was snapped back to the present when Wilde abruptly lowered her skirts and said, his forehead wrinkling, "Jesus, I hear a dog barking!"

"So? You said yourself if anyone happened by they would see only the parked carriage. They'll just suppose that we've gone for a walk. Everyone knows that you and I are out for a ride this afternoon with my father's blessing."

It was true.

They had waved to several acquaintances on their way out of the fort. Lois was clever. She knew how to take full advantage of any opportunity.

It was a quiet Sunday afternoon, but her father was tied up with the fort's Indian agent. She had interrupted the two and complained that she was "bored to tears." The colonel understood and sympathized and suggested she go for a walk. He said he would enlist his aide-de-camp to escort her so that she would be safe. She promptly told her father that she had a better idea; she would like to take a nice, long carriage ride. It was such a warm, lovely day and she really hadn't seen much of the fort. Her indulgent father had quickly agreed.

And now she and her lover were at the far southern edge of the big reservation, enjoying the warm, still day.

"That barking dog is getting closer," said Wilde nervously.

Lois laughed off his concern. She lifted her skirts back up and provocatively parted her legs. Then she looked into Daniel Wilde's eyes and commanded, "Take me, Danny. Take me now, lest I change my mind."

Wilde nodded and fumbled anxiously with the buttons of his trousers. Lois laughed and helped him. When he moved between her spread legs, he murmured, "Lois, Lois, you thrill me like no woman ever has."

"Even more than your little wife down in Texas?" she taunted.

"More than any other woman."

"That's so sweet," she whispered, then softly sighed, wishing that he thrilled her more than any other man.

He didn't.

At first he had excited her. But their relationship was rapidly growing stale. Lately there were occasions when Danny was thrusting into her and grunting with exertion that she had to stifle a yawn of sheer boredom. Their lovemaking had taken on a too familiar pattern. She easily anticipated every move before it was made. He was not particularly imaginative.

"Lois, my love, yes, yes." He was panting hard as he hammered into her.

He was, she knew, already on the verge of climax. How predictable. How tiresome. How disappointing. She wanted more than he was capable of giving. She wanted a powerful but controlled lover who could hold an erection until she had tired of playing.

The handsome, half-naked Shanaco instantly flashed into her mind. Lois closed her eyes and envisioned the dangerous, copper-skinned Comanche chieftain taking her. Forcing her to be his sexual captive. Keeping her locked up and naked. Making fierce animal love to her hour upon hour.

"Aah!" Daniel Wilde groaned out his release.

Lois sighed with disgust.

And Maggie Bankhead, out for a romp with her dog on this warm Sunday afternoon, topped a rise, saw a parked carriage rocking violently and heard a man moan loudly as if in pain.

"Shh!" she warned Pistol, snapping her fingers to keep him silent. Puzzled at first, then horrified as she recognized the buggy and the terrible truth dawned, Maggie spun about and raced back the way she had come, desperate to get away, to not be seen or heard.

For a half mile, Maggie, barefoot, ran as fast as her weak legs would carry her. Soon she got a painful stitch in her side and had to stop and catch her breath. Hands clasping her side, she frowned with dismay. Now she was certain of what she had only suspected before.

Lois Harkins was having an illicit affair with the very married Captain Daniel Wilde!

Seven

In the cool gray of the breaking October dawn, a solitary soldier came out of the silent, darkened barracks.

Brass bugle tucked under his arm, campaign hat on his head, uniform neatly pressed, the young trooper yawned, then stepped down off the barracks porch and into the empty quad.

He turned and headed in a northwesterly direction, passing the rows of darkened sandstone troopers' barracks. Opposite the barracks, directly across the wide quadrangle, was officers row. In the center of the line of the officers' quarters stood the commanding officer's residence.

At the southernmost end of the parade ground were the administration, quartermaster and clerk's offices. And, set alone and apart from the offices but bordering the parade ground, was the one-room schoolhouse.

The various buildings formed a rectangle around the fort's large parade ground, where, at the center, a flagpole rose to meet the Oklahoma sky.

Behind the enlisted-mens' barracks was the schoolteacher's cottage. The bakery. The regimental hospital. The post surgeon's residence. The chapel. The mess hall. The ordnance, quartermaster and commissary warehouses. In back of the warehouses was "Suds Row," where the laundresses were quartered.

Farther on out were the stables. A big hay field. A well-tended garden patch that supplied fresh fruits and vegetables to the troops and the officers' wives. Many of those wives could frequently be seen out in the garden, hoe in hand, bonnet on head, weeding the various vines. Or, down on their knees, skirts ballooning, basket over one arm, picking produce.

Directly outside the fort was a growing civilian community. A general mercantile store that doubled as the stage station. A tailor shop. A blacksmith. An apothecary. A card-and-billards parlor. An undertaker.

No saloons.

Saloons were strictly against government policy on a reservation. But liquor was readily available nonetheless, no matter how hard the Indian agent, Double Jimmy, and the army tried to put a stop to its flow.

In a couple of back rooms in the false-fronted businesses lining the wooden sidewalks, shot glasses of whiskey were served to paying patrons on makeshift rough plank bars that could be easily dismantled and hidden away at the drop of a hat.

Drunkenness was not all that uncommon. Occasionally there were knife fights and shootings, usually involving the shiftless, ne'er-do-well white trouble-makers who hung around the fort.

East of the fort were the buildings of the Comanche-Kiowa Indian agency. Double Jimmy lived there in a small two-room cottage. Similar dwellings housed other agency employees. Near the modest residences were a corn grinder, a sawmill and an Indian goods warehouse.

Still farther out and stretching in every direction as far as the eye could see were the conical buffalo-hide tepees of the reservation tribes.

On this very early Monday morning, the fort, the civilian community, the agency and the vast reservation were all quiet. Everyone was sleeping.

Private Preston Calame, bugle in hand, stepped into position beneath the parade ground's flagpole. He licked his dry lips, drew a long, deep breath, raised the bugle to his mouth and blew the rousing notes of reveille.

The fort was bugle-blasted to life.

Maggie's eyes flew open after the first couple of notes from Private Calame's horn. Her cottage, just around the corner of the bakery, was near the parade ground. Pistol, dozing before the door, instantly awakened, jumped up and barked a cheerful good morning to his sleepy mistress.

"Be quiet!" Maggie scolded, then groaned and snuggled farther down into the warm bedcovers. She closed her eyes and sighed. Then yelped and sat up straight when Pistol raced across the room, leapt onto the bed and made himself comfortable, placing his head on her stomach. Maggie laughed and affectionately rubbed him behind his left ear. Pistol growled his pleasure. "Okay, boy," she soon said. "Get down now and I'll let you out."

Pistol barked, jumped off the bed and beat Maggie to the door. When she opened it a crack, he shot out, a streak of silver disappearing into the dawn darkness. Maggie called after him, "You be right here on the porch waiting for me in an hour, you hear?"

Maggie closed the door and shivered. The early mornings were getting chilly. She considered building a fire in the grate, but soon dismissed the idea. When the sun came up, the cottage would quickly warm. Until then she would just get back in bed.

Maggie crawled between the covers, turned onto her side, folded her hands beneath her cheek and closed her eyes. And frowned, troubled. She could not forget seeing Harkins's parked carriage shaking and bouncing and creaking in yesterday afternoon's brilliant sunshine. Nor the unsettling sounds of a woman's sighing shrieks and a man's deep groans coming from inside the jolting, jiggling buggy.

Half the population of the fort had seen Captain Daniel Wilde and Lois Harkins set out together for a seemingly innocent Sunday drive. Poor naive Colonel Harkins; foolishly supposing that he could trust his hand-picked aide-de-camp to look after his only daughter.

Maggie wondered if anyone else knew about the

pair's shameful indiscretion. She didn't think so. She sure wouldn't tell anyone. Maggie prided herself on not being a gossip. She never spread rumors. She paid little attention to those she heard. She disliked women who tattled and talked unkindly about others, saying hurtful, harmful things even when they had no proof.

Maggie rolled onto her back, raised her arms and folded them beneath her head. Her brows knitted and she exhaled heavily. She should, she knew, keep the whole tawdry affair to herself. Tell no one. That's what she had to do. But how could she possibly keep it from Katie?

An officer's wife and Maggie's dearest female friend, Katie Atwood was tiny, attractive, talkative and a totally likable young woman who loved her husband passionately and enjoyed every minute of her life at the fort.

Katie Atwood was one of the first people Maggie had met upon her arrival at Fort Sill. Katie had been a one-woman welcoming committee, meeting Maggie's coach and immediately inviting her to tea. The two of them had been close ever since.

Maggie suddenly threw back the covers and bounded out of bed. She *had* to tell Katie. She would tell her everything—and make Katie promise to keep it a secret—when she saw her this afternoon. She and Katie had volunteered to hang new curtains in the house being readied for the half-breed leader, Shanaco.

The dwelling had been thoroughly cleaned. All it

lacked was the new curtains and a few finishing touches. The Comanche chieftain was scheduled to move into the secluded cabin Wednesday morning, just forty-eight hours from now.

Maggie smiled as she shed her nightgown.

Truth to tell, she could hardly wait to see the look on Katie's face when she shared her shocking secret.

Eight

The school bell was clanging when Maggie, in a freshly pressed navy cotton dress with white collar and cuffs, crossed the quadrangle at ten minutes of eight that crisp Monday morning. Pistol walked slowly at her side.

Students were streaming toward the schoolhouse from every direction, chattering happily in their native tongues. Maggie searched for and quickly spotted her favorite student, the adorable little Bright Feather. The lame six-year-old Kiowa was lagging behind the others, unable to keep up. He tried gamely to overtake the laughing boys who rushed on ahead, but it was impossible.

The child was left too far behind to make it on his own. Struggling. But, as always, uncomplaining.

Bright Feather was smiling sunnily, his well-scrubbed young face glowing with excitement. He loved school. He loved being with the other children. And, amazingly, he never felt sorry for himself. Never whined or cried even when the other children refused to let him play games with them because of his infirmity.

Maggie's chest tightened as she watched the sweet little boy hobble toward the schoolhouse. Bright Feather had been dealt more than his share of adversity. He had lost both his parents in a battle with white settlers when he was three years old. Such a shame. He was a beautiful child with his gleaming raven hair and huge dark eyes and sweet mouth that was constantly stretched into a pleasing smile.

Each time she saw him, Maggie wanted to grab him and hug him tightly. Just squeeze him to pieces. She refrained. And she tried to conceal the fact that she was more than a little partial to him.

Maggie swallowed hard and hurried forward to meet the laboring little boy.

"Bright Feather," she called to him.

He turned, looked up, saw her, and his smile grew broader. Pistol raced forward, skidded to a stop at Bright Feather's feet, barked eagerly and pressed his big furry body against the child's thin chest.

But Pistol didn't leap up on the boy. The dog was invariably gentle with Bright Feather. The little boy laughed, threw his short arms around Pistol's neck, hugged him tightly and rubbed his cheek against the dog's great head.

"That's enough, Pistol," Maggie warned, and the dog gently pulled free and moved back.

"Good morning," Maggie said, and smiled down at Bright Feather.

"Miss Bankhead," he said politely, grinning. Then proudly displayed his growing skill in the new language he was learning by adding, very slowly, "How are you today?"

Maggie couldn't stop herself. She laid a hand atop his dark head, cupped it gently, leaned down and brushed a quick kiss to his smooth, coppery cheek. "I'm very well, thanks, and you?"

Bright Feather continued to smile, but he shrugged narrow shoulders, unsure. She prompted, "Very well."

"Very well," he repeated, and grinned happily when she laughed her approval.

Just outside the schoolhouse door, Pistol stopped and barked loudly. Maggie snapped her fingers and he immediately stretched, panted and lay down, knowing he was not allowed to enter. Maggie and Bright Feather went in together.

Inside the crowded classroom, noisy children were not yet in their seats. They were milling around, talking, laughing, playfully wrestling with one another, shouting across the room at one another. Being children.

Bright Feather, tired after the long walk from the tepee he shared with a half-dozen other reservation orphans, took his seat in the front row. Maggie nodded her approval. Then she began to look about for her friend, the aged Kiowa chief, Old Coyote. He was not in his usual place in the front row.

Each morning he sat in the same chair, directly in front of her and directly beside Bright Feather. He never missed classes. Maggie was momentarily concerned. Was the old Indian sick and unable to come to class? She continued to scan the sea of young bronzed faces.

Most of the students were standing, so her view was somewhat obscured. A number of the Indian children were fifteen, sixteen and older, and many of the boys—once young braves—were quite tall.

Maggie stood on tiptoe, glanced about, and finally got a fleeting glimpse of Coyote's white hair and wrinkled face. He was seated at the very back of the room. Odd.

Relieved that he was well and present, Maggie clapped her hands for attention. "Class! Class, it is time to begin our lessons. Please sit down."

It took a few minutes for the energetic boys and girls to quiet down and take their places. Maggie waited patiently. At last all were seated and Maggie had a clear view of the entire room.

That's when she saw him.

Seated at the very back of the room beside Old Coyote was the half-breed Comanche chieftain. Dressed in white man's clothes this morning, but looking just as dangerous, just as rebellious as when he had ridden into the fort. His presence filled the room with a kind of crackling excitement. He dominated the space so completely it was hard to get a breath.

He was, no question, quite magnificent. So imperial. So imperious. So physically beautiful. Big and tall. Broad-shouldered and leanly muscled. Harshly handsome face with the high, flat cheekbones of an Indian, but so refined as to add to the perfect symmetry of his classic features. Arresting silver eyes fringed with night-black lashes. Proud, high nose. Wide, sensuous, but strangely cruel-looking mouth.

For a brief moment Maggie was held powerless by some undefinable force he exuded, unnerved by his intimidating presence. But she quickly regained her composure and began the morning's lessons. All business now, her only interest was that of teaching the eager students to speak and write English. She pointedly ignored the imposing half-breed.

With interest, Shanaco noted her disinterest. He was not accustomed to being ignored. Especially by women. White or Indian. This pale-skinned, flame-haired teacher's nonchalant disregard was oddly refreshing. It was novel to be in the same room with a beautiful young female and have her take no notice of him. He was both surprised and intrigued.

He wanted to know her better.

Maggie calmly taught the students, calling on first one, then another, to come up to the newly mounted blackboard, take a fresh piece of chalk and write the latest English word that he or she had learned to spell. All the students were eager to be called on. They raised their hands and waved them about, hoping to have her call on them.

One in particular attracted her attention above all the others.

Shanaco.

Shanaco had his hand raised. Maggie pretended not to see it. Shanaco knew better. She saw him. The fact that she pretended she didn't and refused to call on him told him more about her than if she had acknowledged him. Maggie Bankhead was, Shanaco felt certain, as aware of him as he was of her.

Maggie continued to conduct the class with the same commanding calm she always demonstrated. But she was relieved when at long last the noon bell rang, signaling the end of the day's schooling. The restless children leapt out of their chairs and dashed for the door. Bright Feather trailed after them. A scattering of adult students moved toward the door at a slower pace.

Maggie bid them all a good day with the reminder, "Don't forget the Friday evening picnic. Be sure you memorize a short poem to recite after the meal."

When the room had emptied, she glanced up to see Old Coyote, making his careful, creaking way toward her. When he reached her, Maggie eagerly grabbed his hand.

Gripping the bony fingers, she said, "Give me a minute to gather up the primers and I'll walk with you."

The old chief shook his head and apologized. "Sorry, Miss Maggie. Have big domino game. Am late." And he left.

One student remained.

Shanaco.

Still lounging in his chair at the back of the room,

Shanaco's long legs were stretched out before him. Maggie could no longer pretend that he didn't exist. She looked directly at the chief and frowned, unsure how to handle the situation.

She folded her arms over her chest, took a few steps toward him and spoke to him in Comanche, a difficult language that Double Jimmy had taught her. Shanaco made no reply. Just continued to sit there unmoving, looking at her.

Maggie uncrossed her arms and pointed to the clock above the blackboard. Then she gestured to the door. Shanaco nodded. He rose to his feet and leisurely made his way to the front of the room.

He stopped when he reached Maggie. He slowly turned to face her. Then took another step toward her. He stood so close and was so tall and broad-shouldered that he filled the entire scope of her vision. So close she could see the pulse beating steadily in his bronzed throat.

Maggie got the distinct feeling that Shanaco expected her to be afraid of him and to show it. Too bad. Not about to be cowed or frightened by anyone, Maggie stood right where she was, toe-to-toe with him, tipped back her head and looked squarely at Shanaco.

And found herself staring, transfixed, into a pair of gleaming silver-gray eyes unlike any she'd ever looked into. Shanaco stared back, his gaze intense and unblinking, long dark lashes lowered slightly, a muscle working in his coppery jaw. Maggie felt her stomach flutter with an unfamiliar sensation.

She again pointed to the open door. Unsmiling, Shanaco nodded, stepped back, turned and walked out. Maggie frowned after him, and a chill of apprehension skipped up her spine. She raised her arms and hugged herself defensively.

Then her lips fell open in surprise when the handsome, long-legged chieftain overtook the limping Bright Feather, scooped him up off the ground and swung the laughing child up atop his broad shoulders.

Nine

Shanaco carried the laughing Bright Feather across the parade ground.

Maggie couldn't keep from smiling. The pair disappeared around the corner of a barracks and Maggie turned away.

Humming now, she erased the blackboard, collected the chalk, gathered up the childrens' books, stacked them neatly in a bookcase and went outside.

Pistol jumped up and barked excitedly. He raced ahead when Maggie set out for the general mercantile store. The weekly stage, due at straight up noon today, carried passengers and delivered the mail.

Maggie looked forward to letters from home. Her mother and father wrote regularly, her sisters occasionally. She treasured every missive. She would, on this particular Monday, collect her own mail and that of Katie Atwood's.

Katie had suggested that while Maggie was picking up their mail, she would be fixing a nice lunch for the two of them. It sounded like a good bargain to Maggie.

Now as Maggie approached the mercantile store,

she saw that the stage had already arrived. She was glad that it was on time for once. She didn't want to be late for lunch. She was undeniably eager to tell Katie about the misbehaving Lieutenant Wilde and Lois Harkins.

The mercantile store was crowded. Everyone always turned out, hoping for news from home. Maggie exchanged pleasantries with several officers' wives, then smiled when she saw Lieutenant Finley making his way toward her.

The lieutenant greeted her warmly and they fell into easy conversation. They commented on the welcome change in the weather, discussed next week's monthly ration day, and talked about whether the fort's newest arrivals were adjusting well. Dave said he'd heard that Colonel Harkins and Major Courteen had scheduled a meeting with Double Jimmy and Chief Shanaco this afternoon. High time, if you asked him. Maggie fully agreed.

One of the things she most liked about Dave Finley was his consideration of others, his heartfelt compassion toward his fellow man. On more than one occasion, she had witnessed his kindness to the displaced Indians.

"Shanaco won't be staying on the reservation," the lieutenant mentioned casually. "The chief told Double Jimmy he'll be gone by Thanksgiving. Soon as he sees to it that the tribe has settled in, he'll disappear."

Maggie nodded but made no comment. If the tales

she'd heard about the hell-raising half-breed were true, his People might be just as well off without him.

Maggie was disappointed to find that there was no mail for her this week. Nor was there any for Katie. She shrugged slender shoulders, turned and motioned toward the door. Lieutenant Finley nodded and followed her outside.

"May I walk you home?" he asked.

"Thanks, Dave, but I'm not going home. I'm having lunch at Katie Atwood's."

"Well, I'm free later this afternoon, perhaps we could..."

"Busy. Katie and I are going out to the little house the army assigned to Shanaco. We're hanging new curtains in the cottage, getting the place ready for him. He's due to move in on Wednesday."

"That's neighborly of you," he said with a smile. "Need any help?"

"Thanks, but no. We can manage."

He knew it was true. The independent Maggie rarely required help from anyone. Bristled if you hinted she might not be able to manage something. But then that's one of the things he so admired about her. That and her flaming red hair. He smiled as they fell into step on the wooden sidewalk. They commented again on the perfect fall weather, discussed the upcoming annual officer's ball and made plans to attend together.

Dave asked how things were going at school and

Maggie explained that her class had grown considerably since the arrival of the Kwahadi Comanches.

"Why, even the chief is a pupil," she said. "Shanaco attended class this morning."

The lieutenant laughed. "You're teasing me."

"No, I'm not. He was in class all morning and he...he...what? What is it?"

The lieutenant rolled his eyes heavenward and shook his head. "Maggie, Shanaco is totally fluent in English. Speaks, reads and writes it better than I do."

Maggie stopped walking, tilted her head to the side and frowned, puzzled. "Are you sure?"

"Very sure. It's said his white mother, now deceased, insisted he learn English. Taught him from the time he was a baby. Guess she suspected that one day he would want to live in the white world."

"Speaks perfect English. Then why...?"

"I don't know," Dave said. "If not to study the subject, perhaps to study the teacher."

"Don't be ridiculous," Maggie said with a smile, but felt her pulse mysteriously quicken.

"Maggie, you're going to kill me," Katie Atwood declared when finally she opened the door to Maggie's impatient knocking.

Katie was still in her robe and gown. Her hair was uncombed and tangled. Her pretty face was pallid, eyes dull.

Looking her over, Maggie gently teased, "Sure you're not already dead?"

Katie managed a weak smile. ''I know I look a fright. I've an upset stomach, lost my breakfast.'' She said, ''I haven't fixed anything for our lunch. Haven't done anything.''

''You poor dear,'' Maggie sympathized, urging Katie back inside. She turned, snapped her fingers at Pistol and he obediently lay down outside. Inside, Maggie said, ''Now, you get right back in bed and I'll fix you a cup of mint tea and get you some soda crackers.''

Katie made a face. ''No, don't bother. I'm not hungry.''

''I know, but you need something to settle your stomach.''

''I suppose,'' Katie said, then shed her robe and got back into bed.

In minutes Maggie brought a tray to the bed. She placed it on Katie's lap and pulled up a chair. ''Drink the tea while it's hot. Have you any peppermint in the house?'' Katie shook her head. Maggie said, ''I'll go back to the store and—''

''No, the tea and crackers will do the trick.'' Katie picked up the cup, took a drink and said, ''Maggie, I feel so bad about this afternoon. I'm letting you down and I—''

''Nonsense,'' said Maggie. ''I can fix myself a quick lunch right here, and afterward I'll go on out to the chief's cottage and hang those curtains.''

''You can't do that! You can't go all the way out

there alone. You'll have to go directly through the Comanche camp and..."

Maggie raised a hand to silence Katie. "No one is going to bother me and the nice long walk will do me good. It's not like I'll be carrying the curtains. They're already at the cottage, ready to be hanged. I can go out there, hang the drapery and be back by sundown."

Katie made a face. Raising a well-arched eyebrow, she said, "You're not the least bit afraid of those devilish Comanches? I tell you that Chief Shanaco looks awfully dangerous to me and—"

"I'm not afraid of the chief nor his People. I have roamed freely all over this reservation by myself since I first got here. I've gone out and helped tend the sick when called on, sometimes in the middle of the night. No harm has ever come to me."

"I know, but that handsome Comanche chief..."

"Will be nowhere near the cottage. He isn't moving in for another couple of days."

"I guess you'll be okay," Katie finally conceded. Then asked hopefully, "Will you stay with me for a little while?"

"I'll stay right here until you're feeling better."

"You're a good friend, Maggie."

"As are you." Maggie smiled then and added, "And if you promise to tell no one, and I do mean no one, I have a juicy secret to share with you."

"Tell me," said Katie, her upset stomach temporarily forgotten, her eyes growing round with interest.

* * *

Colonel Harkins came to his feet when Shanaco, dressed as a white man, and Double Jimmy walked into his office at shortly after two o'clock.

"Thank you so much for coming this afternoon, Chief Shanaco," Harkins said, leaning across the desk and firmly shaking Shanaco's hand. "I don't believe you've met Major Miles Courteen," he said, indicating a frail-looking, impeccably groomed man with iron-gray hair and warm brown eyes. Slapping Courteen's shoulder, Colonel Harkins explained, "The damned Bureau of Indian Affairs keeps Double Jimmy and me away from the fort so much of the time I've come to rely heavily on Major Courteen."

"A pleasure to meet you, sir." Shanaco was polite to the slender, courtly officer.

"Chief Shanaco," said Major Courteen with a friendly shake of his head.

"Double Jimmy, always good to see you," said Harkins.

"Thank you, Colonel," Double Jimmy replied. "Major Courteen," he said, acknowledging the soft-spoken southerner for whom he had great respect.

"Shall we all sit down?" said Colonel Harkins. "We've a lot to talk about."

When Shanaco, Double Jimmy and Courteen were seated, Colonel Harkins dropped back down into his chair and the meeting began.

"Chief, I'm aware that you are a young man of much influence with your People," said Colonel Harkins. "I'm grateful that you were able to impress upon them the necessity of coming in to Fort Sill."

Shanaco quickly corrected him. "I had nothing to do with it, Colonel. My grandfather, Chief Gray Wolf, was entirely responsible."

"Yes, of course. Sorry to hear of Gray Wolf's passing," said Harkins. "You know your grandfather was the last holdout of all the signatory chiefs and—"

"I know that, sir," Shanaco cut in.

Colonel Harkins smiled. "Look at it this way, Chief Shanaco, you can consider yourself civilization's advance guard opening the way for generations of—"

"Colonel, I've no intention of staying at Fort Sill," Shanaco again interrupted. "It was only out of respect for my grandfather that I led the People onto the reservation. As I have told Double Jimmy, I do not intend to remain."

Again Colonel Harkins smiled. "I hope we can change your mind about leaving. We need you here, Shanaco. For the time being, I am eager to hear what your thoughts are on how to make this transition as painless as possible for your People. Major Courteen and I sincerely want to do what's best for them, I hope you know that."

Shanaco leaned back in his chair and laced lean fingers over his waist. "The first thing you have to do is allow the People to keep at least a portion of their horse herd. If you know anything about the Comanche, you know that their horses are everything to them. You cannot expect proud young men who are some of the best horsemen on the plains to give up their mounts."

Colonel Harkins nodded thoughtfully but said, "I understand that, and I will return the horses to them if in turn you will give me your guarantee that the mounted braves won't be riding away from the fort, crossing the river into Texas."

"No," Shanaco said flatly. "I can give you no such guarantee. I *can* guarantee that if you do not return their horses, they will take them back in the dead of night and flee this reservation." He fixed the colonel with cold gray eyes and added, "They have lost enough. A short time ago, when I was a boy, all the Comancheria—" he lifted his hands, made a wide circle in the air "—belonged to the People."

Colonel Harkins silently nodded his understanding. The Comancheria—the Comanche country—was vast, stretching for hundreds of miles and including great portions of New Mexico, Colorado, Kansas, Oklahoma and especially Texas. For centuries the Indians had been free to ride across the open reaches of the rolling prairies that were lush with grass and carved with deep creeks and flowing rivers.

Colonel Harkins finally spoke. "I know that, Chief, and I—"

"This fort sits squarely in the Comancheria, Colonel. It is you and the troopers who are on our land, not we on yours."

Colonel Harkins looked to Double Jimmy for help.

The Indian agent said softly, "We cannot turn back the clock, Shanaco, but the colonel, the major and I will do everything we can to help your People adjust to this new way of life." He glanced at the colonel and, without asking permission, said, "Some of the horse herd—they can take their pick—will be immediately returned to the young Comanche braves."

Shanaco nodded and swiftly moved on to another subject. "Beef issues. You will deliver our beef on the hoof and allow the men to do the slaughtering. They have to retain some semblance of independence."

"Agreed," said Colonel Harkins. "Now what about…?"

The meeting continued for more than an hour. When it was over, much had been discussed and determined. They all shook hands. Colonel Harkins suggested that Shanaco ride out and have a look at the cabin he was soon to occupy. Shanaco nodded, said he might do that.

Double Jimmy and Shanaco walked outside and stood for a moment on the shaded sally port. Double Jimmy reached into his breast pocket and took out the makings to build a cigarette. Shanaco leaned a muscular shoulder against a porch pilaster and gazed out over the quadrangle. The two men talked quietly for a time.

Finally Double Jimmy, blowing out a plume of smoke, said, "Well, I'm off to the agency storehouse to inventory the supply of flour and cornmeal and dried beans."

Shanaco's dark head swung around. "The Comanche do not like cornmeal and beans."

Double Jimmy exhaled heavily, flicked a long ash from his cigarette. "That's all we have to feed them with until the next beef ration arrives next week." Quickly changing the subject, he said, "The colonel's right. You really should ride out and have a look at the new cabin."

Shanaco pushed away from the pilaster. The yoked, pale-blue shirt he wore stretched across his shoulders as he shoved his hands deep into the pockets of his dark twill trousers and rocked back on his heels.

"Maybe I will."

"It's a nice little place, you'll see. You can move in in a couple of days. Shall I show you where it is?"

"Thanks. I can find it."

Ten

Shanaco was thirsty.

He stayed where he was until Double Jimmy was out of sight, then turned and headed directly for the civilian village on the outskirts of the fort.

In minutes he climbed the steps to a wooden sidewalk that stretched the length of the false-front buildings.

He passed the undertaker's, the Federal Land Office, the tailor's shop. A couple of men stood outside the general mercantile store. Civilians. One was a big brawny fellow with a shaggy brown beard and blackened teeth. The other was totally bald and quite short, but muscular and strong-looking. The pair exchanged glances as Shanaco approached.

Unfazed, Shanaco walked up to them and asked, "Where can a man buy a drink of whiskey?"

The big, ugly one snorted. "A *man* can buy a drink in Jake's card parlor. But you ain't no man. You're a mixed-blood, so you'll just have to go thirsty." He smiled broadly, showing his blackened teeth.

Grinning, his short companion repeated, "You

ain't no man, you're a mixed-blood.'' The pair went into spasms of guttural laughter.

Shanaco shrugged, stepped between them and walked on down the sidewalk. He stopped before the bat-wing doors of Jake's card parlor. He stepped inside the smoky, noisy room and looked around. The place was full. Players at both billiard tables. Every seat at the half-dozen poker tables was taken. There was laughter and loud talk and the striking of billiard balls with long wooden cue sticks. The flicking of cards being dealt and the clinking of coins being tossed to the center of the tables.

One of the players at a poker table near the door, a tobacco-chewing man with bushy eyebrows and ruddy cheeks, looked up and saw Shanaco standing in the doorway. In seconds the noisy room went totally silent. A dropped pin could have been heard. Every eye was on Shanaco and every mouth was agape.

Shanaco walked through the crowded poker parlor to the very back. There he parted, then ducked through the shabby curtains covering a narrow door opening into the back room. Three men were there drinking whiskey. Shanaco went to the opposite end of the makeshift plank bar and waited until the little, nervous-looking barkeep finally came over and asked him what he wanted.

''A glass of your best bourbon,'' Shanaco said.

The barkeep swallowed hard but reached for the whiskey bottle and a shot glass. Shanaco took a bill from his pants pocket and paid for the liquor. Then he stood flat-footed, tossed down the rotgut whiskey in one swallow and motioned for a fill-up. The barkeep poured another. Shanaco drank it down. He made a face, wiped his mouth on the back of his hand and turned to leave.

But he didn't quite make it.

Standing in the curtained door, blocking his way, was the short, muscular fellow he'd seen outside the mercantile store. His big, beefy companion stood directly behind him, grinning.

Shanaco drew a slow breath.

He knew what was coming next. He hoped he was wrong. He wasn't. Without a word, the shorter man stepped forward and threw a punch, landing a glancing blow to Shanaco's left jaw. Shanaco never flinched. But the man squealed in pain and darted behind his larger companion when Shanaco's lightning right fist connected with his nose, sending blood splashing all over his startled face and down his soiled shirtfront.

The big man shoved his bleeding friend out of harm's way and stepped in to take over. He took a swing. Shanaco raised a defensive left, deflected the blow and clipped his opponent on the chin. He roared like a lion through his blackened teeth.

The fight spilled out into the card room. Pool sharks and poker players stopped their games to watch and cheer and place wagers. Most bet on the big, bullying man they knew well.

Willie ''Big Boy'' Carson was a regular around the village and everyone steered clear of him as best they could. He was as mean as a snake and had mopped the floor with more than one hapless opponent.

But there were those who had heard of the half-breed's reputation. It was said that whether he was riding and raiding with the Comanche or living among the whites who hated him, Shanaco was fearless. He had faced death numerous times and had the battle scars to prove it. If anybody could put Big Boy Carson away, it was the reckless half-breed. So several gents took tempting odds and placed their money on Shanaco.

A wise decision.

When the brutal brawl ended, it was the beaten Willie Carson who lay on the floor, spiting blood, struggling for breath. All the half-breed had suffered was a rapidly swelling right eye. The spectators were amazed. Shanaco was in such great physical condition he wasn't even breathing hard.

Shanaco walked out of the card parlor amid whistles and hoots and grudging applause. He went directly to the sandstone barracks where he was temporally billeted with the troopers. The quarters were deserted at this hour of the afternoon.

Shanaco stripped off his blue shirt, tossed it on his cot. He found a wash pan and filled it with water from the drinking keg against the wall. He picked up a cloth, dipped it into the water and carefully bathed his face. He leaned close to the cracked shaving mirror mounted on the wall. He frowned. His right eye was already turning purple and was swollen almost shut.

Shanaco pressed the damp cloth to his battered eye for several minutes, then looked into the mirror again. He exhaled heavily. Anyone who saw him would know he had been in a fight. And, of course, he would be labeled the troublemaker. Everyone knew it was the Indians who caused trouble on a reservation. Never the whites.

Shanaco drew on a clean white shirt, buttoned it midway down his chest and left the barracks. He walked to the stables, went inside the tack room and took his bridle down off the wall. The bridle draped over his left shoulder, he went back out, leaned his arms over the top board of the wooden corral and whistled for his stallion.

The black lifted his head, looked around, whinnied and galloped eagerly toward his master. He stuck his head over the fence and rubbed his jaw against Shanaco's face and shoulder.

Shanaco laughed and stroked his sleek neck. "Want to take a little ride, boy?"

The black neighed his reply. Shanaco opened the corral gate and the stallion trotted out. Eschewing a saddle, Shanaco haltered the mount and swung up onto his bare back. It was a warm, sunny day and Shanaco felt fine, despite the bruised eye. A short ride was just what he needed.

Leaving the fort behind, Shanaco put the black into

a fast gallop. The wind on his face felt good. Having the powerful horse between his legs felt better. He loved to ride. All Comanches loved to ride and were expert horsemen. He had learned to ride almost before he had learned to walk.

By the time he was no more than thirteen, he had ridden on raids with his father, Chief Naco, and the warriors. They had traveled hundreds of miles to execute surprise attacks against their enemies, the whites. Their prowess in battle had made them rich with captured horses. Brave warriors owned as many as two hundred horses apiece. His father, the chief, had had more than a thousand!

Shanaco smiled, recalling how tired he had been at the end of the day when they had ridden seventy or eighty miles before stopping. But he had been careful to conceal his discomfort from the warriors. Especially from his father, who seemed never to tire or to be afraid.

Shanaco drew a deep, invigorating breath of the crisp, clear air, reached up and untied the leather cord holding his hair in place. He stuffed the cord into his breast pocket. His shoulder-length hair streamed out behind him like the black's long tail. Horse and rider were as one as they raced across the grass-covered Oklahoma prairie.

Shanaco drew rein on a low hill overlooking the newly settled Comanche encampment. He was, as always, amazed at the resilience of the People. They were going about their lives as if they had lived here forever. Their buffalo-hide tepees dotted the rolling plains and there was much activity in the camp.

Shanaco kneed the black. He rode down into the village. Laughing children dashed out to meet him and run alongside. Dogs barked and women waved. Shanaco guided the black toward a gathering of men outside a tepee. On seeing him, most of the assembled warriors nodded and smiled a greeting. A few looked at him coldly, judging him, disliking him. Most of the braves idolized him. A small minority detested him.

It had always been thus.

Shanaco dismounted, dropped the reins to the ground and joined the men. He crouched down on his heels and motioned for them to do the same. When all were crouched in a circle, Shanaco told them, in their native tongue, that he had, this very afternoon, met with the fort's commandant, Colonel Harkins. The white leader had agreed to let them keep most of their horses. A loud cheer went up from the braves.

Shanaco stayed with the men for the next hour, listening to their complaints, promising to do what he could to make things better, informing them that ration day was but a week away when they would have a big celebration with horse races and games for the children and fresh beef to be slaughtered and roasted over open fires. An event they could all look forward to enjoying. He also reminded them that the Indian agent was a good man who had their interest at heart.

When finally Shanaco rose to his feet to leave, one of the young braves who admired him pointed up at his black eye and teased him about it. The others joined in and he left them all laughing, some with him, some at him.

The sun was beginning to slip toward the western horizon when Shanaco reached the southern edge of the reservation. Near the banks of Cache Creek sat the secluded cabin that was to be his. Shanaco's eyes narrowed when he saw that the front door stood ajar.

Someone was inside.

Shanaco dismounted and moved closer. He whistled to alert the intruder.

Alone inside, barefoot and humming a song, Maggie Bankhead was gathering a muslin curtain onto a long brass rod. The sudden whistle startled her, causing her to jump. Eyes gone round, she dropped the curtain and went running to the door.

And found herself face-to-face with the feared halfbreed, Chief Shanaco. She started to step past him. He shifted and stood in her way. They stared at each other, saying nothing. It was as though time stood still.

Snared by those strange silver eyes, one of which was discolored and swollen half shut, Maggie gazed at Shanaco. He was so large and powerfully built and they were alone way out here away from anyone. Yet she felt no fear of him. She knew he wouldn't hurt her.

His raven hair was loose. It fell to his shoulders, and a stray lock rested on his high bronzed cheekbone. His nose was straight and proud. His wide, full mouth had a cruel set to it, giving his features a satanic look. Yet he was handsome, incredibly handsome. He was dressed as a white man but was the incarnation of wild savage beauty.

Maggie was fascinated.

So was Shanaco.

Shanaco stared unblinking at the slender, pale-skinned beauty whose unbound red hair was ablaze in the dying sunlight. Her vivid blue eyes were fixed on his face. He was surprised to see that there was absolutely no hint of fear shining from their indigo depths. Only healthy curiosity and frank interest. Her nose was small and cute and turned up slightly at the tip. Her mouth was full and soft-looking, the lips parted to reveal perfect white teeth. The pulse at the side of her ivory throat was beating rapidly as if she had overly exerted.

Or was overly excited.

Jolts of electricity passed between them. Both felt it. Both fought it. But not that hard.

Shanaco reached for Maggie, pushed her back inside the cottage. For a moment, Maggie struggled at arm's length to free herself. Wordlessly Shanaco reeled her in, pulled her flush against him, wrapped a long arm around her, bent her backward, lowered his head and kissed her.

Maggie involuntarily responded to the hottest, most invasive kiss she had ever known. Her weak arms hanging at her sides, head falling back, she stood unmoving in Shanaco's close embrace while that cruel-looking mouth slanted across hers, tasting, molding, persuading.

Her trembling lips opening beneath his, Maggie felt his sleek tongue immediately slide between her teeth to spread incredible fire. When his tongue touched and toyed with hers, the heat of the kiss spread far beyond their joined mouths.

At once Maggie became aware of the strong arms wrapped tightly around her, pressing her close against his tall, lean body. Her soft breasts were flattened against the hard plains of his broad chest, her nipples tightening and tingling from the intimate contact.

She couldn't help herself, she lifted a hand and tangled her fingers in his silky blue-black hair and sighed. Shanaco drew her closer, deepened the kiss and urged her arm up around his neck.

For a long, thrilling minute they stood there in the dying sunlight kissing as if they were lovers too long parted. Until finally Maggie gathered her wits, realized what they were doing, anxiously pulled away and smacked Shanaco hard across his arrogant face.

"I will do all the deciding when I wish to be kissed!" she told him heatedly.

"Then you had better stay away from my cottage," Shanaco calmly replied.

Eleven

The wolfhound hadn't barked.

It had not occurred to her at the time, but now Maggie was puzzled by the dog's mysterious silence.

Pistol was always responsive. He barked a warning anytime a stranger approached her. So why, Maggie wondered, had the faithful watchdog remained totally quiet this afternoon when Shanaco had come into the cabin?

Pistol had been just outside, lying near the front door. Yet he hadn't made a sound and had meekly allowed Shanaco to walk right past him. Had the Comanche chieftain put some kind of Indian sign on the wolfhound? Had he put some kind of hex on her as well? The fine hair rose on the nape of her neck.

Maggie shook her head and laughed. Hardly! She had yet to meet the man that could hypnotize her.

Night had now fallen over the fort. Maggie was safely back in her own cottage. She was ready for bed in a white cotton nightgown, hair brushed a hundred strokes and held back off her face with a ribbon. She sat on the floor before the dying fire, knees raised, arms wrapped around them. She stared into the flickering flames and thought back over the events of the afternoon.

She couldn't very well be angry with Pistol and not herself.

Pistol hadn't barked when Shanaco stepped inside and she hadn't uttered one word of protest when the imposing half-breed took her in his arms and kissed her. And oh, did he kiss her! She had been kissed before, of course, but *never* the way Shanaco kissed her.

Maggie raised a hand, touched her fingers to her bottom lip and involuntarily trembled. She would never have let Shanaco—or anyone else—know, but when he kissed her she had practically swooned with pleasure! Never in her life had she felt the way she had when she'd stood in Shanaco's close embrace while he passionately kissed her. The hard strength and awesome heat of his tall, lean body pressed against hers had taken her breath—and apparently her intellect—away.

She'd had to summon every ounce of the self-control she possessed to make him stop. To make herself stop. It had been so tempting to simply surrender and stay right there in his powerful arms with those masterful lips melded to hers for the rest of the afternoon. For the rest of the evening. The rest of the night.

Maggie sighed. She was being silly. Behaving like a daydreaming schoolgirl. She should never have allowed the Comanche chief to kiss her in the first place. What on earth was she thinking? She wasn't thinking, that was the problem. When she had come to her senses, she had firmly warned Shanaco that he had better leave her alone.

He said he would. She believed him, despite the gossip about him. He was, it was whispered, a danger to decent white women. A handsome but heartless savage who took what he wanted, when he wanted. A menacing primitive in white man's clothing. A charming scoundrel who was an untamed animal at heart.

There were, admittedly, enough bad stories about Shanaco to condemn him. Obviously he had already gotten into mischief here at the fort. His blackened eye was evidence of his misdeeds. And he had, without her consent, brazenly kissed her. Was she the only one? Or had he kissed others?

The fire had died. Only faint embers remained.

Maggie began to scowl, her forehead wrinkling. To her knowledge, she and Lois Harkins were presently the only unmarried females at the fort. Had the vain, flirtatious Lois met Shanaco? Had they ever been alone? If Shanaco kissed Lois the way he kissed her, would Lois make him stop? Doubtful. A troubling vision of Lois in Shanaco's arms caused Maggie to experience a sharp throb of jealousy.

Her disturbing thoughts were interrupted by the sound of the lone bugler playing the notes of tattoo, calling the troopers to sleep. It was time she was in bed herself. She shot to her feet.

Maggie snapped her fingers at the dozing Pistol. "You're in big trouble, my friend." Pistol gave her a hurt, questioning look. She smiled, patted his head and led him to the door. When he went out, she cautioned, "All right, I'll forgive you just this once. But if you see a tall handsome man with long black hair lurking around here, you bark your head off, you hear me?"

Pistol yapped his response.

Maggie laughed, closed the door, yawned and headed for the feather bed in the corner of the room. She lifted the globe on the kerosene lamp beside the bed and blew out the flame. She slipped between the covers. The nights were growing chilly and the warm blanket felt good.

Maggie snuggled down, sighed and continued to think about the mysterious man whose burning lips had so dazzled her. He was young, vigorous and brutally masculine. And his kiss had been thrilling beyond belief. But Maggie realized she had best keep the encounter—and the kiss—a secret. Tell no one. Not even Katie. The last thing she wanted to do was cause trouble for Shanaco.

Or for herself.

Maggie sighed and closed her eyes.

She fell asleep to the sound of the bugler blowing the last mournful notes of taps.

The rest of the week passed uneventfully for Maggie. She didn't see Shanaco again, although each morning when she stepped into the classroom she quickly scanned the faces, half expecting him to show up. She was relieved that he didn't. She wasn't sure how she would feel when next she saw him.

Maggie heard that he had moved into his cottage. She considered that to be a bit of good news. With a place of his own perhaps he wouldn't spend so much time in the civilian village, drinking in the back room of Jake's and inviting trouble.

By Friday afternoon Maggie had too many other things on her mind to give much thought to Shanaco.

This particular Friday was to be a very special one. All week the students had eagerly looked forward to this afternoon's promised outing, which Maggie referred to as the "poetry picnic." The event had been planned for more than a month and was often the topic of discussion among the students.

Maggie had decided that it would be beneficial for the children to begin learning and appreciating poetry. She had come up with the idea of making the learning easier for them by making it fun. And what could be more fun than a big picnic after which each child would recite a portion of a poem he or she had learned.

When Maggie had broached the subject in the classroom, all the students were instantly enthusiastic. The prospect of a picnic excited them so much they zealously agreed to learn a bit of poetry. Maggie suggested that if each would memorize at least eight lines of a poem, they would be rewarded with the outdoor feast.

All had immediately turned to her for advice and help. Help which she was delighted to give. She spent hours going through her precious leather-bound books with the children, making suggestions, helping each to choose a poem. Then patiently coaching them as they struggled to memorize a few lines.

Now at last, it was time for the poetry picnic.

It was a perfect autumn day. The lowering sun was warm and the air was clear and crisp. Birds sang musically in the treetops as if they knew that this beautiful sunny day was one of the last before the winter winds began to blow and the leaves began to fall.

With Pistol running on ahead, Maggie and her excited students walked down to the banks of Cache Creek to share a sumptuous spread that had been generously provided by the officers' wives.

The children helped Maggie spread blankets on the grassy creek banks and unpack wicker hampers filled with delicious foods. There was laughter and joy and much discussion about the poetry they had worked so hard to memorize.

After the food had been devoured and the dishes cleared away, Maggie had the group move about until they were seated in a large circle. Then she announced that it was time to begin the poetry recitations. All were eager to go first. To make it fair Maggie took a piece of paper from her satchel and wrote numbers on it. A number for each child in attendance.

With the help of two Comanche girls, she tore the paper into tiny bits, each containing a number. She gathered each numbered piece, folded them, dropped them into her straw bonnet and passed the bonnet around the circle.

"I'm number one!" cried a young Kiowa girl, and shot to her feet, eager to show what she had learned.

Maggie listened as the girl laboriously recited from a Wordsworth poem. Maggie nodded her approval, then applauded vigorously when the girl finished without missing a word. Another child—a tall, gangly Paneteka boy—came to his feet and began quoting from Ralph Waldo Emerson. The next student had chosen Keats. Another Walt Whitman. Emily Dickinson. Lord Byron. Alfred Lord Tennyson.

The recitation continued as the sun sank steadily lower. Bright Feather was the last. He had drawn the highest number. When his turn finally came, he struggled to his feet, cleared his throat and stood nervously facing the group with his hands behind his back.

The sun had now slipped completely below the horizon. Only a golden gloaming of light remained, the soft illumination giving everything a strange surreal quality, as if it were all a dream. As if *they* were all a dream.

The tiny copper-skinned Bright Feather stood in the center of that seeming illusion and started to quote from a poem by Edgar Allan Poe.

When he began to speak in his sweet, soft voice, Maggie felt her heart swell with pride and affection.

Bright Feather spoke slowly, distinctly, pausing as he struggled to recall the poem's lines, then pressing on.

"...That my days have been a dream;
Yet if hope has flown away..."

He frowned suddenly, bit his bottom lip, and repeated,

"Yet if hope has flown away..."

Again he stopped speaking. He looked pained. Maggie held her breath, hoping the last few lines would come to him. Her eyes on his anguished face, she heard the other children begin to quietly snicker and her heart ached for Bright Feather. She drew a deep breath and was about to scold the children.

The laughter abruptly stopped and an eerie silence fell over the crowd.

And out of that silence a deep baritone voice that Maggie instantly recognized softly began reciting the last lines of the beautiful Poe poem.

"In a night, or in a day,
In a vision, or in none,
Is it therefore the less gone?"

Like an apparition, he stood on a hill above, silhouetted against the last spectral glow of twilight.

Every eye turned and clung to him, and Maggie was as spellbound as the children when he recited the final lines of the poem.

> "*All* that we see or seem
> Is but a dream within a dream?"

Twelve

While Maggie had warned Shanaco that he was to leave her alone, Lois Harkins was bent on doing everything she could to get the Comanche chief's attention.

The spoiled seductress's affair with her father's married aide-de-camp was growing stale. Lois was bored with Lieutenant Wilde. She needed a new lover. Someone handsome and thrilling and forceful.

And forbidden.

Shanaco.

The Eagle.

From the moment he had ridden onto the fort, Lois had daydreamed of lying naked beneath the handsome half-breed. She could imagine the kind of wild, animal loving he would provide. The prospect of such a taboo tryst had her plotting and planning before she'd stepped down off the review stand that sunny October morning.

Shanaco didn't know it, but he was no longer the hunter, she was. She was the huntress, he was the prey. And she fully intended to snare him in her trap. Once he was caught, they could change places. She'd be his helpless captive, he her vengeful captor. What exciting possibilities that fantasy conjured up.

Lois grew more impatient with each passing day. Shanaco had been at the fort for more than two weeks and she had yet to meet him. Apparently it wasn't going to be as easy to instigate an affair with the Comanche chieftain as it had been with Lieutenant Wilde. Wilde was right there under her nose and all she'd had to do was reach out and take him.

But how, she wondered, could she possibly gain access to Shanaco? She knew they intended to provide him with a private cabin, but the last she had heard he was still billeted in a barracks with the troopers. As far as she knew he slept there every night.

In the daytime he was out on the reservation with his People. Or with Double Jimmy and her father.

Or in the civilian village.

Impatient to get her hands on him, Lois decided to start spending her afternoons in the village. Perhaps she would run into him. She could do that without arousing suspicions. Should anyone ask, she could claim she was shopping.

Lois dressed in her finest and sauntered up and down the wooden sidewalks. No luck on the first day. Or the second. But her heart began to pound when finally, after three fruitless afternoons, the object of her desire walked out of Jake's card parlor and headed down the wooden sidewalk. Coming in her direction.

Lois drew a shallow breath, reached out and grabbed the colorful barber pole for support. She stood there waiting, her blond hair gleaming in the sunlight, her pretty face glowing with good health. She was totally confident of her feminine allure. Certain that Shanaco would take one look and instantly desire her.

She saw that today he was dressed as a white man in a cotton shirt and snug twill trousers. But he looked just as handsome, just as menacing as he had when he'd worn nothing but a skimpy breechcloth. He moved with an easy, fluid grace and effortlessly exuded a strong masculine self-confidence. Just looking at him made Lois tingle from head to toe.

He was almost to her. She wet her lips, thrust out her chest and bent a knee forward. Shanaco glanced at her. She smiled coquettishly and lowered her lashes. Then blinked in surprise when he dismissed her with a cold, impersonal nod. He never slowed. Walked right past her.

Lois was stunned. Absolutely incredulous. She couldn't believe it. Was the Comanche blind? Did Indians have a different standard of beauty than their white counterparts? Did he not yearn to hold her in his arms? Such an obvious snub from a male had never happened to her before.

Shaken, Lois stared after him, wanting him more than ever, insulted but fascinated. She was intrigued by the catlike way he moved. And by the way his white shirt stretched across his wide, powerful shoulders. And especially with the way his tight twill trousers hung so appealingly on his slim hips.

Lois sighed and bit her lip in disappointment. She had assumed that the minute he saw her he'd want her. Well, he *would* want her, she was determined that he would. She had only to get him alone. Once she'd accomplished that she knew what to do with him. To him. She'd let him feel her burning touch on his nakedness and arouse him so completely she would take his breath away.

But damn him, she hated to wait. She wanted him now. This afternoon.

Seething, Lois angrily headed back to the quarters she shared with her father. In her room, she shed her saucy hat, kid gloves and light woolen wrap, tossing all on the floor. She climbed onto the feather bed, stretched out on her stomach and beat the mattress with her small fists, cursing the indifferent Shanaco.

She had to come up with a foolproof scheme wherein she and the imperious half-breed would be thrown together and…and… Lois began to smile like the cat that got the cream. The annual officers' ball!

To show his respect for Shanaco's position as leader of his People, the post commandant—her father—should invite the chieftain to the ball as the honored guest.

Lois turned over onto her back and giggled happily. She would put a bug in her father's ear that very evening. She'd insist he should invite Shanaco to the ball. Shanaco would feel obligated to attend.

The officers' snooty wives would shun him, of course, but she wouldn't. She would make him feel welcome, would offer him a glass of punch. Would dance with him. And once she had him on the dance floor, she would work her magic.

Lois smiled, pleased with herself. By the end of the dance the haughty half-breed would be so hot for her he wouldn't say no to anything she proposed. She'd work him up into a lather and then carefully whisper to him where he was to meet her later that night.

The smile left Lois's face as quickly as it had come. She sighed heavily. The officers' ball was two weeks from tomorrow night. How could she ever wait that long to be in Shanaco's arms?

She fretted and frowned until she remembered. Tomorrow was ration day! Lois sat straight up and her eyes began to gleam. She wouldn't have to wait for the officers' ball to see Shanaco. He was a Comanche chieftain. He would definitely be present at ration day.

She fell onto her back laughing happily. He'd be there and he would be dressed in that skimpy little breechcloth that covered nothing but his groin.

Thirteen

On ration day the entire population of the fort turned out for the fun and festivities. Ration day took place every fortnight and was always on a Saturday. For whites and Indians alike it was a day-long carnival and an occasion not to be missed.

All the tribes came into the agency from their scattered, far-out settlements. In tepees all across the huge reservation, the People awakened with the dawn. Excited. Eager to get dressed and to go to the agency. Indian braves, squaws and children rode in under the watchful eye of armed troopers.

The cavalcade began in the early morning. Long columns came in a steady stream from the furthermost reaches of the preserve. Well before noon everyone had arrived and the fun and merriment had begun.

This particular Saturday was a perfect fall day. A chill to the air, but a bright sun shone down from a cloudless indigo sky.

Maggie attended, as she did each fortnight. Regretfully she had to make Pistol stay behind at the cottage. She hated to do it, but she had taken him to ration day once and he had worn her out. When he'd seen the Indian children running about with their dogs, he had chased anxiously after them, barking incessantly and darting away from her. So now he had to stay home.

Maggie went with Katie Atwood, since Katie's husband, Blakely, was away from the fort on patrol.

Dressed in light woolens, Katie carrying a wicker picnic basket and Maggie, a blanket, the two young women walked freely among the Indians, laughing and talking as they made their way among the men. The onetime warriors were dressed in buckskin shirts, leggings and moccasins. Some sported pipe-stem bone breastplates, others had bright-colored bandannas knotted around their necks. Their thick black hair was smoothed back with grease and neatly braided down each coppery cheek.

Most of the men were standing about, talking and gesturing. Others were crouched on the ground in circles, gambling. Some played cards, others tossed dice. They had quickly learned such vices from the white men. Maggie clucked her tongue. Too bad they couldn't learn to read and write as quickly as they had learned to wager on games of chance.

The excited gamblers shouted and argued and slapped one another on the back. Hearing the Comanche tongue being spoken, Maggie looked curiously around.

She didn't see Shanaco.

She mentally shrugged. Since he seemed to have little interest in showing support for his People, he probably wouldn't bother coming out today. An omission for which he should be ashamed of himself. If there was ever an occasion when the Comanche leader should be present, it was on ration day.

And, furthermore, he should be there dressed as a Comanche, not a white man!

Maggie and Katie waded on through the throngs of Indian men. They reached a row of makeshift booths that were manned by officers' wives. The good-hearted ladies were giving away cakes, cookies and candy to the Indians and soldiers alike. Maggie had made a cake for the event, but had ended up leaving it at the cottage. Her culinary efforts left a great deal to be desired. When she'd shown the lopsided cake to Pistol, he had given her a sad, pitying look. So she'd donated fresh fruit instead.

Maggie smiled now when she caught sight of the shy Bright Feather, standing before a booth, several feet back, gazing yearningly at a big glass jar filled with peppermint sticks.

Without a word to Katie, Maggie hurried toward him. Katie saw the child and followed. When Maggie reached Bright Feather and greeted him, he smiled that heart-tugging smile of his.

She asked, "Would you like a peppermint stick?" His smile grew broader and his big dark eyes flashed. She said, "Practice your English. Ask the nice lady if you may have a peppermint stick."

Bright Feather limped forward. He reached the booth. He was so little his face was on the level of the plank board where the candy jar sat. He peered over it at a tall, rawboned woman with graying hair and asked politely, "May I have a peppermint stick, ma'am?"

Margaret Tullison laughed, reached out, ruffled his hair and said, "You sure can, darlin'!" She reached in the jar, took out two sticks and handed both to him. He took them and stood there with a peppermint stick in each hand, so pleased with his good fortune he was speechless.

"Remember what you say when someone gives you something," Maggie prompted.

"Thank you very much," Bright Feather said to Margaret Tullison.

"You're mighty welcome," she said. Then added, "Tell you what, if you eat those up and want another, you come right back over here."

"Bright Feather" came the soft voice of the Kiowa woman he lived with. Morning Sun was the patient, motherly, middle-aged widow who was raising Bright Feather and five other orphans. Those five were with her now. She gently scolded Bright Feather in their native tongue. "You must not wander away from me. You could get lost in the crowd. Now come."

He nodded, but proudly held up his peppermint sticks. Margaret Tullison was already lifting the glass top from the big jar, taking out candy for the other five children. Maggie acknowledged Morning Sun and bid Bright Feather goodbye.

Turning to Margaret Tullison, she said, "We'll be back to relieve you at three o'clock."

"Good enough," said Margaret.

"We better start looking in earnest for a place to spread the blanket," Katie said.

"Yes, I agree."

They had volunteered to help out by manning one of the booths from three o'clock until six. Until that time, they were free and they wanted to find just the right spot. A place where they wouldn't miss anything and could most enjoy the festivities.

"What about over there close to the main agency building?" Katie suggested, pointing. "That's where all the rations will be distributed, so most of the activity should take place around there."

Maggie nodded but declined. If they settled in near the agency buildings, they would see only the Indian women and children.

"Wouldn't you rather go on out beyond the buildings to the pasture where they'll race the horses this afternoon?" Maggie asked. "That's where most everyone goes, and if we're not there early, we won't get a front-row spot."

"Well, all right," Katie was agreeable. "We can eat our picnic lunch before they start running their horses and kicking up dirt."

"Of course. Let's go now and…and… Wait, I see Double Jimmy. Let's say hello."

The ruddy-faced, white-haired Double Jimmy stood beside one of the big, heavily loaded agency wagons.

In the crook of his arm was a tiny Indian baby and at his side was the infant's proud young mother. Double Jimmy was making silly faces at the baby and teasing the mother. The baby was cooing. The mother was beaming and laughing.

The travois ponies were lined up close to the large wagons from which the rations and clothing would be distributed. The Indian women stood about waiting, visiting, talking together, showing off their new babies and discussing the big meal they would have once they were issued their supply of fresh beef.

Double Jimmy looked up and saw Maggie and Katie coming toward him. He waved them forward, gave the squirming baby a kiss on the forehead and handed it back to its mother.

"You two lovely young ladies gonna help us hand out supplies?" he asked, giving both a hug when they reached him.

"I suppose we could," Maggie said with a smile. But she hoped it wouldn't be necessary. She didn't want to stay here. She wanted to watch the horse races.

"Naw," said Double Jimmy. "Not necessary. I was just teasing you." He raised his white eyebrows at Maggie. "I figure I know where you'll spend most of the afternoon."

Maggie playfully punched him on the shoulder. "You think you know everything, don't you?"

"This much I know. When the horse racing starts,

you'll be there cheering 'em on or my name's not James W. James."

Maggie laughed. "You know me too well." And he did. Over the years, Maggie's father had owned many sleek Thoroughbreds. Maggie had learned to love horses and horse racing from the time she was a toddler. "You coming out there?"

Double Jimmy shook his head. "Got my hands pretty full right here."

"Don't you have several hands to help you?" asked Katie, looking about for his assistants.

"Of course he does," Maggie answered for him. Then to him, "When are you going to quit working so hard? Let the others handle some of the tasks?"

"What? You mean this agency could operate without me?" he said with mock horror. "Well, I'll be switched!"

The women laughed. Maggie said, "This agency could *never* do without you and neither could I. Come for supper some night soon?"

"Just tell me when."

"Make it a week from Tuesday."

"I'll be there," said Double Jimmy. He made a face then and said, "You're not meaning to try your hand at biscuit-making again, are you, child?"

"I promise not to," she said, and laughed at herself. The last batch of biscuits she had made had been a disaster. Didn't rise at all, were burned nearly black and were as hard as rocks. "Pistol and I are still playing toss and fetch with the last ones I made."

Fourteen

"My goodness, I'm so full I need a nap," Katie said an hour later.

"I know what you mean," Maggie agreed with a yawn.

They had found the ideal spot for their picnic lunch. A long line of live oaks grew at the edge of a broad, grass-covered pasture. They had spread the blanket in the shade of a big oak. There they had an unobstructed view of the pasture where the horse racing would take place.

Full and drowsy from their lunch, Maggie and Katie now watched with lazy interest as the Indians began bringing their prized horses onto the straightaway track. The race would be a quarter of a mile. A lightning-fast sprint. The horses would thunder directly past them.

Maggie sat leaning back on stiffened arms, legs stretched out before her, feet crossed at the ankles. Her head felt heavy. So did her eyelids. She idly wondered why she had been so all-fired keen to come out here and spend the afternoon. Right now she'd much prefer being back at her cottage, where she could climb up onto her soft feather bed and sleep for an hour or two.

She was about to suggest that they leave when she looked up and almost lost her breath. Shanaco was coming onto the track, leading his shiny black stallion.

"There he is!" exclaimed Katie in a stage whisper.

"Who?" Maggie pretended ignorance.

"You know very well who," Katie said. "The chief of the Comanches. The Eagle. Shanaco. The rebellious half-breed everyone's talking about." She paused then, shaded her eyes with a hand and added, "Lord, he *is* good-looking, isn't he?"

Maggie shrugged slender shoulders. "I suppose."

Katie chattered on, but Maggie didn't hear a word she said. Her full attention was focused on Shanaco.

The tall, handsome chieftain wore fringed, tight-fitting leggings and soft moccasins. But no shirt. His broad, coppery chest was bare, and it must have been lightly greased because it gleamed in the bright sunshine. A scarlet bandanna was knotted at his throat, and a wide copper band was wrapped around his right biceps. His raven hair hung loose around his shoulders; his scalp lock was adorned with red ribbon and tiny silver bells.

He turned abruptly, the movement exposing his beautiful, deeply clefted back as well as the gentle curve of his lean buttocks and long, muscular legs. If ever a man looked good bare chested and in a pair of tight buckskin leggings, it was Shanaco.

He turned back around and he was smiling broadly. It was, Maggie realized, the first time she had ever seen him smile. Really smile. She was amazed at how it softened his stark, sharply cut features. She wished she was closer so she could see his metallic eyes twinkle with that radiant smile.

Maggie quietly ground her teeth when a cluster of young men crowded around the smiling Shanaco, partially blocking her view. He was taller than the others, so she could still see his dark head, but not his lean, powerful body.

"...and I'd bet my bottom dollar she will," Katie was saying.

"What? I...I'm sorry." Maggie reluctantly turned to look at her friend.

"I said, 'Look down there at the far end of the pasture. Right near the finish line. Lois Harkins, all gussied-up, seated queenly in a parked buggy. She's staring at Chief Shanaco as if he were some tempting dessert.'" Katie leaned closer to Maggie and whispered, "Think she'll try to get The Eagle in her bed?"

"Katie Helen Atwood!" Maggie exclaimed under her breath.

Whispering still, Katie said, "Mark my words. If what you told me about her is true, and I have no reason to doubt it, then what would stop her from going after an exquisite masculine prize like Shanaco?"

Maggie exhaled with irritation. "For one thing, she won't get the opportunity."

"Women like Lois make their own opportunities, you know that. She'll find a way to meet him. And then..."

Over my dead body. "What if she does? Who cares? The races are about to start. Let's watch."

Along the sidelines, whites and Indians alike were making bets. The Indians had little with which to wager. No money. Only small keepsakes and articles saved from their old way of life, things that were valuable to them and no one else. The troopers bet money they had saved from their meager wages. There was much laughing and shouting as the betting grew fierce.

Maggie glanced again at the track. Riders were now mounted and exercising their horses. Trotting them up and down the straightaway. She glanced again at Shanaco. He was not yet mounted. He stood beside the nickering coal-black stallion, rubbing the creature's sleek neck and whispering into its pricked ear. Finally he climbed astride the pony's bare back with the easy grace of an acrobat.

He put the black into a canter, then kneed him into a gallop. The stallion stood out from the crowded field, just as his rider did. Watching, Maggie frowned suddenly. This race was unfair. The other Indian ponies didn't have much of a chance against Shanaco's magnificent black. She knew enough about horses to recognize that the stallion was a superior creature. Perfectly configured and bred for speed and stamina.

And while most everyone had turned out specifically to see Shanaco race the mighty stallion, she found it less than noble of him to enter the race knowing he would be the sure winner. He was supposed to be the leader of his People, the one they looked to for guidance, the chief who put aside his own ego so that they might glean the glory.

Selfish, selfish man!

Maggie was shaken from her reverie by the sound of the bugler blowing a warning to the riders to return to the starting line and take their places. The contestants called to one another, laughed and trotted toward the start line. The last one to move into place was Shanaco and the black.

Fourteen riders and their mounts had filed into position behind a chalked line. The nervous horses snorted and stomped the ground. One reared up, almost unseating his rider. Shouts and whistles came from the sidelines. Everyone, including Maggie and Katie, were now on their feet.

A uniformed trooper stepped up to the line and raised his .45 Colt pistol. The anxious riders hunkered down close to their mounts' necks, moccasined feet poised to slam into the beasts' bellies. Maggie stared directly at Shanaco. He wasn't moving a muscle. Wasn't leaning forward. Wasn't hunkered down. His moccasined feet were not raised or poised. He was seated astride the stock-still stallion with his back regally straight and his right hand loose on the reins.

The trooper fired his Colt into the air.

The horses shot away.

The black easily moved to the front of the pack. The others galloped after him. Maggie bit her bottom lip. She knew the outcome already. Shanaco was going to win. The others didn't stand a chance.

The race was half over. A young Comanche riding a small, speedy paint was gaining on Shanaco. A couple of lengths back, a little wiry mustang was laboring hard to catch up. Behind the three front-runners raced the thundering herd.

Nearing the finish line of the fast quarter mile, Shanaco and the black were a neck ahead and bragging bettors were already counting their winnings.

But just as the race was about to end, Maggie saw Shanaco loosen his hand ever so slightly on the reins in a silent signal to his mount. The black changed strides, fell back just a hair, and the paint shot ahead, crossing the finish line first.

There were groans all around from puzzled bettors.

Maggie wasn't puzzled.

She knew a great deal about horses and even more about riders. Shanaco had purposely lost the race to his young tribesman. Maggie felt her heart throb in her chest. Although she'd chosen to forget, this was not the first time she'd witnessed the supposedly cold, uncaring Shanaco make a truly admirable gesture. Apparently there was *some* good to the man.

Maggie was thoughtful as she watched the laughing chieftain congratulating the race's proud young winner. Shanaco warmly embraced the shorter, younger man and Maggie caught herself smiling her approval.

A fresh batch of horses were already lining up for the start of another race. A horse and rider could enter only one race. The contestants in the first were finished for the day. Now it was the Paneteka tribe's turn. After them, the Kiowas. But Maggie found that she was no longer terribly interested in the races.

From beneath lowered lashes she watched as Shanaco led the black off the track.

She involuntarily stiffened when she saw the simpering Lois hastily alight from her carriage and step directly into Shanaco's path.

He stopped. He towered over Lois.

Lois was tipping her head back, looking up at him, and asking him something. Shanaco nodded, then stepped around her. Maggie saw Lois watch him walk away. And she was smiling as if pleased.

Maggie quietly fumed.

Fifteen

Three o'clock that afternoon.

Maggie and Katie now manned the booth vacated by Margaret Tullison. The foot traffic had thinned out considerably. They knew the reason. The horse races had ended and the rations were being issued over behind the agency buildings. Double Jimmy and three of his helpers had set up folding tables directly in front of the loaded wagons.

The Indian women had patiently lined up to collect their share of badly needed supplies. Coffee and sugar and corn and salt and soap and clothing for their families. The laughing women packed the allotted treasures on the travois horses. They were eager to get over to the large holding pens where the beef would be distributed.

The beef issue was the climax of every ration day. The cattle were given to the Indians on the hoof, making it great sport for everyone. Just as they had for the horse races, the Indians crowded around, cheering and waving as a soldier or agency employee released the cattle, one at a time, into a huge pen.

As the frightened steer bolted across the corral, a

mounted brave with quiver and arrow would race after the startled creature, taking aim, releasing an arrow, pretending he was still out on the open plains hunting buffalo.

After the cattle were slain, the Indians made quick work of skinning their kill. Once that was done, the women finished the butchering and hauled the fresh meat away. While their men stayed behind to watch the rest of the slaughtering, the women headed home to start preparing the big feasts.

Steaks and roasts and ribs would be cooking over blazing fires when the men returned. The joyful feasting would go on until well past midnight, and the People, young and old alike, would go to bed with full bellies for a change.

At their booth on the parade ground, Maggie and Katie could hear the shouts and laughter coming from the pens where the beef was being issued. Maggie wondered if Shanaco was out there, joining in the merriment.

She didn't have to wonder long.

She got up out of the folding chair in which she had been sitting, leaned her elbows on the booth's plank counter and glanced at the sparse crowd milling up and down the quadrangle.

Shanaco was approaching.

He was walking slowly because Old Coyote was at his side. The aged chief was saying something to Shanaco, gesturing with his hands, likely telling a tall tale. When Coyote finished speaking, Shanaco threw back his head and laughed. Maggie found herself smiling foolishly.

She caught herself, stopped, straightened and crossed her arms over her chest. And felt her knees go weak when Coyote pointed directly at her. Shanaco nodded, took the old chief's arm and propelled him toward the booth.

"Is he coming over here?" Katie Atwood asked, rising to stand beside Maggie.

"He is," Maggie replied, hoping she sounded casual.

Old Coyote was smiling as he made his slow, sure way toward the booth. "Miss Maggie," he said when he reached her, "so happy you still here. Need your help."

"You have it," she assured him, and reaching out, took his hand and squeezed it. Then said, "Chief Coyote, you know Katie Atwood, I believe."

The old Kiowa looked puzzled but nodded to Katie, then addressed Maggie. "You know Chief Shanaco?"

"Why, yes, I...yes," Maggie said, and finally looked up at the tall Comanche. With a slight shake of her head, she said, "Shanaco, this is my good friend, Mrs. Katie Atwood. Katie, Chief Shanaco."

"Nice to meet you," he said politely, and the overwhelmed Katie could only nod. His gaze quickly returned to Maggie. "We have this minor problem and the chief tells me you can help us solve it."

"I'll certainly try," said Maggie.

"Have done it again, Miss Maggie," Old Coyote said, sheepish. "Cannot remember where I live. You know?"

"Yes, I do," she said, and smiled kindly at him.

It wasn't the first time the old chief had forgotten where he lived. Several times Maggie had had to escort him to his tepee because he couldn't recall exactly where it was. His was the tepee nearest to the fort and agency buildings, so it was no trouble to walk him home when he was lost.

"Could we impose on you to show us?" Shanaco said in a deep, well-modulated voice.

"Well, I could just tell you where—"

"Show us," said Shanaco. It was more command than request.

"Go on, go with them," prompted Katie. "I can hold things down here while you're gone."

Maggie was trapped. "All right, then." To Katie, she said, "I'll be back in fifteen minutes."

"Take as long as you need," Katie replied.

Maggie released Coyote's hand, ducked under the makeshift counter, rose and took his arm. "We'll see you home, Coyote."

The trio walked slowly up the parade ground past the many booths and officers' quarters. Soon they left the buildings behind. At Maggie's direction, they turned due west just beyond the fort. Within minutes they reached the eastern border of the Kiowa reservation. Coyote's tepee was right on the line.

"Here we are," Maggie said, pointing to the conical, buffalo-hide covered dwelling.

"You sure?" asked Old Coyote. "This where I live?"

"It is. Shall I go inside with you and make sure?"

"Please," he said. He looked up at Shanaco. "I see you later. Thank you."

Shanaco nodded and held the tepee's flap open while Maggie stooped and ducked inside. The old chief followed. Shanaco stayed outside.

"See, this is your home. These are your things," Maggie said. "Look around. This is home."

Coyote's eyes lighted and he nodded when he saw his clay pipe, his fur-covered pallet, his meager personal possessions. "Yes, is my home. I live here."

"Now that you remember where it is, do you want to stay? Or shall I take you farther out onto the reservation where your People will be having their big feast in a couple of hours?"

"I stay here for now, take nap. Will go to feast later," he said. "Young men from tribe promise to come get me when feasting starts."

"Then I'll leave you to get some rest," she said.

"Thank you, Miss Maggie," he said, and clumsily patted her back.

"You're very welcome, Chief."

Maggie left him, ducked back outside and was half surprised to find herself standing face-to-face with Shanaco.

"Still here?" she said with a shake of her head, as

if annoyed. "No need for you to walk me back to the fort. While I appreciate the gesture, I need no escort. I'm perfectly capable of returning alone."

Shanaco stared at her, the slightest hint of mischief appearing in his silver eyes. "You, Miss Bankhead, are a touch too presumptuous."

Maggie frowned. "I beg your pardon?"

"I've no intention of walking you back."

Without another word he turned and strolled away, leaving Maggie puzzled and put out. The man was truly exasperating. He *never* behaved as expected.

Sixteen

Weeks prior to the officers' ball, the ladies began planning what they would wear for the momentous occasion.

Katie Atwood and Maggie were no exception. The ball was an annual event to which everyone looked eagerly forward. Especially the females. Life at the frontier fort was often hard, lonely and monotonous. There were no luxuries. No theaters, no restaurants, no museums. No indulgent families and childhood friends. The officers' wives were often bored and homesick, eager for any distraction.

A child of privilege, Maggie had several lovely ball gowns that had never been worn. She had realized, shortly after arriving at Fort Sill, that she'd have no need for such finery here.

This year's officers' ball would be her first opportunity to wear one of the stylish gowns. A generous person, she insisted that Katie choose one.

"I couldn't," Katie weakly protested.

"Of course you can," Maggie persisted, and Katie had hugged her and eagerly looked through the array of beautiful gowns.

Now, on the evening of the ball, Maggie was alone in her cottage, preparing for the gala. The dress she'd chosen, a lush lilac velvet with high banded collar, tight long sleeves and full skirts, lay spread out on her bed. Next to the dress was a pair of sheer silk stockings and soft kid dancing slippers.

Earlier in the afternoon she had carefully washed her hair, using the last of her scented shampoo. Dusk was falling and she was hurrying to get ready. Sensing her excitement, Pistol anxiously followed her around, barking, wanting to know what was going on.

"Pistol, will you please lie down and leave me alone," Maggie finally scolded. "I am trying to get ready for the ball."

The dog's ears shot forward and he stared at her.

"I want to look my best," she explained softly. "You see, Shanaco will be there and...and..." Maggie stopped speaking, shook her head, dismayed. She couldn't believe what she had just said. But it was true. It was foolish she knew, but she was undeniably excited by the prospect of seeing Shanaco tonight. Each time she saw him she felt a thrill unlike any she'd ever experienced.

Maggie laughed abruptly and assured herself she would soon get over this outlandish schoolgirl crush. There was nothing complex or worrisome about the situation. It was easily explained. She was attracted because Shanaco came from a very different world from hers. He was unlike any man she'd ever known, therefore mysterious and compelling.

Maggie shrugged bare shoulders, dismissing Shanaco from her thoughts. He would be gone from the reservation no later than Thanksgiving. Double Jimmy had told her that the half-breed chief was anxious to leave.

Maggie trembled. She had better get dressed.

Wearing a satin chemise and lace-trimmed underwear, she stood before a framed mirror mounted atop the fireplace. Bottom lip caught between her teeth, she painstakingly dressed the clean red tresses atop her head. When finally she was finished with the laborious task, she frowned at herself. She had never quite gotten the hang of fixing her own hair.

Maggie sighed heavily, yanked the decorative pins from her hair, and let it cascade down over her bare shoulders and around her cheeks. She turned around, hurried to the tall bureau and picked up an oyster-shell comb. She smoothed the heavy hair back off her forehead and secured it with the comb. She returned to the mirror and looked at herself. Again, she made a face. She should have accepted Katie's offer to dress her hair.

Maggie shrugged. Too late now. Dave Finley would be knocking on the door any minute. Maggie rushed to the bed, yanked up the stockings and shoes and crossed to the armless rocker before the fireplace. She sat down and began to hum as she drew on the sheer stockings.

Across the quadrangle, in the private quarters she shared with her father, a totally naked Lois Harkins was in her room. She was also pulling on a pair of sheer silk stockings. She smiled with anticipation as she playfully snapped the saucy satin garter just above her left knee.

Lois sighed, sank lazily back in the easy chair and lifted her flowing blond hair up atop her head. She stretched her stockinged leg out and admired the shapely calf and slender ankle. She would, she felt certain, be the most beautiful woman at the ball.

Lois shivered deliciously.

This was to be the night she would finally get to officially meet the handsome half-breed, Shanaco. Lois laughed gaily as she recalled how easy it had been to convince her father that he simply had to invite the Comanche leader to the ball.

Days after Shanaco's arrival at the fort, she had, after waiting for just the right moment, teased and flattered her father, and finally said, "Father, as the fort commandant, you must show your respect for Chief Shanaco's position as leader of his People."

"Why, I do show my respect and—"

"Invite him to the officers' ball. Invite him as the honored guest."

"Well, now, I don't know if he would want to come and—"

"You'll insist he attend."

"I will?"

"Yes, as the honored guest."

"I suppose it would be the polite thing to do."

"Absolutely," she'd said, and kissed his cheek.

Now, lounging here naked before the flickering fire, Lois was pleased that her plan had worked so well. On ration day she had stopped Shanaco after the races and told him about the ball. Promised him that he would be invited. She had kept that promise. Her guileless father hardly realized that the idea to invite Shanaco had been hers. He now thought it was his and she made it a point to praise him for being so clever and thoughtful.

The groundwork had been carefully laid. Now she would take over. In less than an hour she would be face-to-face with the chief. She would be formally introduced as the fort commandant's daughter. That's all she needed. She would take it from there. She could hardly wait to get her hands on the Comanche chieftain. Tonight was her opportunity to begin the seduction.

The half-breed would easily succumb to her charms. How could he not?

"Lois, dear, are you dressed?" Her father's voice came through the closed door. "It's time we go."

Lois stayed where she was. "Almost ready, Father."

She smiled wickedly as she lifted a hand to her pale right breast. She plucked at the nipple, coaxing it into a pebble-hard point. She repeated the exercise on her left nipple. As she worked at it, she frowned with frustration.

She wished she had some ice. Back East when she

was going out for the evening, she always brought a glass of ice to her room and rubbed the ice on her nipples just before dressing. She liked the way the cold made her nipples rigid, made them stand out visibly against her tight bodice. Men liked it too. She'd seen them gaze at her bosom with barely disguised hunger.

She wanted the handsome Shanaco to look at her like that. Damn this backward frontier settlement where a lady couldn't get her hands on a bucket of ice.

Continuing to urge her nipples into firm points, Lois rose from the chair. She stepped over to the bed and reluctantly picked up her lacy underwear. She'd much prefer wearing nothing at all under the ball gown, but it was rather chilly outdoors. She stepped into the underwear and then drew the blue satin ball gown over her head and let it fall down her warm body. She positioned the low-cut bodice down as far as she could and smoothed the shimmering fabric snug against her full breasts. "Ah, yes," she said aloud as she looked down and saw that her nipples were pressing provocatively against the shimmering blue satin. She would, if need be, once she was at the ball, excuse herself, duck into a cloakroom or somewhere, and tease the nipples back into titillating tips no man could miss. Especially not Shanaco.

"Father," she called, "could you give me a hand, please?"

"Aren't you ready yet, child? Come on out here."

Lois swept out of the room, hurriedly turned her back and ordered, "Fasten those hooks down my dress, Father."

The colonel frowned. "Your back's bare. Where's your chemise, Lois?"

"Couldn't wear one under this gown, Father. Hurry, please. We don't want to be late."

Colonel Harkins shook his head with resignation and hastily fastened the dress. "Now, Lois, you behave yourself this evening, you hear me?"

"Why, Father, don't I always?"

Seventeen

A hush fell over the crowd as everyone turned to stare.

Shanaco walked through the door and paused just inside the entrance.

The Comanche chieftain was dressed like a white man in dark, well-cut evening clothes, snowy white shirt and black silk cravat. His black leather shoes were neatly polished and his long raven hair was tied back off his cleanly shaven face. He was well groomed and as handsomely dressed as any cultured, aristocratic gentleman. A patrician prince of the Plains. Handsome, aloof and noble.

Yet as he stood there unmoving, allowing the curious crowd to examine him, there was about him a definite wildness, a barely leashed intensity that made men nervous and frightened ladies. An appearance of cold hostility. He was young, vigorous and brutally masculine. Hard, lean and ruthless. A murderous Comanche warrior underneath the white man's clothes.

Shanaco was unbothered by the crowd's curiosity. He was used to making people uneasy. When he walked through the fort or down the sidewalks of the civilian village, people watched him as he passed. He could feel them watching him. He took perverse pleasure from making the whites jittery.

Still, this dance was the last place on earth he wanted to be. He would stay only long enough to pay his respects to the fort commandant, then he'd duck out and head to Jake's card parlor.

Devoid of expression, Shanaco looked around the room. But when he spotted Maggie Bankhead's flaming hair, he felt a quick surge of unexpected pleasure. His first impulse was to go to her, smile at her, talk to her. He took a step forward, then stopped himself.

"Chief," said the approaching fort commandant, his hand extended, "welcome. Welcome to the officers' ball. So glad you could make it this evening."

"Thank you, sir." Shanaco shook the offered hand.

Colonel Harkins slapped him on the back. "Come, I want to introduce you to my daughter."

The grand ballroom was actually a fort warehouse that had been emptied and then carefully decorated for the occasion. The floor had been waxed and polished to a high sheen. Low burning gaslights cast a soft illumination over the spacious hall. Boughs of freshly cut cedar tied with bright ribbons sweetened the air.

At one end of the dance floor was a long table covered in white linen. On that table were dishes of tempting foods and bottles of brandy and wine and champagne that were being chilled in buckets of cold water.

At the opposite end of the room a small hired orchestra played. The six-piece ensemble consisted of two fiddles, a coronet, a piano, a bass and a violin. Dressed in evening garb, the talented group had come over from Lawton to play for the dance.

Shortly after eight o'clock the room had begun to fill with smartly uniformed officers and their well-turned-out wives. Greetings were exchanged and gossip was shared. Most of the whispers concerned the arrival of the ball's guest of honor.

Shanaco.

By half past eight the dance floor was filled with dancers and laughter rang out as couples spun about in a waltz. On the sidelines Maggie stood beside Dave Finley, making conversation, observing the dancers. She smiled when she saw Katie and Blakely Atwood coming toward them.

Katie and Maggie hugged while Blake Atwood and Dave shook hands. The women nodded yes when Blake asked if they'd like champagne.

"Stay here, I'll get you ladies a glass," Blake said.

"I'll go with you," Dave said.

Once the men walked away, Katie whispered to Maggie, "Can you believe Shanaco actually showed up? I mean, why would he want to come to the officers' ball?"

"I doubt he wanted to come, but Dave said Colonel Harkins insisted. Said the colonel told Shanaco he was to be tonight's honored guest and that he should at least put in a brief appearance."

"All the same, I'm surprised and...and..." Katie paused, grabbed Maggie's arm. "Maggie, Shanaco's looking straight at you!"

"Don't be absurd," Maggie replied, then smiled at Dave Finley as he and Blake Atwood returned.

Shanaco cast one last appreciative glance in Maggie's direction. She looked particularly pretty in a high-necked lilac velvet dress. Her glorious hair was spilling down around her shoulders and Shanaco imagined those silky tresses falling across his bare chest.

She turned to accept a glass of champagne from her escort. She was smiling up at the officer. Shanaco turned away, allowed his host to guide him through the crowd. They were heading directly toward the bold blonde who had intercepted him at the horse track on ration day.

She had stepped out of a carriage and into his way, stopping him. She had introduced herself and told him that her father wanted him to come to the officers' ball. Said she would be there and looked forward to seeing him.

She was now flanked by two officers. One was the elderly, distinguished Major Miles Courteen, whom Shanaco had met at the meeting with Harkins and Double Jimmy. The other, a young sandy-haired man of medium height and build, was scowling.

''Chief Shanaco, I'd like you to meet my only daughter, Lois.''

Dimpling while she looked directly into his cold silver eyes, Lois did not mention that they had met before. She lifted her hand to be kissed. Shanaco shook it instead, then quickly released it.

He bowed slightly, ''Miss Harkins.''

''Chief Shanaco, I'm very pleased to meet you,'' said Lois sweetly. ''I do hope you'll save at least one dance for me.''

Shanaco gave no reply. He could tell by the way she was looking at him that she wanted more than a dance.

''You remember Major Miles Courteen,'' said Colonel Harkins.

''Yes, of course. Nice to see you again, sir,'' Shanaco said, and shook Major Courteen's hand.

''Happy you could make it this evening,'' Courteen replied with a friendly smile.

''The major has spent the past couple of days in the regimental hospital,'' Colonel Harkins commented. ''Just released yesterday.''

''Sorry to hear that, Major,'' said Shanaco. ''I hope you're feeling better.''

''Yes, yes, I'm fine,'' Major Courteen assured him, but he looked wan and drawn.

''And this young man is my trusted aide-de-camp, Captain Daniel Wilde,'' the colonel said, directing Shanaco's attention to the sandy-haired officer at Lois's side.

"Captain Wilde," Shanaco acknowledged.

Daniel Wilde nodded but said nothing, and his eyes flashed with hatred.

"Excuse me, Miss Harkins," Shanaco said as her father led him away for more introductions.

Her brows knitted, Lois looked after Shanaco, puzzled and angry. He had not responded to her as she had expected. Was the Comanche blind? Hadn't he noticed that she was beautiful? He *would* notice before the evening was over, she'd see to that!

"What the hell's that dirty savage doing here?" Wilde whispered to Lois, his jaw rigid.

"Now, you knew very well Shanaco was coming this evening," she said. "Father thought it would be a good idea to invite him and I wholeheartedly agreed."

"Yes, well you better stay away from him. He's dangerous, mark my words."

"Don't be silly, Danny."

"Don't let the fine clothes fool you. That Indian's a barbaric bastard and no white woman is safe around him."

"Really?" Lois murmured, hoping that it was true.

The dance continued.

Maggie and Dave Finley spun about the floor, laughing and talking. Warm from the champagne she'd downed—and from the mere presence of the Comanche chief—Maggie felt breathless and gay. As if she could dance forever. Again and again as they turned about, Maggie kept getting glimpses of the tall, imposing Shanaco, and just the sight of him made her feel flushed and overly warm.

He was not on the dance floor. He stood, arms folded, against the wall, looking bored and uncomfortable.

A half hour into the ball, Maggie looked across the room at Lois Harkins. She saw Lois hug her father's arm and whisper something in his ear. The colonel shook his head no and Lieutenant Wilde looked angry.

Maggie decided, "She's a Lorilie up to her old mischief."

"Father, I think we are being rude to Chief Shanaco," Lois had whispered to her father. "Look at him. Our guest of honor is standing over against the wall all alone. Nobody will have anything to do with Shanaco and that's a shame. I feel that I should dance with him since no one else will."

"Well, now, Lois, I don't...I..."

"For God's sake, Miss Harkins," Captain Wilde muttered under his breath.

But Lois was gone.

Satin skirts lifted, she anxiously made her way through the crowd. Her heart was beginning to beat rapidly as she approached Shanaco. He stood at the edge of the crowd, arms crossed over his chest, a faraway look in his eyes.

Lois hurried up to Shanaco, smiled and said,

"Chief Shanaco, my father thinks it would be wise for you and I to dance. Show everyone, including the officers' wives, that the whites and Indians can coexist peacefully."

"I appreciate the gesture, Miss Harkins," Shanaco said politely, uncrossing his arms, "but I don't dance."

"Of course you do. Why, everyone knows that even Indians dance."

"I don't."

"You will. With me," she said, then took hold of his right hand with both of her own. "You're going to dance with me and you'll enjoy it, I promise."

Refusing to take no for an answer, the determined Lois dragged the reluctant Shanaco onto the floor. Other dancers stopped dancing and stared. The officers and their ladies whispered, surprised and disapproving.

Lois never noticed. She had eyes only for Shanaco.

"I knew it," she accused as they turned about the floor. "You do dance. And you dance divinely!"

And he did.

Shanaco moved with the unconscious grace that was so much a part of him. Lois was in heaven. She draped an arm around his shoulder, clasped the strong column of his neck with possessive fingers and pressed her voluptuous body close to his.

For a time she made small talk, asking questions, but getting no response. Finally she stood on tiptoe, put her lips near his ear and whispered, "Feel me moving against you, Chief? Wouldn't you like to feel me moving against you when I'm not wearing clothes? When you're not, either? When you're hot and hard and I'm soft and wet?'' Her eyes flashed when she added, ''I know you would. And you can. My father's duties often take him away from the fort for days at a time.''

''Miss Harkins,'' Shanaco said through thinned lips, ''behave yourself.''

''I don't want to behave and you don't want me to. Do you, Chief?'' No reply. Undeterred, she murmured, ''When my father is gone, I'm alone in our residence. And, oh so lonely.''

Shanaco did not encourage her. Did not respond to her brash overtures. But Lois was used to getting what she wanted and she wanted Shanaco. She continued to tease him, moving her body suggestively against his, insinuating her gowned knee between his long legs in an attempt to arouse him. She was quite adept at playing provocative games. She could make the most outrageous moves on her dance partner while outwardly appearing to be circumspect.

The dancers who had paused to stare and whisper were now dancing again, supposing that the commandant's young daughter had her father's blessing and was only attempting to make the half-breed chief feel welcome.

Not Maggie.

She knew better. Watching the pair over Dave's shoulder as they spun about, Maggie bristled. Astute, she had a very good idea of what Lois was saying—and doing—to Shanaco. She knew as well that if he responded, it could cause all kinds of trouble.

As if he had read her thoughts, Dave Finley said, "Shall we help out Shanaco?"

"Someone needs to," Maggie said.

Dave Finley maneuvered Maggie across the crowded floor to Lois and Shanaco.

"May I cut in?" Dave said, tapping Shanaco on the shoulder. Before she could object, Dave took Lois in his arms and danced her away. Maggie automatically stepped into Shanaco's arms. He held her at arm's length and thanked her with his eyes. Unnerved by him, and more attracted than she would ever have admitted, she immediately began lecturing him.

"You had better be careful, Chief Shanaco. Lois is lovely, I know, but she's the commandant's daughter and she will get you into serious trouble."

Shanaco easily replied, "And you? Will you get me into trouble, Maggie?"

She blushed hotly. "That's Miss Bankhead to you, and no, there is no chance of that *ever* happening."

Eighteen

She purred and stretched like a lazy cat. And she realized, with a small degree of surprise, that she was no longer dressed. She didn't recall discarding her elegant ball gown, lacy underwear, shoes and stockings. But they lay on the floor by the bed and she wore only a nightgown.

Perhaps he had undressed her. If so, she would return the favor. It would be, she decided, a sensual delight to strip him bare.

"You are *going to get me in trouble," he smilingly accused, his voice low and with a dark resonance that sent chills up her spine.*

"Perhaps," she said with a teasing laugh, and, looking into his hypnotic silver eyes, added, "but it will be worth it, I promise you."

"Then go ahead," he urged, "get me in trouble. Do what you will to me." And as he spoke, his dexterous fingers tugged at the delicate ribbon tied at her throat.

She lay on her back atop her soft feather bed. He sat on the edge of the mattress, leaning over her, his fierce eyes burning with an intense light that made her heart throb.

He was still fully clothed. His dark evening jacket stretched across his wide shoulders, the silk cravat untied and hanging loose, white shirt open at the collar, exposing his bronzed throat.

Across the room, the fire in the grate was slowly dying, the low-burning flames casting deep shadows on the hard planes of his handsome face.

The yoke of her nightgown was now open. He brushed back both sides of the delicate fabric, lowered his face and placed a kiss in the sensitive hollow of her throat. She thought her heart would beat its way out of her chest when she felt his lips open and his sleek tongue lightly paint her flesh with searing liquid heat.

He lifted his head and looked at her. His pale eyes flashed in the shadows, like a hungry wolf's. "Unbutton my shirt," he ordered. "Touch me. Feel my heart beating."

Mesmerized, she lifted both hands and began unbuttoning his shirt. When it was open down his coppery chest, she pushed it apart and laid eager fingers on the hard band of muscle. His flesh was satiny smooth and incredibly hot to the touch. His heart beat heavily against her open palm.

"Let me feel your heart beating against mine," he commanded as he roughly took hold of her upper arms and drew her into a sitting position facing him.

He swept her opened gown apart. She clasped his

hard biceps and pressed her bared breasts against his naked chest.

"Like this?" she asked, and provocatively brushed her left breast back and forth against the solid wall of his chest.

Loving the touch of his warm, bare flesh against her own, she inhaled deeply of his clean, unique scent and sighed with rising pleasure. After a few seconds she pulled back a little, looked into his eyes and said, "Oh, please. Kiss me. Kiss me now."

Shanaco's strong arms went around Maggie and his lips captured hers. Just as it had been that day at his cottage, the kiss was hot and invasive and incredibly stirring. Maggie responded with a passion that rivaled his, and when finally the prolonged kiss ended, she sagged weakly against him, gasping for breath and shaking with emotion.

She winced when Shanaco grabbed a handful of her flowing hair at the back of her head, yanked her face up and stared hungrily into her eyes. "I am," he warned, "going to make love to you right here in this bed until you are mine and mine alone. If this is not what you want, tell me now."

"It is what I want," she replied breathlessly, captivated but mildly fearful of that elemental savagery that was surely so much a part of him.

His long fingers tangling tightly in her hair, he ground his hot mouth down on hers again and Maggie felt his heart pound against her breasts. She trembled. When he tore his lips from hers, she was again lying on her back. She held her breath when he laid his cheek against her naked breast and asked, his voice vibrating against her, "Are you afraid of me?"

"No, I'm not," she whispered.

But she shivered and her breath came out in a whoosh when he turned his face inward and kissed her left breast. Her eyes slid closed and she dug her fingers into the muscles along his wide shoulders. She murmured his name.

Shanaco's mouth moved back up to hers and he kissed her trembling lips. He kept kissing her, over and over, and soon Maggie became aware of his lean fingers pulling at the long tail of her nightgown. She felt the soft fabric sliding up to her knees. Then higher. She stiffened slightly but made no attempt to make him stop.

Her weak arms lifted and wound tightly around his neck; her lips opened and moved beneath his as Maggie was carried away on a rising tide of passion. When Shanaco impatiently shoved the gown up to her thighs, she tore her lips from his and buried her face in his throat.

She shuddered when she felt his hand go beneath the bunched gown to touch her bare stomach. When his spread fingers began to slide possessively down her quivering belly, Maggie whispered, "Yes, oh yes." Her breathing became shallow and labored and she was so hot, she felt as if she would burst into flame. "Oh, oh, oh..." She squirmed and thrust her pelvis forward.

"Shanaco, Shanaco, Shanaco..."

Calling his name, Maggie awakened with a start.

Eyes opening wide, heart hammering, she lunged up in bed and looked anxiously around, expecting to see Shanaco. She swallowed hard. She saw that she'd kicked all the covers off. Worse, her long nightgown was wadded around her thighs and her bare legs were slightly parted. Maggie slammed her knees together and shoved her nightgown down.

Her face scarlet, her entire body perspiring, she sat there shaken and trembling. The dream had been so real. Too real. It was as if he had actually been in the room with her. She could feel his hot lips on hers, feel his warm hand on her stomach.

Never in her life had Maggie had an erotic dream. She was disturbed by the dream's sexual content and intensity. Shocked at herself. The carnal dream had been so incredibly real, it had left her feeling drained. Yet at the same time, aroused. A feverish, almost painful yearning lingered.

She wondered if the shameful dream was a manifestation of an unconscious desire she harbored for the Comanche chieftain. No, of course not, she assured herself. Yet she was burning hot in the coldness of the room. So uncomfortably feverish, she had to check the strong urge to strip off the choking nightgown and toss it to the floor.

Heart pounding, she rose from the bed, crossed to the armless rocker and sat down. Her knees together, bare feet planted firmly on the floor, she hugged her arms across her breasts. She rocked back and forth, gritting her teeth, willing herself to calm down, to relax and forget the appalling dream. That's all it had been, a dream. Just a dream. She was not to blame for what she had dreamed.

Nothing to worry about. No one knew what she had dreamed. No one would ever know. It was only natural that such a graphic sexual dream about a particular person would leave her feeling flushed and uneasy. The effects would be gone within minutes and the dream soon forgotten.

Not so.

The fire in the grate had totally died and turned to cold ash before the night's deepening chill drove Maggie back to the warmth of her bed.

And even then the dream was as vivid as ever.

There was a burning in the blood that Shanaco could not deny. Long after he'd briefly held her in his arms at the ball, he continued to think about her, to smell the perfumed hair, to feel the softness of her small hand in his, to hear her musical voice.

Shanaco harbored a carefully suppressed passion for the independent young woman with the flaming red hair and flashing blue eyes. Why, he didn't know. But from the first moment he'd seen her running across the pasture with the wolfhound at her heels, he had wanted her. Desired her. Yearned to hold her in his arms.

Maggie Bankhead fascinated him, enchanted him,

excited him. She was incredibly appealing, and not just because she was beautiful, but because she did not behave as other women. She was neither afraid of him nor attracted to him. She was not uneasy in his presence, never flinched when his eyes met hers. Had no qualms about scolding and lecturing him. Hadn't hesitated to tell him that "she would do all the deciding when she wanted to be kissed."

Shanaco smiled at the recollection.

He lifted the glass of whiskey to his lips and took a long pull. He sat leaning comfortably back in the only upholstered chair at his secluded cabin. He stared into the dying fire. He had been sitting there alone since leaving the officers' ball a couple of hours earlier.

His custom-cut evening jacket tossed aside, his white shirt open down his chest, leather shoes kicked off, Shanaco reflected on the events of the evening. The few fleeting minutes with Maggie had been enjoyable, even though she had spent all her time warning him to stay away from Lois Harkins.

Maggie was perceptive. And right. The commandant's blond daughter worried him. Lois Harkins had made no bones about the fact that she wanted to make love to him. The voluptuous blonde had an overly developed body and underdeveloped morals. She had, with her father looking on, brazenly propositioned him on the dance floor. Had he given the nod, he would have her here right now. With no more than the snap of his fingers, she'd have quickly agreed to spend the night in his bed.

Shanaco shrugged and took another drink of whiskey.

The woman he'd really like to have here with him was the fiery, flame-haired Maggie Bankhead. The thought of making love to her made his lower belly tighten and his groin stir. He wanted her. But he would never make any attempt to seduce her. Shanaco smiled sardonically.

He wouldn't dare touch Lois Harkins because she would cause him too much trouble. He wouldn't dare touch Maggie Bankhead because he would cause her too much trouble.

Shanaco shook his head and poured himself another shot of whiskey.

When the ball finally ended, Captain Daniel Wilde had, like the loyal aide-de-camp he was, escorted his commanding officer and the colonel's daughter back to their residence.

Colonel Harkins was yawning sleepily by the time the trio went inside. "I hope you won't think me rude, Captain," said the colonel, "I'm utterly exhausted. It's off to bed for me."

"Good night, Colonel," said Daniel Wilde.

"Lois will see you out," said the colonel. "Or pour you a nightcap if you wish." He kissed his daughter's cheek. "Good night, dear."

"'Night, Father," she said.

Captain Wilde waited barely long enough for the older man to get out of the room before he crossed to Lois, put a spread hand on her bare throat, urged her head back with his thumb and said, "I'll go now and leave my door unlocked." He grinned then and added, "I'll expect you in five minutes." He bent, started to kiss her.

Lois turned her head. "I'm not coming tonight."

"What do you mean?"

She pushed on his chest, turned away from him. "Exactly what I said, Danny. I'm tired."

Wilde's jaw hardened. He took Lois's arm and spun her to face him. "What are you trying to pull, Lois?"

She smiled sweetly, laid her hands on his chest and said innocently, "Nothing, Danny." She slipped her arms up around his neck and playfully bit his chin. "I'm very sleepy, that's all."

"Well, all right, baby," he said, finally softening. He kissed her, then lifted his head and smiled at her. "Lois, I don't think you realize just how desirable you are."

"Oh, Danny, you're sweet."

He pressed her close. "Listen, darling, I know you're a friendly girl and that's one of the things about you I find so charming. But, Lois, you're not aware of just what you do to men."

"I know what I do to you," she teased.

"Dammit, listen to me. You need to watch your step around that sullen half-breed Comanche. You should never have danced with him tonight. He might well have gotten the wrong idea.''

''I seriously doubt it,'' she said, keeping a straight face despite the double meaning of her statement.

''All the same, I want you to stay the hell away from him, you hear? It's not safe for you to have anything to do with him.''

''You'll protect me, won't you, Danny?'' Lois took his arm, propelled him toward the door.

''That's what I'm trying to do.''

''I know and I do appreciate it.'' She opened the door. ''Now, good night, Danny. Dream of me.''

''I will and you—'' The door closed in his face before he could finish the sentence.

Lois leaned back against the door and sighed wearily. Daniel Wilde had become a terrible bore. She wanted something different. Someone different.

Shanaco.

Nineteen

The flag was stirring in the breeze at the top of the pole when Shanaco crossed the parade ground at eight o'clock Monday morning. Soldiers were lined up outside the paymaster's door. The troopers watched Shanaco as he passed. They made remarks meant for him to hear. He heard. But he paid no attention. He was accustomed to be stared at and talked about.

Shanaco was resented by the troops. A man who catered to no one, he offended the enlisted men and officers alike with his arrogance and pride. They wanted to see him humbled and put in his place. But he moved about the reservation and outlying village as if he were a feudal lord.

He drank in the back room of Jake's, played poker with anyone who would sit down with him and generally caused a stir wherever he went. In other words, he behaved like a white man. And the white settlers and soldiers didn't like it.

The one white man who didn't resent him, the one who had befriended Shanaco from the start, was the Indian agent Double Jimmy. The two respected and genuinely liked each other. And, they had the same goal: to see to that the Indians were well fed, had blankets and warm clothing for the coming winter, and were as content as possible under the circumstances.

On this blustery Monday morning Shanaco was scheduled for yet another meeting with Double Jimmy and Colonel Harkins. He was never really satisfied with the progress made in the lengthy councils. He was not convinced that the fort commandant was overly concerned with the welfare of the Indians. It was becoming increasingly evident that Colonel Harkins didn't like Indians any more than the troops he commanded.

Skeptical of Harkins's intentions, Shanaco had voiced his opinion to Double Jimmy. Ever the diplomat, Double Jimmy had assured Shanaco that Colonel Harkins cared about the Indians and could be trusted.

"You must understand, Shanaco," Double Jimmy had reasoned, "the colonel lost many a good man, many a good soldier, fighting the Indians here in the West."

"He's not the only one who lost men," Shanaco replied with a rapt, steady-eyed gaze. "And women."

Aware that Shanaco's parents had been slaughtered in a surprise raid during the long Red River campaign, Double Jimmy said, "I know, I know. There was much bloodshed on both sides. But the colonel is trying to do the right thing by your People, son. Give him a chance. You'll see."

Shanaco looked up now and saw Double Jimmy standing on the sally port outside Colonel Harkins's office. "'Morning, Chief,'' Double Jimmy called out, a wide smile on his face.

"Good morning,'' Shanaco replied, then stepped up onto the shaded porch and shook hands with the older man. "You doing all right?''

"No complaints whatsoever,'' said the man who seemed to be eternally cheerful. "How about you?'' Before Shanaco could reply, Double Jimmy said, "Say, I hear you attended the officers' ball Saturday night.''

"I didn't have much choice,'' Shanaco said.

Double Jimmy laughed and slapped him on the back. "No, not really. But it wasn't that bad, was it?''

"Who told you I was there?''

"Who didn't?'' Double Jimmy said with a wink. "Maggie Bankhead, for one. I saw her a few minutes ago on the way to morning classes. Already old news, but I asked her how it went, what happened. She said she danced with you.''

Shanaco nodded. "She was very kind.''

"I'm not surprised. Maggie's a sweetheart and she always...she is so...say, wait a minute, I have an idea! Maggie's fixing supper for me tomorrow evening. Why don't you come with me?''

"I don't think so,'' Shanaco declined.

As if he hadn't spoken, Double Jimmy said, "Maggie will be pleased to have you join us, I know she will.'' He laughed heartily then and warned, "Now, don't expect a mouthwatering meal. I love Maggie like a daughter but she's not much of a cook. Bless her heart, she tries, but..." Double Jimmy shook his head, shrugged his shoulders. "Maggie grew up in a house full of servants. Never had to turn a hand until she came out here."

"She seems to have adjusted well."

"She sure has. She's always enjoyed a challenge," Double Jimmy said with frank adoration. "So say you'll come for supper tomorrow evening."

"Yes. I'll come. Why not?"

"Good enough. Now, I guess we better get on inside and meet with the colonel."

Three hours later, after much discussion and heated debate with Shanaco making demands and Colonel Harkins attempting to placate him, the meeting ended. Double Jimmy and Shanaco parted ways outside. Shanaco headed for the civilian village. Double Jimmy went directly to the fort's one-room schoolhouse.

At straight up noon the bell rang and rowdy children poured out of the classroom. The last to leave, as usual, were Bright Feather and the aged Old Coyote. Maggie followed them out and watched as Pistol rose off his haunches and affectionately nudged Bright Feather. The little boy laughed and petted the wolfhound's great head. Maggie smiled and her smile grew broader when she looked up and saw Double Jimmy.

''What a pleasant surprise,'' she said, stepping forward to kiss his cheek. ''How did this morning's meeting go?''

''I feel we made some real progress,'' he said. ''I'll tell you about it on the way to your cottage.''

''Oh, sorry. I'm not going straight home. Katie Atwood sent word for me to come by her quarters. Said she has something important to tell me.''

''That's fine. I have plenty of work to do myself. Need to inventory supplies at the agency warehouse. Been putting it off too long.''

Maggie arched an eyebrow. ''You might consider letting your hired hands do it.''

''Nah, I better get on over there and help. At least supervise.''

''In that case, I have to run. I told Katie I'd be there as soon as classes ended.''

''Want me to walk you over?''

''No, Pistol's a great escort. See you tomorrow evening?''

''I'll be there.'' Maggie nodded and turned to leave. Double Jimmy called after her, ''Be okay if I bring a guest?''

''Certainly. Anytime. I'm planning on cooking my precious supply of fresh beef, so it'll be a good time to bring someone.''

She hurried away without bothering to ask who the guest would be. She crossed the parade ground and made her way down Officers' Row to Katie Atwood's quarters. When Katie answered her knock, Maggie took one look at her and knew something was wrong.

"Dear Lord in heaven, what is it, Katie? Are you sick again?"

"Oh, Maggie, you're not going to believe it! We're leaving Fort Sill!"

"No!" Maggie exclaimed.

"Blake got the orders this morning and came right home to tell me. He's to report to Fort Richardson in Jacksboro, Texas, in two weeks."

"Two weeks? That means you'll be leaving right away!" Maggie said, frowning. "It can't be true. It can't."

"It is. The fifteenth of November is our last day at Fort Sill." Tears spilled down Katie's cheeks.

"Don't cry," Maggie said, and put her arms around her friend. "I can't help it," Katie wept. "I'll be so lonely down in Texas. I'll miss you so."

"And I you," Maggie said. "But you'll meet officers' wives there. You'll make friends."

"It won't be the same," said Katie.

Maggie set Katie back, looked into her tear-filled eyes and said, "No, it won't. But I'll write to you regularly, tell you all the news." Katie sniffed, nodded. "Now, cheer up and let's make the most of the time we have left," Maggie said.

Katie nodded and dashed the tears from her cheeks with the back of her hand. "Is it too cold out to fix a picnic lunch and walk up to Cache Creek?"

"No, it's brisk, but the sun's out and it's a beautiful day. Let's do it."

Twenty

Late Tuesday evening.

Maggie was frazzled. And tired. And wishing she hadn't invited Double Jimmy to supper.

Maggie's heavy hair was pinned haphazardly atop her head and she was still in the plain cotton shirtwaist dress she had worn all day. While classes officially ended at noon, she had stayed and spent the long afternoon helping three of the newly arrived Comanche children who were having difficulty learning English.

The three boys were older than most of the students. Aware that the younger the child, the easier he learned a new language, Maggie's heart went out to the boys. Tall, gangly and shy, they were embarrassed that the younger children could read and write and they couldn't.

Maggie was afraid they would stop coming to class, and she didn't want that to happen. If they were to have any chance in their new life, they had to learn English. So one day she had instructed the three, in their native tongue, to stay behind after the other students had gone. She asked the boys if any or all of them would be interested in attending private lessons for just the three of them. A couple of afternoons each week. All had eagerly said yes.

Now, after spending this Tuesday afternoon with the three young Comanches and then visiting Katie, Maggie was finally home. She stood before the cast-iron cookstove, forking sizzling meat and watching a pan of potatoes boiling. She was running late. Double Jimmy was due to arrive for supper any minute. And he was bringing a guest.

Maggie sighed.

She should have cleaned up and started cooking earlier. But after tutoring the three boys she felt that she needed to go by Katie's instead of coming home. Once there, she had, knowing that their days together were numbered, stayed longer than intended.

Too long.

When finally she had realized it was beginning to get dark, she had raced home. A glance at the clock beside her bed and she grimaced. Twenty minutes of seven! No time to freshen up. Only time to put on the meat, peel some potatoes and rush to set three places at the wooden eating table.

When the loud knock came, Maggie uttered an oath under her breath and poked one last time at the three thick steaks browning in the skillet. She wiped her hands on the dish towel draped over her left shoulder, shoved a wayward lock of hair behind her ear and went to answer.

She yanked the door open and said, "You must be early because I...I...ah, I..." Maggie stopped speaking when she caught sight of the tall, broad-shouldered man standing behind Double Jimmy.

Shanaco.

Maggie felt her cheeks grow hot and knew she was blushing. It was the first time she had seen the handsome Comanche chief since having the erotic dream about him. She could hardly look at him. She felt as if he could tell what was going through her mind, as if he knew exactly what she had dreamed.

"You not feeling well, child?" asked a concerned Double Jimmy. "If you're not up to having company this evening, we'll understand. Won't we, Shanaco?"

Avoiding Shanaco's eyes, Maggie waved a dismissive hand and said, "I'm fine. Do come in. Both of you."

Double Jimmy nodded and walked inside.

"I believe, Miss Bankhead," Shanaco said as he ducked his head and stepped through the low doorway, "something's burning."

"Oh, good Lord!" she said, and her hands flew up to her flushed face. "The steaks!" She whirled about to rush across the room. Shanaco caught her arm and stopped her.

"Allow me," he said, and, stepping past her, went directly to the cookstove. He picked up a long handled fork and turned the blackened beef. "Just the way I like my steaks," he said. "Charred on the outside, pink on the inside."

"You're just being nice," Maggie accused as she stepped up beside him. "I hope Double Jimmy warned you about my cooking."

"I sure did," Double Jimmy laughingly admitted, closing the cottage door and moving toward the horsehide sofa.

Shanaco said nothing. Just smiled at her. He eased the dish towel from her shoulder, lifted it to her face and blotted a spot of chalk from her turned-up nose. Their eyes met. And held for a long tension-filled moment.

Finally Maggie took the dish towel from his hand, stepped around him and checked the boiling potatoes. Now they stood side by side at the cookstove, he tending the steaks, she the potatoes. Each knew it was unnecessary. The steaks had been turned, the potatoes poked. Shanaco could have moved away, could have taken a seat on the horsehide sofa or in the armless rocker. Maggie could have turned away and finished setting the table.

Neither moved.

Maggie's arm brushed his as she jabbed at the boiling potatoes. Shanaco's shoulder grazed her upper arm as he needlessly turned the steaks again. They stole glances at each other. They smiled as if they shared a delightful secret. Communicating without saying a word, both silently acknowledged the pleasure derived from the simple act of cooking a meal together. There was a curious intimacy about it they both experienced and treasured.

"You two ever going to finish cooking supper?" said Double Jimmy from across the room, breaking the spell. "How long does it take to fry a steak?"

"Almost done," Maggie said. She looked up at

Shanaco and then took the pan of potatoes off the stove and moved away.

Minutes later the three sat at the square eating table enjoying the meal and one another's company. Shanaco quickly learned that Maggie was as smart as she was pretty. She also had a great sense of humor and entertained both him and Double Jimmy with tales of what went on in the classroom. He listened with interest. He smiled with delight. He tilted his chair back and laughed out loud when, at Double Jimmy's urging, Maggie told of how she had fallen in a deep mud puddle on her very first day at Fort Sill. She didn't mind being laughed at. She laughed at herself. A rich, warm musical laugh that enchanted Shanaco. A laugh he knew he could never forget.

Shanaco found that he liked being here. He felt unusually comfortable in this cozy one-room cottage that had been made homelike and hospitable by its beautiful, spirited occupant. Colorful curtains covered the windows and hooked rugs were scattered about on the plank floors. The horsehide sofa and the armless rocker were pulled up close to the fireplace.

Shanaco covertly glanced around. Maggie's touches were everywhere. Delicate knickknacks and framed pictures and leather-bound books were stacked neatly on shelves. In the far corner of the room was a low bureau atop which a lone lamp cast diffused light on decorative bottles of varying shapes and sizes. Shanaco supposed the bottles were filled with perfumes and oils to care for Maggie's pale, flawless skin.

There was a small clock on the bureau,.a box of stationery, a piece of blue ribbon. But the item that really caught his eye was a gold-handled hairbrush. Its bristles held a few gleaming strands of Maggie's flaming hair. He would, he mused, like to watch her brush her hair. He'd like to brush it for her.

Next to the bureau was a neatly made bed with warm blankets and an abundance of soft feather pillows. It was easy to envision Maggie in that bed with those fiery red tresses spilling across the snowy white pillows.

Too easy.

Shanaco quickly looked away. His heavy brows knitted with curiosity when he spotted a baseball bat leaning against the wall beside the back door. He wondered what...

Maggie snapped him out of his reveries with a direct question. "Tell the truth, Shanaco. Just how long do you intend to stay here at Fort Sill?"

Shanaco's dark head swung around. He fixed her with those metallic eyes and shrugged his shoulders. "A couple more weeks at the outside."

"A couple more weeks!" Maggie repeated. "That's not nearly long enough and you know it!"

"I will have done all I can do by then. Besides, I made it clear the day we rode into the fort that I would not be staying permanently."

"Well, I for one think it's unforgivable that you refuse to..."

Her blue eyes flashing with indignation, Maggie began berating the Comanche chieftain, speaking her mind, not mincing words. He should not leave the reservation! It was selfish and callous of him to desert his People when they needed him. Surely, as their leader, his responsibility was to remain here permanently. How could he expect them to settle down and live here in peace if he refused to do so?

Shanaco took her blistering reprimands with good grace. He did not defend himself. He did not argue or make any attempt to present his side of the situation. Instead he gazed at her with admiration and interest. She was passionate in her beliefs and not shy about stating them. He liked that. He liked her. And she liked him. He could tell. Liked him more than she wanted to like him.

Too soon the meal was finished. The three of them lingered over their coffee. Double Jimmy was beginning to yawn, ready to call it a night. Maggie and Shanaco were not. Each was afraid that an evening such as this might never come again. Shanaco knew it was unlikely that he would be seeing much of Maggie before he left. Maggie realized that Shanaco would soon be gone from the reservation and she would never see him again.

He'd leave without saying goodbye.

Finally Double Jimmy said, ''It's been a long day, time I was getting home to bed.'' He pushed back his chair and stood up. ''You coming, Chief?''

Shanaco and Maggie glanced at each other across the table. He wanted to stay. She wanted him to stay. He knew he shouldn't. She knew he shouldn't. He wondered what would happen if he stayed. She wondered what would happen if he stayed.

Shanaco swallowed hard.

Maggie cleared her throat.

Shanaco guiltily longed to yank Maggie up out of her chair and kiss her the way he had kissed her that day at his cottage. Maggie guiltily yearned to have Shanaco snatch her up out of her chair and kiss her the way he had kissed her that day at his cottage. His eyes fixed on her, Shanaco rose to his feet. Watching him intently, Maggie pushed back her chair and stood up.

She saw the two men to the door. Double Jimmy hugged her and stepped out into the night. Shanaco thanked her and told her he had enjoyed the evening.

''In that case you must come with Double Jimmy again,'' she said, and offered her hand.

He took it warmly in his and gently squeezed her slender fingers. With the hint of a smile, he warned, ''If I'm still here.''

A pain of near panic shot through Maggie's chest. ''Saturday. Come back Saturday night.'' She paused, then anxiously added, ''I mean, come with Double Jimmy, just as you did tonight.''

Shanaco nodded. ''I wouldn't think of coming alone.''

''No, certainly not.''

Twenty-One

Shanaco said good-night and stepped out into the chill November darkness. He glanced at the wolfhound stationed by the door. Pistol's gleaming golden eyes were instantly riveted to the tall, lean stranger.

But to Maggie's dismay, the faithful guard dog didn't move nor did he make a sound. Shanaco snapped his long fingers and Pistol went barreling past Maggie into the warm cottage. Shanaco slowly raised his eyes to meet Maggie's. She stared at him, the fine hair rising on the nape of her neck.

"How did you do that?" she asked. "Pistol barks at everyone but you. Why?"

Shanaco said nothing—just smiled, turned on his heel and left her.

Maggie slowly closed the door. Pistol was already across the room, stretched out before the fire, dozing. She shook her head, nonplussed by Pistol's response, or lack thereof, to a stranger's presence in her home. It was as if Shanaco could control the wolfhound with just a look.

Maggie leaned back against the door and sighed, the dog's puzzling laxity quickly forgotten. Her thoughts were only of Shanaco—the handsome half-breed, the last Comanche chieftain, the mysterious mixed-blood no one really knew.

Maggie sighed again. And then she began to smile involuntarily. She had thoroughly enjoyed the evening. She had found the enigmatic Shanaco to be good company. He was charming and intelligent and entertaining. And while she had heard all the negative talk about him, she knew there was another side to the man.

Maggie pushed away from the door. The truth was, that despite his faults, she couldn't help liking Shanaco. She liked hearing him speak, liked hearing him laugh. Liked seeing him seated across the table from her, as if he belonged there. She liked looking up to find his arresting silver eyes fixed on her and she liked watching the play of firelight across his starkly chiseled face. And she liked watching the muscles work in his smooth bronzed throat when he swallowed.

Climbing up onto her mattress, Maggie stretched out on her stomach and placed her chin on her folded hands as she continued to reflect on the evening with the fascinating chieftain.

Shanaco was taller than the other Comanches by a good three or four inches. He looked older than his twenty-six years, and his strongly cut features bore the stamp of his mixed blood. It was clear he was not pure Comanche, nor was he all white. His striking countenance was perfectly refined by his mother's aristocratic blood. Yet his powerful body had the look of repressed savagery, which his well-fitting white-man's clothes could not conceal.

Maggie flopped over onto her back, flung her arms above her head and shivered. The simple act of standing at the stove beside Shanaco had been incredibly pleasurable. The entire evening had been enjoyable and exciting. He possessed the power to thrill her by just being in the same room with her.

His strong masculine presence had filled her little cottage to such a degree that she had, at times, found it difficult to breathe. And that troubled her. Shanaco was a powerfully magnetic force to be reckoned with and Maggie knew in her heart that it wouldn't be wise to be around him too often.

She had always prided herself on not behaving a simpering, swooning fool where the opposite sex was concerned. She had no intention of losing her head or her heart to any man, no matter how compelling. Yet she couldn't forget the feel of Shanaco's smooth, warm lips on hers. What a kiss that had been.

Maggie felt her heart skip a beat.

She frowned and scolded herself for acting impulsively by inviting Shanaco to come back Saturday night. Why on earth had she done such an imprudent thing? And why had he agreed to come? Surely a worldly man like Shanaco had better ways to spend a Saturday night.

Too late now. She couldn't very well withdraw the invitation. That would be unforgivably rude. She fretted as finally she got up and turned down the bed.

* * *

Maggie needn't have worried.

Double Jimmy showed up alone on that cold Saturday evening. Maggie's welcoming smile slipped slightly as she looked curiously around, expecting the tall Comanche to step out of the shadows and into the light.

"Shanaco sends his regrets," Double Jimmy quickly said. "He couldn't make it this evening."

Maggie was stunned by the degree of disappointment that instantly swamped her. She had made a special effort to look her best. Now she realized it had been solely for Shanaco's benefit. She'd had Katie help dress her hair atop her head and she had worn one of her most attractive dresses. She had counted the hours until she saw him again. Had waited impatiently for him to arrive.

"It's just as well," she managed, and smiled once more. "Now we can have a nice long visit, just the two of us."

"That we can, child, and I'm pleased that I won't have to share you." Double Jimmy reached out and patted Pistol's head. He stepped inside and added, "Besides, it's going to be a while before we can get together again."

"Oh? Why's that?"

"I'm heading back up to Washington come Monday morning."

"Again, so soon?" Maggie frowned. "I'll miss you. How long will you be gone?"

"Not as long as the last time, I hope. But I need

to spend more time with those Washington bureaucrats, see if I can't set them straight once and for all. These Comanches are going to starve this winter if the rations are not increased."

Maggie exhaled wearily. "It's going to be awfully lonesome around here," she said over her shoulder as she headed for the cookstove. "You'll be gone. And my good friend, Katie Atwood, is leaving on the stage Monday morning."

"I know. I'd heard Katie's husband has been transferred to Fort Richardson down in Texas," Double Jimmy said. "That's a shame. I know you two young women spent a lot of time together."

The weather had turned.

The nights had grown bitter cold as blue northers, one after another, blew across the desolate plains and low hills of the reservation. Maggie took down an extra quilt and spread it across the foot of her bed.

A week had passed since the night Shanaco had come for supper. Maggie hadn't seen him since. But she had heard the usual stories about him. He had been seen swaggering down the sidewalks of the civilian village, drunk and sullen. He'd been in another fight after one of the locals pulled a knife on him in Jake's card parlor. A female going into the mercantile store swore that Shanaco had looked at her lasciviously and she'd been terrified.

Maggie supposed that some of the stories were undoubtedly true. But not all. She had known since the morning Shanaco had ridden through the fort gates that he would inherently attract trouble. And that he would not always be to blame.

Maggie undressed, slipped between the icy sheets, turned onto her side and drew her knees up. She snuggled down into the mattress and was soon fast asleep.

Just past midnight a loud knock instantly awakened her. Heart hammering, Maggie lunged up, threw on a robe and hurried to the door.

"Who is it?" she called out.

"Coyote" came the old man's response.

Maggie threw open the door. Shivering, the aged Kiowa chief said, "Miss Maggie, is Bright Feather. The boy is sick. Bad sick."

"Oh, no," Maggie said, clutching the lapels of her robe. "What is it? What's wrong with him?"

"Think it is the influenza. Child very hot, but freezing cold."

Maggie nodded. "I'll go right over. Won't take me a minute to get dressed."

"I wait right out here," Coyote said.

A few minutes later, Maggie, bundled up against the cold, hurried toward the Kiowa reservation with Old Coyote at her side and Pistol on her heels.

Outside the tepee, Maggie turned to Coyote and said, "You go on home now and get some rest."

"I stay if you need me."

Maggie patted his stooped shoulder. "You've done enough. I'll take over."

He nodded, turned and left.

Maggie folded back the flap of the big tepee, ducked her head, went inside and shrugged out of her warm wrap. She straightened, squinting in the dim light, then her heart squeezed in her chest when she saw a big, broad-shouldered man with his back to her, sitting cross-legged on a fur-skin bed, holding the sick Bright Feather in his arms.

Silently, Maggie approached. She sank down onto her knees beside the pair. She sat back on her heels and laid a gentle hand on Bright Feather's dark head.

She and Shanaco exchanged worried looks.

"What can I do?" she whispered.

"Stay here with him. Hold him," Shanaco said softly. "Love him."

Maggie nodded, sat flat down on the soft fur bed and allowed Shanaco to place Bright Feather in her arms. The boy's sick eyes opened. He saw Maggie's bright hair and managed a weak smile.

"I'm here, sweetheart," she murmured, and pressed him close against her breasts. "Right here with you."

Expecting Shanaco to leave now that she had arrived, Maggie gave him a questioning look when, instead of rising to his feet, he moved around behind her. He stretched a stiffened arm out, placed his palm flat on the floor and said, "Lean against me so your back won't get tired."

"You're staying?"

"We'll take turns holding him," Shanaco said. "Now, lean back."

"No, that's not necessary. I'm fine," she said. "I'm not tired."

"My chest is yours when you do tire" came his low, well-modulated voice.

"Look in my reticule," she instructed. "There's a tin of pain tablets."

Shanaco shook a couple of pain tablets from the small tin box. Morning Sun, the quiet Kiowa woman who looked after the tribe's parentless children, promptly brought forth a cup of water. While Maggie held Bright Feather, Shanaco gave him the pills with a couple of sips of water.

"That should do the trick soon," Maggie said.

She continued to sit there on the floor with Bright Feather cradled in her arms. She soothed him, she whispered to him, hummed a lullaby and prayed that he would be all right.

A full hour passed before Maggie began to feel as if her tired back was breaking. Through veiled lashes, she glanced over her shoulder at Shanaco. He said nothing but moved closer and again stretched a stiffened arm out behind her.

Maggie finally gave in and leaned back against him. She sighed and closed her eyes for a moment in silent gratitude. Shanaco's solid chest braced and supported her as she crooned to the precious little boy who was burning with fever and trembling violently.

Through the long cold night Maggie and Shanaco took turns holding Bright Feather. Finally, with dawn not far off, the boy's fever broke. His temperature went down and he was sleeping peacefully. Out of danger.

The grateful Morning Sun thanked them both for coming and promised to keep a close eye on the child.

"I'll be back to check on him later in the day," Maggie told the Kiowa woman.

"I'll tell him when he wakes," said Morning Sun.

Outside, Pistol looked up. He started to bark, but when he saw Shanaco the dog fell silent. Pistol eyed Shanaco warily and moved closer to Maggie, pressing his head against her knee. Both Maggie and Shanaco laughed.

Shanaco asked, "May I walk you to your cottage?"

"Yes. I'd like that," she said honestly.

The stars were beginning to fade, but the first pale streaks of gray light had not yet appeared on the eastern horizon. The reservation and the fort were silent, sleeping.

"Looks like we're the only ones awake," Maggie commented.

"Yes. Just you and me. Awake and alone in the night."

"And no one knows that we are."

"No one."

They looked at each other and smiled. When they reached Maggie's cottage, she slowly turned to face Shanaco. She had the strongest urge to reach out and touch his handsome face. She wondered what he would do if she did. She didn't dare.

"Would you like to come inside and have a cup of hot coffee?" she asked.

Shanaco shook his dark head. "No thanks."

Taken aback, longing to have him seated at her kitchen table, she asked bluntly, "Why not?"

Slowly Shanaco lifted both hands, took hold of the collars of her woolen wrap, pressed them together beneath her chin and looked into her eyes for a long moment. His thumbs brushed her cold cheeks and she was sure he was going to kiss her. Abruptly he dropped his hands away and stepped back.

Then he shocked her when he said, "Maggie, if I come inside with you, I might never want to leave."

Twenty-Two

Shanaco was strongly attracted to Maggie, but he wasn't sure that the attraction was mutual. Maggie was never nervous or giddy around him the way other women were. And she'd thought nothing of inviting him inside in the middle of the night.

Her nonchalance where he was concerned made her all the more captivating. And challenging. He was vain enough to believe that if he tried very hard, he could make her respond to him as a man.

He had no intention of doing so. He would never again attempt to kiss her as he had that day at his cottage. He wouldn't have kissed her then had he known her better.

He had come to admire Maggie. He knew, by the way she treated the Indian children, that although she was a bit too fiery and bossy, she was a caring, tenderhearted person. That made her all the more appealing. And untouchable. He couldn't—wouldn't—take advantage of such a good woman.

Concerned for her reputation and knowing how the whites regarded him, Shanaco made it a point to never acknowledge Maggie if anyone other than Double

Jimmy was present. The majority of the fort's population had no idea they even knew each other. He had told no one. Would tell no one.

By unspoken mutual agreement, Shanaco and Maggie behaved like strangers when they met. But anytime Shanaco caught sight of Maggie's flaming red hair he felt his heart thump against his ribs. Just a fleeting glimpse of her and he experienced a deep yearning to hold her in his arms. A longing to embrace her that was so powerful it had become almost a physical pain.

He knew it could never happen.

Just days after Double Jimmy's departure, Lois's father, Colonel Harkins, got orders to accompany General Sherman on an inspection tour of the frontier forts scattered across the vast Texas frontier. Major Miles Courteen, the ranking subordinate, was to be left in command of the fort in the colonel's absence.

When Lois heard the news she could hardly contain her glee. Two whole weeks to do what she pleased. And what she pleased was to seek out the handsome Comanche chieftain and make up for lost time.

Ever the actress, Lois stood in the cold winter rain to bid a tearful goodbye to her father on the Thursday afternoon he was to ride away. The colonel had chosen a handful of officers to go along. One was Maggie's friend, Lieutenant Dave Finley.

Maggie was there to bid the lieutenant adieu. She hated to see him go. She depended on Dave Finley and Double Jimmy and didn't like the idea that both would be away from the fort at the same time.

"You take care of yourself, you hear," Maggie said when the lieutenant squeezed her hand.

"You do the same," Finley replied as he brushed a kiss to her cheek before turning away to mount up.

Maggie heard sniffling, frowned and turned to see who was crying. Then rolled her eyes heavenward when she saw Lois Harkins clinging to her father and pretending to weep. What a fraud! Lois Harkins was probably delighted that her father would be away for two weeks.

"Lois, there, there, dear, please don't cry," Colonel Harkins said, consoling his daughter. "I hate to leave you, but I'll be back before you know it."

Lois managed to make her eyes well up and tears slipped down her cheeks when she threw her arms around her father's neck and said, "Oh, how I shall miss you, Father. I'll just be lost without you."

Maggie could no longer stomach the spectacle. She turned and hurried away after waving one last time to Lieutenant Finley.

"I know, I know, baby girl," the colonel was saying, patting Lois's back and trying to comfort her. "You know you can call on Major Courteen if you need anything." The colonel paused, exhaled heavily and added, "I do wish you'd take my advice and stay with Mrs. Tullison while I'm away. She's a fine woman and a fine cook and she'll be lonely, too, what with her husband going on the tour with us."

Lois made a face of distaste against her father's wool-covered shoulder. She wasn't about to stay with the nosy Margaret Tullison and be watched every moment like a prisoner.

"Now, Papa, you know I can't sleep in any bed but my own."

"Well, I suppose you'll be safe enough. I've asked both Mrs. Tullison and Lieutenant Wilde to look in on you."

Lois gave her father a hug and raised her head. "That's so sweet and thoughtful of you. Don't you worry for a minute. I'll be just fine."

"I hope so," he finally said. "You get frightened, you go right to Mrs. Tullison's. Anybody bothers you in any way, you tell Major Courteen. He'll set them straight."

Struggling to maintain her melancholy demeanor, Lois stood waving sadly as the detachment rode away. When the last mounted trooper cantered out through the fort gates, Lois turned away. Shoulders slumping, cheeks wet with rain, she slowly made her way back toward her private quarters. Aware that there were curious eyes on her, she continued to play the part of the despondent daughter until she was safely inside.

Once there she closed the door, gave a great whoop of joy and began stripping off her damp clothes. Leaving the discarded garments where they fell, she trekked, totally naked, into her father's small study where a fire burned in the grate and a half-full bottle

of whiskey sat in a crystal decanter on the shelf behind the desk.

Lois poured herself a shot of bourbon and downed it in one swallow. She made a face, coughed, poured another and sank down into her father's high-backed leather chair. She put her bare feet up on the desk, crossed her ankles, leaned back and sighed with satisfaction.

And she began to make her plans for the evening. An evening that was to last on into the night if she had her way. Indeed, she intended to be in Shanaco's arms and in his bed when tomorrow's sun came up.

The prospect caused her bare belly to flutter and her nipples to tighten.

Sipping the bourbon and considering what she should wear and what time she should venture out to his cottage, Lois frowned when she heard a loud knock on the door. Annoyed that someone was already intruding on her precious privacy, Lois exhaled as she rose from the chair, gathered up her dropped clothes and hurried to her room.

There she drew on a satin robe, tied the sash at her waist and slipped her bare feet into a pair of delicate bedroom slippers. When she opened the front door, Captain Daniel Wilde hurriedly shoved her back inside, came in after her and immediately started stripping.

"What on earth do you think you're doing?" Lois asked, hands on her hips.

"What does it look like?" he replied, yanking the

tails of his blue uniform blouse up out of his trousers. ''I'm getting ready to spend the afternoon in bed with you.''

''No, you are not.''

''Why not?'' he said, and unbuckled his belt. ''Daddy's gone, remember? Now, slip out of that robe. I know you're naked underneath and I know why. You were waiting for me, weren't you? Admit it, baby.''

''I was not waiting for you,'' she said. ''My clothes were wet and I had to get out of them before I caught my death.''

Daniel Wilde unbuttoned his pants. ''Come now, Lois. You don't fool me. You never have. Can you think of a better way to spend a rainy afternoon than making love with me?''

''Well, no, of course not,'' she said sweetly, determined to get rid of him without raising his suspicions. ''But, Danny, darling, we just can't. It's already half past four and I'm to have supper with that nosy old Mrs. Tullison this evening. I promised Father I would. She'll be expecting me there within the hour.''

''Damn to hell,'' Wilde swore. ''Fine. Go on and hurry back. I'll wait here.''

''No such thing,'' she said, shaking her head. ''Actually, I'm a little under the weather. Soon as I get back from Mrs. Tullison's, I'm going straight to bed. Alone.''

''Sure you don't want me to...?''

"No, Danny. Now, be a good boy and run along. I must get dressed and over to Mrs. Tullison's."

Lieutenant Wilde was grumbling as Lois shoved him out the door. She expelled a great sigh of relief and locked the door behind him. She had lied to Wilde. She wasn't about to join Mrs. Tullison for supper.

Lois had barely closed and locked the door before another knock came. Lois swore through gritted teeth.

"Danny, I told you I..." she said, opening the door, then stopped speaking when she saw the tall, plain woman before her.

Margaret Tullison. "Danny?" Margaret Tullison repeated. "Was Captain Wilde here?" Her eyebrows lifted suspiciously.

"No, no. I was afraid he would come by to check on me, see if I'm all right alone. Father asked him to keep an eye on me."

"Well, I would hope he hasn't been here, what with you going around undressed! And at this hour of the day," said the middle-aged Margaret Tullison. "Why, it's indecent."

"What's indecent about taking a bath, Mrs. Tullison?" Lois defended herself. "I was out in the rain this afternoon bidding my father goodbye. My clothes got damp and I was chilled to the bone. I hoped that a good hot bath might keep me from catching a cold."

"I see," said Margaret Tullison. "So Lieutenant Wilde wasn't here?"

''Certainly not!'' Lois pretended offense.

''Well, then, bless your heart. You do look a bit peaked. Lord knows you don't want to wind up in the hospital like poor Major Courteen.''

''That was last week,'' Lois reminded her. ''He's fine now.''

''No such thing. He was taken back to the hospital less than an hour ago with suspected pneumonia.''

''I'm sorry to hear that,'' said Lois.

''Yes, such a good man,'' Margaret Tullison replied. ''But it's you I'm worried about. Let me come in and fix you a nice hot cup of tea and then—''

''That's most kind of you,'' said Lois, but she didn't throw open the door. ''The truth is, I've not yet had that hot bath. I was planning a nice long soak and then right into bed.''

''You're not coming for supper?''

''I have no appetite, Mrs. Tullison. The only thing I want to do is get in my nice warm bed and get some sleep. You understand.''

''Why, yes. Certainly. You have plenty of food in the—''

''I do. I'll fix myself a little something,'' Lois said, beginning to close the door. ''Thanks so much for stopping by.''

''Sure you'll be all right alone here?''

''Positive. Now, good night.''

Twenty-Three

Lois Harkins could hardly contain her excitement.

Finally she was alone and could go about the serious business of getting ready for the upcoming evening with Shanaco. Shivering with anticipation, she shrugged out of the satin robe, leaving it in the small foyer where it fell.

She hummed happily as she went into her room. From a bureau drawer she took sheer silk stockings and red satin garters. She had purchased the scarlet garters not an hour after seeing the handsome Shanaco ride into the fort on that warm October morning. She had noted how his black stallion was decorated with red trappings, so she supposed red was Shanaco's favorite color.

She wanted to wear his favorite color to please him.

Lois tossed the stockings and garters on her bed and giggled as she took a flaming red silk dress from the very back of her closet. It was one she'd bought in New York shortly before coming out to Fort Sill.

The dress had never been worn. It, like the garters, had been saved for tonight's momentous occasion. She would don both and then allow the handsome savage to take them off. Tear them off if he so desired! She was half afraid of the powerfully built Comanche, wasn't sure what he might do to her once he got her alone. But that made the secret rendezvous all the more exciting.

Reluctantly, Lois reached for a long, lace-trimmed petticoat, tossing it on the bed. She hated wearing any kind of underclothing, but the lovely red gown required the added fullness of a petticoat if it were to show off her figure to the best advantage.

Lois went back to the closet, sank down onto her knees and studied the dozen pairs of shoes lined up on the floor. She chose a pair of delicate golden dancing slippers intricately decorated with tiny beads of red sewn across the instep. Perfect.

Gold slippers, red garters and silk stockings in hand, she sank down onto the vanity stool before her dressing table. Taking her time, making a sensuous exercise of it, she leisurely drew on a sheer stocking, straightening her leg out before her, admiring its smooth flesh and perfect shape. When she slipped the scarlet garter up past her knee, she snapped it playfully and trembled. Within the hour the handsome half-breed would be removing the garter.

And everything else.

When the stockings, garters and shoes were on, Lois swiveled about on the vanity stool to examine herself in the mirror. As always, she liked what she saw. Her breasts were very full, but high, no sagging whatsoever. The nipples were the size of silver dollars, their hue a tempting raspberry shade. No man could look on those twin mounds of creamy flesh and not go wild over her.

Lois rose, kicked the vanity stool back out of the way and studied her exquisite body, full length. Ah, yes, she was unbelievably tempting like this, naked save for the stockings and garters. Her hips flared with just the right amount of feminine roundness while her belly was appealingly flat. Her ivory thighs were firm and strong, perfect for holding a lover. And the springy curls between those thighs were as pale and golden as her long, lovely tresses.

Continuing to stand before the mirror, Lois looked among the many bottles, pots and jars resting atop her dressing table. She finally lifted a small container of rouge she'd never used before, dipped the tip of her little finger in it and stuck it in her mouth to sample. She was pleased; it tasted quite good. She applied a generous amount to the full, ripe lips that Shanaco would soon be kissing hungrily.

At last, Lois turned and hurried to the bed. She picked up the lace-trimmed petticoat and drew it down over her head. In minutes she was back before the mirror, fully dressed. The red silk gown, cut very low over the bosom and fitted very tight beneath, accentuated her full breasts and small waist. Her blond hair, brushed out and lying atop her bare white shoulders, gleamed in the lamp's diffused glow.

Satisfied, Lois rushed from her room. In the foyer she stopped and swirled a long woolen cape around her shoulders. She drew the hood up over her head so that, if she were seen, she wouldn't be recognized. She eased the door open, looked anxiously about and saw no one.

A flickering fire was the room's only light.

A zinc tub filled with hot sudsy water sat directly before that low-burning fire.

Shanaco, as naked as Adam in the Garden, had just climbed out of the tub. Dripping water, he realized he'd forgotten to lay out a towel. He shrugged wide shoulders and pushed his long raven hair back. He needed no towel. He'd let the fire dry him, then get right into bed.

Shanaco's head snapped around when, not bothering to knock, an intruder suddenly rushed inside, slammed the door and threw off a heavy long cape. Lois Harkins stood before him, smiling. Shanaco frowned but made no attempt to cover himself.

Lois stared at Shanaco, unable to believe her good fortune. This beautiful savage, whom she had waited so long to make love to stood there gloriously naked before the fire. Wet from a bath, his bronzed body gleamed in the firelight.

His was the most magnificent male body she had ever seen. And she had seen plenty. His coppery shoulders were incredibly wide, his deep torso narrowing down to a trim waist and slim hips. His legs were long and leanly muscled, the thighs like hammered steel.

His chest was smooth and hairless, while dense raven hair covered his groin. Diamond droplets of water clung to the night-black coils that surrounded the male flesh she had daydreamed of so often. She shuddered with joy—even at rest, it was impressive. And she had no intention of letting it stay at rest for long.

"I'm not receiving company this evening, Miss Harkins," Shanaco said in a calm, low voice.

Lois was undeterred. Mouth watering, she moved quickly forward. "This is just how I dreamed I would find you, Shanaco."

"Now that you have," he replied coldly, "turn around and leave."

Lois didn't turn around. She walked right up to him, boldly reached out and fanned her sharp, red-nailed fingertips across his smooth chest. "You don't really want me to go, do you, Chief? Do you like my red dress? I wore it just for you and underneath I'm as naked as you are." Her hand fluttered down his tight belly to his groin.

"I told you, I'm not receiving company tonight."

Lois smiled seductively, put out the tip of her tongue, licked her rouged lips and said, "I'm not company, Shanaco. I'm your lover." She laughed then and added, "I have come, my beautiful savage. Now I will make you come."

"You, Miss Harkins, are a vulgar, spoiled bitch, and if I wanted you, I'd have let you know. Go home."

Lois smiled and told him, "I refuse to leave until

you put this—'' her hand slipped around the soft, warm flesh nestled in the crisp black hair ''—where it belongs. Deep inside me.''

''In case you haven't noticed, it doesn't want you. Nor do I.''

She giggled and began to work the flaccid flesh. ''It will want me. I'll make it want me. I'll make you so hard, Shanaco, you'll be in agony until you've made wild, hot love to me.''

Shanaco shook his head, wrapped lean fingers around her wrist and moved her hand away. ''You may be something of a novelty here at this frontier outpost, Miss Harkins, but I've known plenty of ladies like you.''

''No, you haven't, Chief,'' she rejoined. ''Let me stay for just an hour and you'll see. I'll do things to you no lady has ever done.''

''Not interested,'' he said, ''and if I…''

Lois anxiously threw her arms around his neck, rose up on tiptoe and kissed him into silence, sucking at his lips and attempting to thrust her tongue into his mouth.

''Jesus Christ, behave yourself,'' he muttered, grabbing a handful of her flowing blond hair at the back of her head and urging her face up.

''Love me, half-breed,'' she pleaded. ''Pull my hair, hurt me. Take me, my beautiful primitive, make me your captive. Keep me here all night. Tie me up if you like. Whatever you want, however you want it.''

Shanaco released her hair, grabbed her forearms and forcefully withdrew them from around his neck. "I'm tired of your nonsense, Miss Harkins. Time for you to leave."

"No, no it's not. Give me a chance and I'll get you so aroused you'll rip my clothes off and—"

"I have never ripped off a woman's clothes," Shanaco said boredly. "I've had enough of this. You are going home."

He took her by an upper arm and propelled her across the room. Lois dragged her feet and begged him to let her stay. Thinking fast, she flipped open the fasteners of her bodice and exposed her lush breasts.

"Look at me, lover," she beseeched him. "Have you ever seen such magnificent nipples? Don't you want to suck—"

"Damn it, woman, cover yourself!"

"No!" Lois angrily protested, and swiftly whirled about to press herself against him once more. "Feel that?" she asked as she brushed her taut nipples back and forth across his chest. "Don't you want me naked beneath you? Or atop you? I know you do because you're getting an erection. Aren't you?" She had a wild look in her eyes as she sensed she was nearing success in breaking him down.

"You are! You are!" she cried, and managed to wedge a hand between their pressing bodies and around his stiffening member. "Ah, darling, yes, yes!

I knew it! Mine, all mine!'' she declared. ''Give it to me, Chief.''

Shanaco tore her hand away, gritted his teeth and roughly set her back. His fingers cutting into her flesh, he gripped her upper arms and said, ''You are going home, Miss Harkins. Right now.'' He turned her around and roughly marched her toward the door.

Lois was growing frantic. She had used all her charms to seduce the naked Shanaco, but nothing was working.

''I want to stay here with you,'' she whined.

''I don't give a tinker's damn what you want.''

She began to fight him. She pounded on his chest with her fists and kicked his shins with her gold-slippered feet, the violent kicking loosening tiny red beads from the golden slippers and scattering some across the plank floor.

Rebuffed, the angry Lois shrieked, ''Why, you dirty half-breed bastard. You'll be sorry you mis-treated me!''

''Fasten your dress and I'll get your wrap'' was his reply.

Crying now, Lois pretended to be fastening her bodice while he retrieved her cape. What she was really doing was tearing the gown's fragile fabric as rapidly as she could. Before he turned back to face her, she had torn off a small piece of the red silk cloth and dropped it behind her to the floor. And, when Shanaco draped the woolen cape around her shoulders, Lois swiftly turned her head and bit his hand, leaving teeth marks on his thumb.

Shanaco yelped in pain, swore and momentarily released his hold on her. Lois seized the opportunity to run her fingertip over her bottom lip and then rub a smudge of telltale rouge on the inside of Shanaco's thigh.

His metallic eyes as cold as ice, Shanaco yanked the door open, shoved her out and said, "Don't come around here again."

Furious, crying, Lois stormed away cursing and muttering under her breath.

And vowing that she would get even.

Twenty-Four

Unseen, an angered Lois slipped through the cold winter darkness and into her father's private residence.

She knew just how to make the arrogant Shanaco pay!

If this savage thought he could coldly reject her and not live to regret it, he was sadly mistaken. Before this night was over the half-breed would wish to high heaven he had played the part of her obedient stud. With Daddy and that damned Double Jimmy in transit, the troop would rally round her. After all, she was the daughter of the regiment!

Lois threw off the cape and immediately went to work on herself. She sat down on the bed, raised her skirts, closed her eyes against the coming pain and pinched the insides of her thighs, squeezing her flesh hard enough to leave bruises. She exhaled heavily and punished her breasts in the same manner.

Lois gritted her teeth, firmed her jaw and slapped herself on the left cheek. Hard.

"Damn!" she swore. Opening her tearing eyes, she hurried to the mirror and examined her face. Blood-red finger marks stood out on her pale cheek. Anyone who saw her wouldn't doubt that she had been viciously struck.

With the tip of her finger Lois smeared her lip rouge all over her mouth, then bit her bottom lip until she drew blood. Pleased, she lifted her hands and mussed her hair until it was a tangled sight.

She then took care of her clothes.

She tore the red silk dress, ripping the fabric until the bodice was hanging in tatters over her bare, pinch-reddened breasts. She yanked at the silk skirts, tearing a section of fabric loose from the waist. When the dress was ruined, she tore lace from her petticoat and, thinking quickly, hurried to the bureau drawer. She took out a pair of naughty French undergarments, tore them as well, then modestly slipped them on as if she'd been wearing them all along.

She smiled at her handiwork.

Lois swept out into the foyer, lifted her torn skirts and looked down at her gold slippers. Several red beads were missing and she knew where they were. She smiled evilly, picturing those missing beads being found on the floor of Shanaco's cottage.

She again donned the long cape and drew a deep breath before she ducked back out into the night and hurried to the darkened quarters of Captain Daniel Wilde.

Weeping now, she banged on the door with her fists and called out. In seconds a sleepy Wilde opened the door to see the crying Lois. "My God, Lois, what…what in the world has happened to you?'' he demanded.

''Oh, Danny, Danny,'' she said, brushing past him and into the shadowy quarters, ''I've been raped!''

''You've been…?'' Wilde was horrified. ''By whom? Who would do such a terrible thing?''

''Shanaco,'' she sobbed, ''the half-breed, Shanaco! He raped me.''

''That barbaric bastard!'' swore Wilde. ''He'll pay for this!''

''Just look at me, Danny!'' Lois wept. ''He hurt me so bad, used me like you'd use a whore. He made me do the most disgusting things with him!''

Daniel Wilde lighted a lamp with shaking hands, sat Lois down on his bunk, knelt before her and carefully examined her. ''Jesus God,'' he swore, upon seeing the split lip and reddened cheek and tangled hair.

Tears streaming down her face, Lois threw open the cape to reveal her torn clothing and bruised body. And she saw, with satisfaction, the building fury in Wilde's eyes.

''See, Danny, how he…he brutalized me.'' Her slender shoulders shook with her sobs.

''Oh, darling, yes, yes…I do, but…but how did this happen? Where were you? Were you in your quarters? Did he break down your door and…?''

''No, no,'' Lois wept, shaking her head. ''I…I was feeling bad, like I was coming down with a cold. I couldn't sleep. I think...I'm sure I had a touch of fever so...I...I...oh, Danny..."

"Go on. You must tell me exactly what happened."

"Well, I...it was foolish of me, I see that now, but I thought if I went to the civilian village and bought a tin of pain tablets, I could...I could..." She sniffed, coughed and continued, "I was on my way back home when I ran into the half-breed. He must have been drunk, I don't know. He saw me and I could tell by the lewd look in his eyes that he...that he..."

"Did he grab you and...?"

"Yes, yes! And I fought him as best I could, but he said he had wanted me from the first minute he saw me and that he was going to have me." Lois dissolved into fresh tears, lifted her hands, covered her face and peeked through her fingers to determine if Wilde was believing her story. He was. "No one else was about, so that filthy Indian swung me up into his arms and forcefully carried me out to his cottage."

"Oh, God, my poor Lois!" swore Wilde.

"Once he shoved me inside he savagely kissed me and tore my clothes. I fought him, but he's so much bigger and stronger..."

"I know, I know," Wilde sympathized. "So he forced you...?"

"I put up a fierce struggle, I swear it. I kicked and kicked him. I'm sure there are red beads from my ruined shoes all over the floor of his cottage. And I bit him, too, bit him on the hand." Again she was racked with sobs when she said, ''But it did no good. The animal used me! If you were to examine him right this minute you would find...you would see lip rouge on his...on his...''

''No! You didn't—''

''He made me, Danny, he made me. Grabbed me by the hair of my head and shoved me down between his legs...and that's not all. He...he...''

''Stay here! I'll get the post surgeon.''

''No!'' she said, immediately frantic at the thought. ''Please don't do that. Please, Danny. I'll be fine, I will, I will. I just want to go home. Promise you won't tell the post surgeon about this.''

''But you might be seriously injured and—''

''No, just the bruises. I'll be all right, please, I don't want to see the doctor.''

''Anything you say, but don't try to stop me from going after Shanaco!''

It was nearing midnight.

Shanaco was sound asleep when the angry Captain Wilde and a quartet of troopers burst into his cottage, awakening him. Wilde snapped his fingers and one of the four, a big stocky man with a deep scar across his left cheek, roughly dragged the sleepy Shanaco out of bed.

Shanaco fought, but there were too many. They managed to quickly restrain him.

''Light a lamp!'' ordered Captain Wilde, and one of the troopers obeyed.

While the soldiers held the naked, struggling Shanaco, Wilde examined him, searching for scratches and bruises. To his dismay, he found none on the half-breed's body. But when he spotted the faint teeth marks on Shanaco's thumb, he knew Lois had told him the truth.

Wilde turned away, picked up the lamp and looked around on the floor. Several tiny red beads were scattered about and a small piece of torn red silk lay just at the edge of the shadows.

His face a mask of anger, Wilde set the lamp down and turned back to the scuffling Shanaco.

"Hold him still!" Wilde ordered as he stepped closer, sank down onto his heels and roughly inspected Shanaco's genitals. Wilde's face grew red with fury when he spotted—on the inside of Shanaco's thigh—a tiny red smudge. He rubbed away the smear, lifted his forefinger, stared at it in disbelief and groaned loudly.

Lois's lip rouge!

Sickening images filling his mind, Wilde shot to his feet. He threw a hard-fisted punch at Shanaco's chin and said, "You will hang for this, half-breed!"

Allowing Shanaco only the opportunity to throw on a shirt and a pair of trousers, they dragged him—shoeless and coatless—out into the cold and to the icehouse prison. Once there they took great delight in beating him senseless.

"Civilized folks don't go about raping helpless white women!" Wilde told the bleeding Shanaco as his big, scar-faced subordinate, Sergeant Sparks, landed yet another punishing blow to Shanaco's exposed midsection.

His face bruised and bleeding, ribs and stomach tender from the merciless battering, Shanaco didn't waste his breath defending himself. He remained silent as they threw him onto the stone floor and locked him up.

He could hear, from inside the roofless icehouse, the troopers congratulating one another on "caging the wild animal."

Shanaco gritted his teeth against the pain. His head was throbbing, his stomach hurting bad, and his chest and shoulders were bruised and sore. He realized that this was a dangerous situation.

The commandant was not at the fort. Double Jimmy, the one man who might believe he was innocent, was also gone. Major Courteen, the second in command, had been taken back to the hospital late this afternoon, so Shanaco had heard in the village.

There was no one to whom Shanaco could turn. No one to hear his side of the story. No one who would believe that Lois Harkins had lied.

He was alone.

Shanaco closed his eyes and clenched his teeth. He didn't need anyone. Wouldn't beg anyone for mercy. He would wait until he regained at least some of his strength. Then he'd break out of this prison, even if it meant getting shot.

Shanaco raised a tired arm and blotted some of the

blood from his battered face with his torn shirtsleeve. The movement exhausted him. His arm fell back to the stone floor. He heaved a great sigh of weariness.

And passed out.

Come Friday morning, the post was in an uproar.

The shocking news of Shanaco's vicious criminal behavior and swift incarceration had spread like a prairie fire throughout the fort and across the reservation.

The entire regiment agreed that the cruel Comanche deserved harsh punishment for daring to lay a hand on the colonel's innocent daughter.

The Indians were furious. They did not believe Shanaco had harmed anyone. Some of the young hot-blooded braves attempted to free Shanaco but were quickly driven back by trigger-happy soldiers. Others fled the reservation, swearing they would never come back.

Maggie heard the gunshots and knew something had happened. On the way to school she saw groups of soldiers gathered and some of the officers' wives standing out in the cold, talking and shaking their heads. Snatches of their conversation carried. "...knew something like this would occur..." "...should have kept him locked up from the start..." "...still an untamed animal..."

A sense of dread swamping her, Maggie hurried on to the schoolhouse. She looked up and saw the Kiowa chief, Old Coyote, waiting for her just outside the classroom. She knew when she saw the look on his weathered face that it was something bad.

She felt her heart flutter.

"What is it?" she asked, taking the old man's arm and ushering him a short distance from the schoolhouse door.

"Shanaco is in prison," he stated simply.

"Again?" she said in disbelief. "They locked him up again? Why? For what?"

Coyote lowered his eyes when he whispered, "He has been accused of...rape."

"Rape?" Maggie repeated without sound, just her lips forming the awful word.

She felt all the blood drain from her face. She listened without commenting as Old Coyote told her all that he had heard. He said that the commandant's young daughter had been plucked off the streets of the civilian village last evening by a drunken Shanaco.

Shanaco had carried the struggling Miss Harkins out to his cottage, where he had made her submit against her will. Later last night the hysterical young woman had gone to her father's aide-de-camp's quarters with her clothing torn and bruises on her body. Captain Wilde and a handful of troopers had gone at once to Shanaco's cottage and arrested him.

Listening to the old man relate the appalling story, Maggie felt physically ill. But she knew that Shanaco had not forced himself on Lois Harkins. She didn't doubt for a moment that it was Lois who had seduced

Shanaco. Lois had eagerly made love with him, then felt guilty afterward. Or was afraid of being found out. So she had made up this damning lie that would endanger Shanaco's very life.

Maggie nervously bit her bottom lip and tried to think what to do. She wished that Double Jimmy was at the fort. She was worried sick for Shanaco. She waited until Old Coyote, tears shining in his eyes, had completely finished speaking.

She then said in a soft but firm voice, "Lois Harkins is lying."

"This is how I feel," said Old Coyote. "Shanaco has never—even on raids against the whites—*never* harmed women or children."

"And he didn't harm this one," Maggie said with conviction. "Surely Major Courteen will—"

Coyote shook his head and interrupted, "Major Courteen very sick. Is in hospital. Unconscious."

"Oh, dear Lord," she said, knowing there was no one to whom she could turn. "Come, we better go on inside."

Maggie was a professional. She warmly greeted the class, smiled at Bright Feather, then enthusiastically drilled the restless students in syntax and the multiplication tables as if nothing were amiss. But her mind was on Shanaco. When the noon bell rang and classes were dismissed, Old Coyote stayed behind.

"We have to do something, Miss Maggie," he said. "The soldiers, they will kill Shanaco."

Maggie patted the old man's stooped shoulder.

"They will kill you if you attempt to free him. Promise me that you will do nothing."

"I am no coward! I will get my old lance and—"

"You mustn't," she warned, then lowering her voice she added, "Let me handle it, please. I will think of something, I promise. Go now and say nothing to anyone. And don't worry."

"I want to help him get away," stated Old Coyote.

Maggie nodded. "When the time is right, I will call on you."

"I will be ready," said the old chief.

Twenty-Five

It was Friday afternoon and Captain Daniel Wilde sat in Colonel Harkins's chair with his feet propped up on the desk and his hands laced behind his head. Opposite him sat the four troopers who had arrested Shanaco. The five were talking about the "yelping mongrel dog" to whom they had taught a lesson.

"I don't feel," said Daniel Wilde, "that it's enough punishment for Shanaco to lie out there resting on the stone floor of the prison."

"Nor do I," said Sergeant Merlin Sparks, thoughtfully scratching the deep scar on his left cheek. "Can't let the red bastard to get off that easy."

The others chimed in their approval. Daniel Wilde smiled and nodded. He had known he could count on Sergeant Sparks. Sparks hated Indians. All Indians. The big man had despised every last redskin on earth since a band of renegade Kiowas had—fifteen years ago—swooped down on a small Texas farm and killed his young fiancée on the eve of their wedding.

"Ideas, anybody?" asked Wilde.

"Tie the son of a bitch to a horse and let it drag him through the res," suggested Sergeant Sparks.

The others eagerly offered their ideas. But none struck Daniel Wilde's fancy. Finally he took his hands from behind his head, moved his feet to the floor and leaned up to the desk.

"Leave it to me. I'll think of something appropriate. You are dismissed, gentlemen."

The troopers rose and filed out of the office. Once they were gone Wilde sat with his fingers steepled, pondering what he should do to Shanaco. At last he smiled as an idea came to him. He sent the orderly for a copy of solar charts.

He laid the tables out atop the desk and, scratching his chin thoughtfully, mused aloud, "Just what time do they lower the colors today?"

Maggie was in the civilian village as sunset approached. She had purposely stayed away from the icehouse prison. She didn't want anyone to suspect that she was concerned about Shanaco's fate.

She busied herself picking up coffee and sugar and other essentials. But she was in no hurry to get her shopping done. She stopped and looked at items she had no intention of buying. The main purpose of her visit to the mercantile was to learn what she could about Shanaco.

She had cautiously avoided discussing the distressing turn of events with anyone but Old Coyote. Only he and Double Jimmy were aware that she even knew Shanaco. She wanted to keep it that way. But she was dying to hear what they were going to do with him. When would he be released? Would he be released?

As she picked up a small sack of flour, she heard the locals talking about Shanaco and strained to listen without looking up or turning her head. "He'll likely be held in the prison till the colonel gets back," said a man in denim overalls and plaid shirt. "It's gonna get mighty cold tonight and that icehouse has no roof," said another. An old-timer tugged on his long gray beard and said, "I figure them troopers will think of something real bad to do to the savage."

Maggie swallowed hard, paid for her items, turned the collar of her wrap up around her ears and left with Pistol at her side. When she reached the fort the sun had just set. Only a pale gloaming of amber light remained. The temperature was already plummeting with the coming of darkness.

The officers' quarters temporarily obstructing her view of the parade ground, Maggie could see the very top of the flagpole rising to meet the winter sky. The colors had been lowered for the day.

She rounded the corner of the building onto the quad and stopped. She didn't believe her eyes. Surely she was seeing things in the fading light. Her arms around her sack of provisions, Maggie took a few steps forward, eyes narrowed, straining to see.

She abruptly stopped short again and involuntarily emitted a soft moan of misery.

Shanaco, beaten and bloody, was lashed to the flagpole, his dark head sagging onto his chest. A guard with a carbine slung over his shoulder marched back and forth across the quad, ignoring the suffering human being tied out in the cold.

As she looked on in horror, Maggie's first inclination was to rush to Shanaco. She checked herself and quickly cautioned Pistol to be quiet. If she were to be of any help, no one must suspect her.

Heartsick, Maggie hurried back around the officers' quarters with Pistol on her heels. She took the long way to her cottage. Once there she paced worriedly, shaking her head, wondering how in the world she could free Shanaco. There was no one to help her. Whatever she did, she would have to do it alone.

Maggie finally stopped pacing and calmly analyzed the situation. Mentally, she began to lay plans. She would, she decided, wait patiently until it was nearing midnight and the soldiers were all in their barracks, the officers in their quarters. Then she would go out there after Shanaco and bring him to the safety of her cottage.

The hours dragged as she waited for the bugler to play taps and the fort to grow silent. But the time was not wasted. Maggie readied her small home for the arrival of the sick, suffering Shanaco.

She spread a freshly laundered sheet out on the floor directly in front of the fireplace. She put clean sheets on her bed and fluffed up the lace-trimmed pillows. She spread the blanket evenly and laid an extra one across the foot of the bed. She carefully folded back one corner of the sheet and blanket, smoothed it neatly, then stepped back to admire her handiwork.

She went to the back door, opened it and brought in spare wood for the fire. Shivering, she stacked the wood beside the fireplace. She tossed a couple of logs on the fire, jabbed at them with the poker and watched the fire blaze up. She laid the poker aside and stood before the fire, staring into the flames, thoughtful, despairing the fact that Double Jimmy was gone.

She was alone.

An old, feeble, forgetful Indian was her only ally.

Maggie mentally shook herself, drew a deep breath, turned about and crossed to the tiny kitchen alcove. She hummed as she cooked a pan of beef broth. She lifted the spoon, tasted it and nodded her approval. Pistol, following her around as she did her chores, realized she was eating something and began to bark furiously.

"Oh, hush, you wouldn't like it," she told him. He didn't believe her. He barked his disagreement. "Very well, you may have a taste," she said.

She took a ladle down off the wall, scooped up a tiny bit of the salty broth, sank down to her heels and poured the steaming liquid into Pistol's bowl. He anxiously lapped at the broth, raised his head, gave her a questioning look, turned and walked away.

"I told you!" she said.

Maggie put tea in the kettle, ready for boiling. She laid out snowy-white bandages, a tincture of iodine and a tin of pain tablets. Then she filled a pan with warm water and placed a half-dozen clean washcloths and a couple of large towels beside it.

Everything at the ready, she paced impatiently, waiting for the middle of the cold winter night.

Finally the time had come.

Maggie drew a dark cape around her shoulders, raised the hood up over her flaming hair and, bending down on her heels, took the curious wolfhound's great head between her hands.

She said, ''Pistol, we are going after Shanaco. You must be very, very quiet when we step outside. You are not to make a sound. Do you hear me?'' Panting, Pistol shook his head excitedly.

Maggie rose to her feet. She looked around for the baseball bat her Indian students used. The large wooden bat rested against the door frame. Maggie picked it up and carefully concealed it inside her long, flowing cape. She drew several anxious breaths and opened the door.

Woman and dog slipped through the winter darkness. They went directly toward the fort's deserted parade ground as the first few flakes of snow began to fly. Warning the dog again, Maggie peeked around the corner of a darkened barracks and sighed with relief.

The one sleepy sentry was slouched against a barrack's wall.

Firmly gripping the baseball bat with both hands now, Maggie motioned for Pistol to stay put. He obeyed. She stole silently forward, praying the guard would not stir and see her.

He didn't.

Head falling onto his chest, he was half dozing. Maggie lifted her eyes heavenward, said a little prayer, stepped up and beaned the unsuspecting guard soundly with the baseball bat. He slumped to the ground, having no idea what had hit him.

Twenty-Six

Maggie turned and softly called to Pistol. The wolfhound silently flashed forward, then waited his turn as Maggie, laying the bat aside, swiftly untied the unconscious Shanaco's hands and feet from the flagpole. He fell forward, despite her best efforts to support him with her body. Maggie winced, hoping she hadn't hurt him further. She sank to her knees beside him and struggled to turn him over onto his back. Pistol sniffed at the unmoving man, his pale amber eyes riveted on Shanaco.

"Old friend, you must help me get him to the cottage," Maggie told the silver-furred creature.

Pistol was so excited he started to bark, but Maggie quickly put her hands to his jaws, silencing him. Thinking fast, she shoved the narrow handle of the bat through Shanaco's belt loop and twisted the bat around, securing it. She then rose and gripped the large end of the bat. By now Pistol had Shanaco's shirt collar firmly between his sharp canine teeth.

"Okay, let's move," Maggie whispered.

Together she and Pistol dragged the unconscious man across the silent quadrangle as the midnight sky opened up and began to furiously spit huge flakes of snow. A heavy snowfall that would mercifully conceal any tracks and leave Shanaco's escape a mystery.

"Thank God," Maggie silently murmured as the snow fluttered down and wet her cheeks.

Out of breath, heart throbbing painfully, Maggie, with Pistol's help, dragged Shanaco across the darkened parade ground. But just when she had almost gotten Shanaco to safety, the silence of the still night was shattered by a drunken baritone she recognized as that of Sergeant Merlin Sparks.

"The rose is red,
The grass is green,
The day is past,
That we have seen."

"Damnation!" Maggie muttered under her breath. Just when she thought she'd pulled it off, the big, drunken Sergeant Merlin Sparks was weaving around the corner of the quartermaster's office and onto the quad not twenty-five feet from them. Quickly lowering Shanaco to the ground, Maggie unhooked the bat from his belt loop, raised it and stood ready to face the approaching Sergeant Sparks.

The excited wolfhound raced away, shot around the quad in the shadows and rushed Sparks from the rear, fangs bared. Pistol pounced with the full force of his two hundred pounds onto the unsuspecting man's back, knocking the drunken brute to the bricked sally port. His forehead striking the brick with a thud, Sparks lay sprawled there facedown, out cold.

Maggie released her breath and lowered the bat. Leaving two unconscious troopers behind, she and Pistol finally got the heavy Shanaco to her cabin and inside. Managing to kick the door shut behind them, she and the wolfhound tugged Shanaco directly to the warming fire and the clean sheet spread out on the floor.

Maggie hurriedly threw off her cape, fell to her knees and drew a labored breath. She put a hand on her hurting chest, sucked her bottom lip behind her teeth and stared at the prostrate Shanaco. Panting rapidly, Pistol sank down onto his haunches and looked from one to the other.

Compassion swept through Maggie as she gazed at this poor, helpless man who had been severely beaten. He was badly hurt. Had been brutally pummeled. All over. Maggie knew that she had to undress him. That presented no problem. No affront to her modesty. She had, after all, on more than one occasion assisted with the infirm and wounded since her arrival at the fort.

Shanaco would not be the first male she had seen sans clothing. Maggie eased the baseball bat out Shanaco's belt loop and thrust it at Pistol. The dog leapt up, took the bat handle in his mouth and raced across the room. He dropped the bat at the door frame and hurried back.

Maggie rolled up her sleeves and went to work. From her sewing box she took a pair of embroidery scissors and began cutting away Shanaco's tattered clothes. With Pistol's help, she managed to swiftly strip Shanaco bare.

Maggie felt her face immediately grow hot. She swallowed hard, sank back on her heels and guiltily examined him.

Battered, bruised and bloody, he remained a beautiful human being. In the prime of his vigor. Physically perfect. Handsomer than any man she'd ever seen, even badly beaten as he was.

The bronzed skin, the broad shoulders, the slim hips, the long legs. The steely muscles in his powerful thighs. The broad, hairless chest rising and falling with his shallow breathing. The washboard stomach. The flat belly and the…the…

Maggie scolded herself and swirled a clean white towel over Shanaco's groin. Tossing his ruined clothing aside, she sprang to her feet and went for the pan of water and washcloths. She threw a couple more logs on the fire. The flames blazed up, snapping and crackling.

Gently, taking great care not to hurt him further, Maggie bathed Shanaco's many fresh abrasions and bruises. She started on his battered face. Using denatured alcohol and boiled water, she cleaned away the dried blood from his temple, his ear, his jaw, his chin. When she applied a clean swab to his mouth, cautiously tracing his cut bottom lip, he moaned softly and she yanked her hand away. Her heart beating in her ears, she waited several long seconds to see if he was waking.

He wasn't.

He lay there unconscious, his eyes closed, his lean, naked body stretched out before her. Maggie tossed aside a blood-streaked cloth and reached for a fresh one. She worked her way down his battered body, sponging his broad, coppery chest with the tender care with which one would bathe a helpless infant.

As she worked, she thoroughly inspected him. There were, marring the perfection of his magnificent body, battle scars from his warrior days. Just below his rib cage on his right side a white slashing scar looked to have been made by a soldier's slicing bayonet. A long-healed bullet wound had left a telltale scar on his muscular left thigh. Many other smaller scars were a testament to his many battles.

No doubt some of the fresh wounds he had suffered at the hands of the troopers would leave their marks, as well. Maggie frowned suddenly. She picked up Shanaco's right hand and stared at it. Fresh teeth marks on his thumb. Had one of the troopers bitten him? Or had Lois Harkins bitten him in the throes of passion?

Frowning, Maggie placed his hand back at his side. She continued with her compassionate ministering, tossing aside soiled cloths, dipping clean ones into freshly poured water. At last she had bathed every part of his body.

Except one.

Hand beginning to shake now, she eased the covering sheet off, pushed it aside. She caught herself holding her breath as she began to bathe the smooth flesh of Shanaco's drum-tight belly. She tried, without success, to keep her eyes off that most male part of him. The soft flesh lay at rest amid a swirl of dense raven curls.

But apparently it hadn't been that way in Lois's presence.

Maggie closed her eyes against the hurtful vision of Shanaco and Lois making love—not rape—love. The two of them writhing naked in Shanaco's bed. Then Lois lying to cover her tracks.

Maggie opened her eyes and sighed heavily.

"How could you?" she asked the unconscious man. "Didn't I tell you she would get you in trouble! Now look what you've done!"

Gritting her teeth so hard her jaws ached, Maggie finished the healing bath and placed bandages where they were most needed. She then rose to her feet, went for a cup of water and came back to him. She attempted to give Shanaco a sip of the water. He did not swallow, so she spread the water over his lips. And shivered involuntarily when his mouth opened slightly and he licked at his gleaming bottom lip.

"Pistol," she said, snapping her fingers, "we have to get him to bed now."

Using the sheet beneath him, Maggie and Pistol dragged Shanaco across the floor to the bed. Once there, Maggie turned about and sat down on the edge of the mattress. She raised her skirts, threw her leg over him and clamped his wide shoulders between her knees. Then groaning, she began lifting him. It took everything she had, but she finally managed to get Shanaco up onto the bed. Only trouble was, she was under him.

Her arms around him, wrists locked across his stomach, she had tugged so hard she had fallen over onto the mattress, bringing him with her. His long, loose hair was in her face and his back was pressing heavily on her breasts. She lay there a minute to renew her strength and allow her heartbeat to slow.

Pistol was now barking his protest and jumping up on the unconscious man, supposing that Shanaco was a threat to his mistress.

As she lay there panting for breath, Maggie suddenly found the situation humorous. She began laughing uncontrollably. Here she was, flat on her back, pinned to the bed by a big, unconscious man who was totally naked. Maggie quickly sobered.

Shanaco was badly hurt and this was no laughing matter.

Straining, she unclasped her hands from around his body, braced them against his upper back, shoved him up a little and scrambled out from under him. Gasping for breath she turned him about on the bed. She scooted off the mattress and lifted his legs from the floor. When finally he was fully stretched out in the bed, she shoved him to the bed's center, lifted his head and put a pillow beneath it. Then she gave a great whoop of joy at a task well done.

Maggie carefully spread the sheet and blanket up over him, tucking both in around his bare, bronzed shoulders. Exhaling with relief, she knelt beside the bed, tilted her head to one side and gazed at him. His long raven hair was fanned out on the pillow, his handsome face in repose, eyes closed, thick dark lashes resting on the high cheekbones, full lips parted slightly. Despite all the cuts and bruises, he looked so young and peaceful he might have been a mere boy who'd been in his first fight.

But Shanaco was no boy. And this was not the first time he'd been in serious trouble.

"You're safe now, Shanaco," Maggie whispered to the sleeping man.

Twenty-Seven

Throughout the cold, snowy night Maggie kept a watchful vigil at Shanaco's bedside. He did not regain consciousness. Did not move. Lay there deathly still and silent.

Worried sick, Maggie was torn between seeking out the regimental surgeon and maintaining her silence. She could be endangering Shanaco's life by eschewing medical aid. But she would certainly be endangering his life if the troopers learned where he was.

After much soul-searching, Maggie decided that she would wait. At least for the night. If Shanaco hadn't awakened by sunrise she would have no choice but to reveal his whereabouts. She couldn't let him die from lack of care.

Her concern for his welfare intensified when, during the night, Shanaco developed a fever. Maggie pressed a hand to his bruised cheek and found him hot to the touch. Within minutes his teeth began to chatter violently and his lean body shook uncontrollably.

"Oh, dear Lord," Maggie murmured. "No, no."

She shot up from the chair, crossed the room and tossed more wood on the fire, poking at it, watching it blaze up. She hurried back to the bed to unfold the extra blanket and spread it up over him.

Still he shook.

Maggie got down every quilt she owned and laid them over him. "There," she said, and sat down on the edge of the bed facing him, bracing an arm across his shuddering body. "You'll warm up now." She cupped his burning cheek in her hand. "You'll be fine, just fine. Any minute now you'll stop shaking."

Shanaco's furious shivering continued. His fever was rising. Maggie was beside herself. She had to do something. She had to get him warm. She considered it for only a moment, then took off her shoes and stockings, lifted one side of the heavy covers and crawled into bed with him.

She draped an arm over his chest, warily edged a knee atop his thigh and pressed herself close against him in an all-out attempt to transfer her body heat to him. Lying close beside him was like hugging a blazing furnace. Yet his teeth were chattering and she knew he was freezing.

"I'll get you warm, Shanaco," she murmured, pressing her lips to his ear. "I will, I promise. I won't let you die."

For the next two hours Maggie lay holding Shanaco tightly as he shivered and quaked. In his troubled sleep he turned more fully to her, snuggling close, seeking warmth, wrapping his arms around her. Maggie felt as if she were being smothered, but she didn't pull away.

The first sign that his fever was beginning to break was when her hand, pressed against his beating heart, grew slightly damp. Then wet. Shanaco was perspiring. Heavily. And he was no longer trembling.

Maggie sighed with relief. She could get up now. She looked at his sleeping face and a faint smile touched her lips. She pressed her cheek to his. His skin was no longer scorching hot, but cool.

"Thank God," she murmured, and reaching a hand up, she smoothed his damp raven hair back off his shiny forehead and temples. She studied him for a long moment, put her lips close to his and whispered softly, "Ah, Shanaco, Shanaco. You bad, beautiful boy. Why did you do it? Didn't I warn you? No matter. I've got you now and it's going to be all right." She smiled and added, "Since you no longer need me, I will get up and leave you to rest."

But Maggie didn't move right away. She yawned sleepily. Then sighed deeply. She decided she'd lie there for a minute before she got off the nice warm bed. That was her last waking thought.

Exhausted, she fell asleep.

Outside the snow continued to fall, covering the ground with several inches of glistening white crystals and creating drifts against the cottage door and beneath the windows.

Inside the man and woman slept peacefully together in the soft warm bed while the wolfhound dozed before the dying fire. Near dawn, the sleeping Maggie snuggled more deeply into the mattress.

Somewhere in her deep subconscious, she became hazily aware that she was pressed against something much warmer than a blanket. Struggling to open her eyes, she finally managed. Slowly she awakened, her lashes leisurely lifting.

And found a pair of sick silver eyes fixed on her. For an instant she was confused, then it all came flooding back. She was, she sleepily realized, in bed with the naked Shanaco.

Suddenly the sound of drumming hoofbeats just outside brought her fully alert. She jumped out of bed, dashed across the room and anxiously wedged a straight-back chair under the doorknob. Shanaco saw what she was doing and asked why it was necessary.

Maggie said, "First I'll get you a drink of water, then I'll tell you everything."

In seconds she was helping him hold his head up while he sipped thirstily. "Want another cup?" she asked.

"No, thanks," Shanaco replied, his voice raspy.

Maggie set the cup aside, drew up a chair and said, "You must be wondering what you're doing here in my cottage and how you got here." Shanaco gave no response, just looked at her. "You're in trouble, Shanaco. Bad trouble. The troopers beat you for what you supposedly did to…to…" She shrugged slender shoulders and hurried on, "You were beaten and tied to the flagpole for punishment of your alleged crime. The troopers fully intended to leave you out there all night in the bitter cold. I couldn't let that happen, so I waited until well past midnight. Then Pistol and I crept out into the darkness and hurried to the parade ground. Once there I....I...well, all right, I admit it, I did a terrible thing," she said.

Shanaco's eyes were riveted on her.

She continued, "I hit the patrolling night guard on the head with a baseball bat, knocked him out cold. But he never saw me, has no idea what happened." Shanaco's cut lips stretched into a hint of a grin. "I clobbered him and then I managed to untie you. Pistol and I had almost gotten you to safety when who shows up but that big brute, Sergeant Sparks, drunk and singing loudly. Before I could make a move, Pistol rushed Sparks from behind, leapt up onto his back and knocked him down. The sergeant hit his head on the brick walk and never moved afterward." She frowned and said, "That's why I wedged the chair under the doorknob. I'm worried. We may not get away with this. The sentry didn't see me, but Sparks might have—"

Interrupting, Shanaco said, "We'll get away with it, Maggie. Do you actually suppose Sparks would ever admit that a dog and a mere waif of a woman managed to put him away? Why, you could pin a note—along with a lock of your hair—to Sparks's tunic telling exactly what happened and he would deny it."

"You think?"

"I know. You're quite a girl, Maggie Bankhead. Thank you for saving me."

"You're very welcome," she said with smile. "Now, I am going to nurse you back to health and then I'll help you escape," Maggie told him. She paused, leaned closer and said, "If Sparks won't tell, there's nothing to worry about. You're safe here with me. Just rest. You need to rest."

Shanaco was too tired and battered to protest. But his split lips again stretched into a small smile of relief and admiration for what she'd done. His coal-black lashes began to lower and in seconds he was again sleeping.

Maggie stayed where she was, watching over him, making sure he stayed covered and was resting peacefully. Gazing at him, she felt a chill skip up her spine. Just minutes ago she had been in bed with this arrestingly handsome man. Had lain in his arms with him stark naked.

Maggie bolted up out of the chair and turned her back on Shanaco. It was quiet out now. The mounted troopers had ridden past and were apparently gone. She crossed the room, took the chair away and cautiously opened the front door to let Pistol out. The sun was just beginning to rise.

Maggie was relieved to see that the ground was covered with several inches of snow. The snow was still falling. Thankfully it was Saturday, so she could stay right here at the cottage until Monday morning without raising anyone's suspicions.

Maggie closed the door and went about her usual tasks, stopping every few minutes to check on Shanaco. He was sleeping soundly. He had turned over onto his side and was facing the wall. His back was to her. This was, she decided, the perfect opportunity to clean up and change out of her soiled, wrinkled clothing.

Hurrying about so she could get the chore done before he awakened, Maggie drew clean underthings from a bureau drawer and picked up her hairbrush from its top. She took the articles to the fireplace and laid them on the hooked rug. She slipped out of her dress while a kettle of water heated on the cookstove. She yanked the pins from her tangled hair and let it fall around her shoulders. With a cautious glance over her shoulder, she stepped out of her petticoats, kicked them aside.

Maggie poured heated water into a basin and carried it to the fireplace. She bent, placed the pan on the floor, took one final look at the sleeping Shanaco, knelt and eased out of her batiste camisole.

Maggie's unbound hair spilled down her slender back.

Shanaco awakened.

His eyes slowly opened. He eased over onto his back and slowly turned his head. He saw fire. Bright, blazing fire. Dancing, moving flames. His eyes widened, then narrowed. He squinted, focused with effort and realized that the fire he saw was a woman's flaming red tresses.

Maggie.

Shanaco licked his dry lips and started to speak, to alert her that he was awake. He didn't make a sound. He stared, fascinated, at the fiery locks spilling around her shoulders and down her back.

His chest tightened when she abruptly swung the gleaming locks around to one side, reached up and began pulling a brush through their silky ends. She was, he realized, naked to the waist. He tried to look away. Wanted to look away because it was Maggie. But he couldn't take his eyes off her. Her back was beautiful. Perfect symmetry, flawless skin, narrow waist.

Shanaco lost his breath when Maggie laid aside the hairbrush and twisted about to more fully face the low burning fire. She reached for a washcloth. She dipped the cloth into a pan of water and began sponging herself.

A guilty voyeur, Shanaco watched unblinking as she pressed the wet cloth to her upturned face and elegant throat. Then slid it lower and slowly swirled it over her bare breasts and delicate ribs. Her eyes were closed with pleasure.

It was a sight Shanaco knew he would never forget. The beautiful Maggie sitting back on her heels wearing nothing but her lace-trimmed undergarments. Glorious red hair spilling down her back, alabaster breasts with their pale pink nipples gleaming wet from the cleansing bath.

When Maggie dropped the cloth back into the water, shot to her feet and began to undo the tape at the waistband of her underwear, Shanaco silently groaned and forced himself to turn away. He closed his eyes and gritted his teeth.

In the quiet of the cottage he could hear the whisper of the gossamer fabric slipping down her legs, knew that she was now naked. In agony he lay there envisioning Maggie standing nude before the fire, the flickering flames caressing her bare, slender body. Beneath the covers, Shanaco clenched his hands into tight fists and reminded himself of what she had done for him. He had the greatest admiration for this brave young beauty who had put her position in jeopardy to save him. He had to remember that at all times.

Shanaco patiently waited until he was sure Maggie had finished with her bath and was again fully clothed. When she tiptoed to the bed to check on him, he opened his eyes and looked up at her.

"Ah, you're awake," she said, and smiled at him. "Hungry?"

He shook his head.

"Nonetheless, you must eat something," she stated emphatically.

She brought a tray to the bed and made him eat a few spoonsful of broth and several soda crackers, saying she realized that it was a strange breakfast, but it would be the best thing for him. She insisted he drink a cup of hot tea. After the light meal was finished, she announced that it was time to change his bandages.

Shanaco objected.

But it did him no good. Maggie built up the fire and came back to the bed with a roll of clean gauze, the denatured alcohol and the iodine bottle. She spent the next half hour removing soiled bandages, cleaning his cuts and bruises, rubbing gently with alcohol and swabbing with iodine. Finally, she dressed the wounds with the clean white gauze.

Maggie was dying to quiz him but knew she had best wait until he was feeling better.

She blinked when she heard him ask, in a low, barely audible voice, "Why, Maggie?"

"Why? Why did I save you? Bring you here?" He nodded tiredly. "Because I know that Lois Harkins lied."

Again he nodded, then smiled weakly and said, "When you save a life, goes the old saying, you are responsible for it."

Maggie shook her head firmly and told him, "I'll be responsible for you until you're well enough to escape from the fort. Then you're on your own."

"Fair enough."

Twenty-Eight

In the anteroom of the officers' mess six men awaited the hearing that had been called by Major Miles Courteen. Outside, an armed provost guard stood, carbine at the ready, in the cold morning air. No one was to be allowed in. No one was to be allowed out.

Five of the six men were seated at a long table.

The sixth man, Captain Daniel Wilde, paced back and forth before the table, muttering to himself. He knew the major to be unconscious with pneumonia. Damn to hell, how could such a sick man be coming here on this cold, snowy morning to conduct a hearing?

"You had better be damned sure—" Captain Wilde stopped pacing to caution Sergeant Sparks and the sentry, Private Henry "—that you have the details of last night's escape ready to relate."

Sergeant Sparks rose to his feet. Eyes bloodshot, uniform damp and scruffy, he'd been roused from his snowy slumber by the sergeant of the guards.

"Captain Wilde, sir, you are not going to believe what happened." His eyes blinked at the hanging coal-oil lamp. "There we were, me and..."

The sentence was never finished. There was a thunderous banging on the door. Sparks swallowed anxiously and pivoted about. The provost guard, carbine slung over his shoulder, yanked the door open wide and two white-clad hospital orderlies bore Major Miles Courteen into the room on a stretcher.

Captain Wilde grew nearly as pale as the sickly major. The hospital orderlies gingerly lifted Major Courteen from the stretcher to the head chair. The chair faced the long table and was near the warmth of a large potbellied stove. The orderlies draped a blanket over the major's shoulders, another over his knees, then moved around to stand behind him.

The major, with visible effort, raised his right hand.

Upon this signal, the provost guard ushered in the company clerk. The clerk took a chair at the opposite end of the long table. He set out his tablets, pens and ink, and opened a large Hunter-case timepiece.

The provost guard shut and locked the door.

The major nodded to the company clerk.

The clerk rose. "This hearing in the matter of the Comanche Chief Shanaco is called to order at 0600 hours on this Saturday morning, the twentieth of November, in the year of our Lord 1875. Major Miles Courteen, ranking subordinate, presiding."

A few feet from the major, an empty chair sat at an angle. Its occupant could easily face both the major and the men seated down the length of the table.

Clutching a blanket close around his thin shoulders, Major Courteen said, "Captain Wilde, this hearing to learn the facts regarding the events of the past thirty-six hours is now officially under way. Present your testimony in detail."

Wilde stood at parade rest, his hands clasped behind his back, and stated his account of exactly what had happened on the two nights in question. He recounted how the hysterical Lois Harkins had awakened him late Thursday night to tell him she had been brutally raped by the Comanche Chief Shanaco. He repeated what Lois had told him, that she had been feeling poorly and therefore had walked into the village.

She had gone into the general mercantile store and purchased a tin of pain tablets and left immediately. It was on her way home from the mercantile when Shanaco, drunk and mean, had seized her, taken her to his cabin, and there forcefully made her submit to his animal hungers.

Major Courteen glanced at the company clerk. The clerk nodded in the affirmative. He was getting it all down.

Captain Wilde continued as he told of his decision to imprison Shanaco for his crime. Finally he concluded, saying Sergeant Sparks would corroborate.

The major nodded to Sergeant Sparks. The sergeant rose, cleared his throat and stated that he and the others seated here had aided their superior in subduing and imprisoning the cruel rapist after the tragic turn of events that had left the commandant's daughter badly injured and in severe physical and mental anguish.

"And you were a party to lashing Shanaco to the flagpole last evening?" asked Major Courteen.

Again the sergeant anxiously cleared his throat, stated that he was, then quickly explained, "But we meant only to leave him out for a very short time because he demonstrated absolutely no repentance for his dastardly crime. I was going out to untie him myself when a swarm of rogue Comanches, silent as snakes they were, overpowered the sentry and me. There must have been at least a dozen of them."

Private Henry leapt to his feet. "More like two dozen, sir."

"Be seated, Private Henry, Sergeant Sparks," said the major. Both men gratefully dropped back down into their seats. But when Wilde made as if to sit down, Major Courteen said, "Continue to stand, Captain Wilde."

"Yes, sir."

"Have you anything more to add to your statement?"

"Sir, I've told you in detail everything that transpired."

"In that case, I have some questions."

"Yes, sir." Wilde was relieved.

"Did you—" Courteen's voice lowered as he was racked with a painful cough "—inform the regimental surgeon?"

"No, sir."

"Did you report this crime to the provost martial?"

"No, sir." Wilde kept eye contact with the major only through force of will. He longed to hang his head.

"Did you call for the sergeant of the guard?"

"No, sir."

"Now, Captain Wilde," said Major Courteen, visibly struggling for breath, "let me sum this up. You did not inform Doc Ledette, the regimental physician, of the rape."

"Correct, sir."

"You did not inform the provost martial."

Wilde was squirming now. He longed to tell Major Courteen that Lois had begged him not to inform the surgeon or the provost martial. But he kept silent.

"Correct, sir."

A long silence ensued.

Major Courteen coughed again, breaking the deadly silence. "And so with no medical proof of penetration and no forensic evidence in support, you served as judge, jury and executioner."

Wilde longed to tell the major that Lois had made him swear he'd tell no one. But he kept his silence. He was already thought of as a fool. He refused to be known as a fool and a poltroon, hiding behind a woman's skirts.

"Y-yes, sir." Wilde's voice quavered.

"And you had the temerity to turn out the troop in search of Shanaco?"

"Yes, sir."

Again a lengthy silence.

Major Courteen coughed. A drop of blood appeared at the corner of his mouth. With difficulty he turned his attention to the sergeant.

"Sergeant Sparks, you were following orders. You bear no responsibility in this and you are free to go." The major waved his hand at the sergeant's men. "The same applies to your troopers and to the sentry."

His gaze returned to Daniel Wilde.

"Captain, you are confined to quarters indefinitely," said Major Courteen.

The company clerk raised his journal.

The major nodded. "This hearing was held in greatest secrecy. The company clerk has prepared an oath of silence for each of you to sign." More blood appeared at the corner of Courteen's mouth. The white-clad hospital orderlies brought forth the stretcher and helped the major aboard.

"Company clerk, have the regimental surgeon and the provost martial meet me at the hospital as soon as possible." He wheezed and clutched his chest, unable for a moment to continue.

At last he spoke, again addressing the company clerk. "When you are satisfied that the oath is signed and witnessed by all present, have the provost guard release the men."

"Major," an orderly pleaded.

"Get me to my sickbed," the major ordered.

Twenty-Nine

Shanaco was fascinated with Maggie. He had never known a woman who was as intelligent, resourceful and fearless. He saw Maggie Bankhead as a remarkably strong person who belonged to herself alone. She had no need for counsel with others before making a decision or taking a chance.

Only the independent Maggie would have dared slip out alone in the middle of a cold winter night, strike the night guard on the head, deal with the brute Sparks and drag a heavy, unconscious half-breed who'd been accused of rape back to her cottage.

Shanaco knew in his heart that anyone else—man or woman—would have been afraid of him. Not Maggie. He had *never* seen the slightest hint of fear in her expressive blue eyes when she looked at him.

Shanaco was both strongly drawn to Maggie and completely puzzled by her. She was so obviously female in everything she did and said and in the way she looked and moved. She was tall and slender and had a wealth of flaming red hair. She was a striking beauty with enormous blue eyes and flawless skin, but it was not just her fair good looks that enchanted him.

It was her total unawareness of his enchantment.

As the hours passed and Shanaco and Maggie remained sequestered in her cottage, Shanaco was struck again and again by the force of her inherent sensuality. Maggie touched his maleness in a way that aroused him as no other woman ever had. Yet she was blissfully ignorant of it.

Shanaco became increasingly annoyed with himself.

Self-control had always been his long suit, but this unwitting young woman had robbed him of his customary composure. Each time she approached the bed he found himself tensing in expectation. When she laid soft hands on him, his heart hammered heavily in his chest.

Maggie never noticed.

Or so Shanaco thought.

Maggie changed his bandages and bathed his wounds with a manner as antiseptic as the alcohol she used, never realizing that her soft hands were spreading incredible heat.

Secretly she thrilled to the touch of smooth bronzed skin stretched tightly over muscle and bone.

''Did that hurt?'' Maggie asked, feeling his body grow taut beneath her fingertips.

''No,'' Shanaco managed, then held his breath as she pushed the covers down past his waist to examine a wound just above his left hipbone. She peeled the gauze back and smiled. ''It's looking so much better,'' she said. ''You no longer need a bandage here.''

Maggie discarded the soiled gauze and cleaned the wound with the professionalism of a trained nurse. But she felt her face grow warm as she noted, with intense curiosity, the thick, well-defined line of coal-black hair running down Shanaco's flat belly starting at his navel and disappearing beneath the blanket.

Shanaco would have been surprised to know that never for a second had Maggie forgotten he was naked. Or that she had seen him naked. All of him. Even that most intimate male part of him. And that she couldn't forget how he looked. Or that each time she got close to him she felt his raw power encompassing her, drawing her to him, thrilling her. She was overwhelmed by his potent masculinity and longed to kiss away all his pain.

Ashamed of her wanton thoughts, Maggie took great pains to conceal her true feelings. She was determined not to reveal her growing attraction to this man who would all too soon be gone from the fort and out of her life forever. She would, she told herself, ignore the fact that he was virile and masculine and the most exciting man she had ever known.

But it was not Shanaco's incredible good looks that touched her heart. He had been wronged, and she knew it was not the first time he had suffered because of his Indian blood. Yet she had never heard him complain about the unfairness of life. Never lamented being a loner of necessity. Never bared his soul; never demonstrated any self-pity.

He was self-reliant, highly intelligent, comfortable

in his own skin, and perhaps more than a trifle cocky. She even liked his innate arrogance; liked the fact that he was strongly masculine and afraid of no one and nothing. She liked the way he walked down the streets as if he owned them, refusing to step aside when the troopers tried to crowd him off the sidewalks.

"Care to sample some more of my special beef broth?" Maggie asked early on that cold Saturday evening.

"Do I have a choice?" Shanaco gently teased.

"You do not," she said, and went about dishing up a hot steaming bowl. Ignoring his statement that he could feed himself, she placed a tray across his lap, sat down on the bed facing him and ladled the broth to his split lips.

"How is it?" she asked after he had slowly swallowed a half-dozen spoonsful.

"Delicious," he said, trying not to make a face.

"Liar," she accused, and they both laughed. Then she said, "Tomorrow you can have solid food. Tonight, it's this or nothing."

Shanaco manfully finished the bowl of broth and drank down a cup of hot tea. Maggie took the tray away, then returned to the bed and asked, "Think you can sleep now?"

"Soon. Sit here with me awhile, please." Maggie nodded and started to pull up the straight-back chair, but he stopped her. "No, here on the bed," he said as he gingerly moved over to make room for her and patted the mattress.

Maggie shrugged, kicked off her slippers, climbed up onto the bed and seated herself cross-legged beside him, tucking her long skirts modestly around her feet.

"Just for a few minutes."

A few minutes stretched into more than an hour. Maggie did most of the talking. She told Shanaco about her students and how she loved them and what a pleasure it was to teach them. She admitted that little Bright Feather was her favorite. She was passionate in declaring that Indians had to speak English in the world that awaited them. She then talked of her home in the Tidewater country of Virginia and of her family and friends.

Shanaco listened and smiled and longed to reach out and encircle a slender ankle that she'd carelessly exposed. That impulse must have shown on his face, because Maggie abruptly shoved her skirts down.

"I've gone on and on about myself," she said. "Now tell me about you."

"What would you like to hear?"

Maggie smiled. "Anything. Anything at all. Your favorite color. The season of the year you like most. Where you'll go when you leave the fort. Whatever you'd like to tell me."

Shanaco smiled, too. "The first thing I'd like you to know is that nothing, and I do mean nothing, happened between Lois Harkins and me."

Maggie's well-arched brows shot up and a slight

smirk twisted her lips. "Nothing? You consider it nothing to...?"

"Lois came to my cottage uninvited," he interrupted. "I was naked when she walked in the door." Maggie screwed up her face. "I had just stepped out of a bath."

"Did you cover yourself?" Maggie blurted out.

Ignoring her question, he said, "She asked me to make love to her. I refused and she promised she would get even." Shanaco paused, waiting for Maggie to speak. She remained silent, her brows furrowed, eyes flashing. Shanaco continued, "Obviously she went straight to Captain Wilde and accused me of raping her. You know the rest."

"But you didn't...you never...?"

"No, Maggie. If I had, none of this would have happened."

Thinking aloud, Maggie murmured, "I'm so glad you didn't make love to her."

"Why?"

"Time you got some sleep," Maggie announced, and jumped down off the bed.

"What about you? Where will you sleep?" he asked.

"On the horsehide sofa."

"Let me sleep on the horsehide sofa."

"No. This is my house and I make the rules."

Shanaco smiled, sighed deeply and fell instantly to sleep.

* * *

Outside, the snow continued falling through the long winter night. Maggie slept on the sofa, or tried to sleep on the sofa. It wasn't that she was terribly uncomfortable there, it was the fact that Shanaco was in bed not thirty feet away. His nearness kept her wide-eyed and restless.

More than once during the night she got up, stole across the room and looked down at Shanaco. She reasoned that she was doing it for his benefit. He was in her care and she needed to check periodically to make sure he was resting. And that his fever hadn't returned.

Each time she tiptoed close, she could hear her heart beating in her ears. Terrified he would wake up and catch her looming over him, Maggie stayed only a few seconds at his bedside. But every time she looked at him it was harder to turn and walk away. His midnight hair was fanned out on the snowy white pillow. His handsome face and bare shoulders were tinted a reddish orange from the flames of the dying fire in the grate.

It was during one of those moments that Maggie realized the elusive thing she had so often yearned for was now right here in her house, in her bed, in her heart.

Maggie turned and rushed anxiously back to the sofa. She lay awake for a long, long time. She was a fool. She was as silly as Lois Harkins. Didn't have a brain in her head. But at least she had enough sense to keep her weakness to herself. Wild horses couldn't pull it out of her. She would never let Shanaco know that she…

Maggie awakened Sunday morning, then stretched, sighed, sat up and peeked across the room.

And laughed.

Shanaco was wide-awake and half sitting up in bed. He had found a length of her hair ribbon on the night table and had tied back his loose raven hair.

Maggie grabbed her robe, slipped it on and hurried to build up the fire. When it was blazing brightly, she turned and approached the bed.

"Good morning," she said, and hoped her guilty thoughts didn't show on her face.

"It is now," he replied in a low, well-modulated voice. Maggie felt her knees go weak.

"Let's hope it will be a good day all day," she said.

It was a good day.

While the storm raged outside and the troopers continued to search for the half-breed who had raped poor Lois Harkins, Shanaco and Maggie were safely ensconced inside her warm, cozy cottage. No one came by to question the respected reservation teacher.

For Maggie and Shanaco it was a long, lazy, pleasant day. Maggie fussed over Shanaco, bathed his wounds, fed him, read to him and skillfully drew him out, asking questions in a casual, diplomatic manner.

Soon he was speaking fondly of his brave Comanche chieftain father, Naco, and his beautiful white captive mother, Sky Eyes. He said they had been happily married and faithful to each other until death.

He told Maggie that his father had been just nineteen when he led a daring raid down into Wise County, Texas. Outside a farmhouse near the settlement of Decatur, he had caught sight of a pretty young girl with flaxen hair in an orchard picking peaches. He pulled the girl up onto his horse and carried her back to Palo Duro Canyon. Then he patiently waited until she turned eighteen to marry her—and during that time they had fallen in love.

Maggie listened, fascinated, as he talked of his life in the canyon, of his parents, of his grandfather. There were so many things she wanted to ask. When had his parents died? How had they died?

But when he paused, she couldn't help herself; the question she asked was "And you, Shanaco? Do you have a Comanche wife?"

Shanaco just grinned wickedly and said, "I'm starving, Maggie. Have any more of that delicious beef broth?"

"Something even better," she said.

"What could possibly be better?" he said with a smile and a wink that dramatically softened his features.

"Ham and mashed potatoes?"

"My mouth is already watering."

Less than forty-eight hours after bringing him to her cottage, Maggie could tell that Shanaco was feeling much better. And she knew that he was enjoying her company, just as she was enjoying his.

The weak winter sun was sinking on that bitter cold Sunday evening as Maggie sat on the bed feeding her patient small bites of cured ham and oversalted potatoes.

Grateful to her, Shanaco was thanking her for all she had done as she fed him a bite of ham.

A heavy lock of her unbound hair fell forward and grazed his cheek, tickling him.

Shanaco laughed.

So did Maggie.

They looked at each other. Their gazes met and held.

Their laughter subsided. It was a long, tense moment. And in that moment Maggie realized that more than anything in the world, she wanted to kiss Shanaco. She wanted Shanaco to kiss her. Wanted him to kiss her the way he had kissed her that afternoon at his cottage.

Maggie wondered if he felt the same. She swallowed with difficulty and carefully set the plate aside on the night table. She laid the silverware atop it. She slowly turned and looked at Shanaco.

And saw in the fathomless depths of his beautiful silver-gray eyes that he shared her feelings.

Without a word Shanaco reached for her and Maggie came into his arms as if she'd always belonged there.

"Ah, Maggie, Maggie," he murmured, and kissed her.

His kiss was slow, gentle, tender. At least in the

beginning. Purposely giving her every opportunity to pull away from him, Shanaco brushed kiss after kiss to her lips, teasing her, tasting her, carefully seeking permission.

But as he kissed her, his powerful arms began to tighten possessively around her. Maggie made no move to free herself. Instead, she lifted her arms, slipped them around his neck and clutched a handful of his blue-black hair.

Shanaco shuddered and his kiss swiftly changed. His heated mouth opened on Maggie's and he coaxed her lips apart. She sighed when she felt his sleek tongue slip between her teeth as he deepened the kiss.

It was a prolonged, invasive kiss and even more thrilling than the kiss in his cottage. Shanaco's mouth was masterful and Maggie eagerly responded, her head falling back, her fingers clasping the strong column of his neck.

Breathless and excited when at last he tore his burning lips from hers, Maggie trembled in his arms when Shanaco said, "I warned you, Maggie."

"You did?"

He nodded, and his nimble fingers went to the buttons going down the bodice of her dress. He leaned her back on his supporting arm, lowered his head and pressed an openmouthed kiss to the gentle swell of her breasts.

His lips against her tingling flesh, he said, "I told you once that if I ever came inside, I might never want to leave." He lifted his head, raised a hand, captured her chin and made her look directly into his eyes.

He said, ''I have no wife, Maggie. Have never had a wife.''

''You haven't?'' she choked, her breath short, heart pounding.

''Let me love you, Maggie,'' he said in a voice that was a caress. ''Let me show you how I feel about you.''

Maggie shivered but said, ''Shanaco, we can't. We mustn't. You're not...you aren't well.''

''Make me well, Maggie.''

Thirty

Maggie didn't hesitate.

She rose from the bed, crossed the room, snapped her fingers at Pistol and sent the surprised wolfhound out the door and into the snow. She locked up behind him, turned and hurried back to the bed.

Wordlessly she began undressing. She was neither reluctant nor doubtful. Nor did she concern herself with the inevitable consequences of her impulsive actions. There would, she knew, be plenty of time for regrets later.

But not now.

Now was a night meant for the kind of passion and pleasure that she would remember for the rest of her life. All the exquisite physical joy and unequaled sensual delight to be found on this earth was surely right here waiting for her. And she was going to reach out and take it without a backward glance.

On this cold, snowy Sunday night she wanted nothing more than to feel this magnificent man's arms around her, his lean, naked body pressed against hers, conquering her, making her his own.

Maggie felt an electric tingling in her arms and legs

as she drew her dress up over her head and dropped it to the floor. Her pulse pounding, she knew that Shanaco was observing every move she made. She found it incredibly exciting to have him watch as she disrobed. She did not feel the least bit shy or reticent, despite the fact she had never before undressed in the presence of a man.

She wanted to undress for Shanaco—she could hardly wait to get her clothes off. Her only concern was would he find her pleasing?

She needn't have worried.

When her clothes had been discarded and she was as naked as he, Maggie watched Shanaco's eyes take on a glittering hotness that made her bare belly contract sharply. At once she felt warm and cold and half dizzy with growing excitement.

Shanaco was dazzled by her startling naked beauty; his erection was swift and sudden and huge. He was grateful for the concealing bedcovers. His only fear was that he couldn't restrain the strong animal hunger she aroused in him. He was afraid he would shock or repel her and that was the last thing he wanted to do.

Shanaco relished the way Maggie proudly stood there before him, inviting him to examine her, challenging him to find fault. He found none. He gazed with wonder on the slender, undraped female form and thought he'd never seen such perfection. Her shoulders were nicely rounded, her skin like fine alabaster. Her breasts, while not large, were high and full, the nipples a shy, virginal pink. She was long-waisted and so slim her delicate ribs showed through the pale, taut flesh. Her waist was so small he could easily scan it with his hands. Her stomach was totally flat and her hips flared with just the right amount of curvature.

Her thighs were firm and well shaped, and between them a riot of blazing red curls guarded the slick feminine flesh he longed to uncover and explore. Shanaco felt his heavy flesh involuntarily stir beneath the covers and he bit the inside of his jaw until he tasted blood.

His intense gaze finally lifted to Maggie's flushed face. He caught the quickening tempo of her breathing and glimpsed the swift pulse at the base of her throat. But her eyes revealed no fear, only anticipation. That pleased him no end.

Maggie was not afraid of him now, had never been afraid of him. Nor was she sexually aroused because he was an Indian and therefore taboo and dangerous. She didn't think of him that way, didn't treat him as if he were a novelty. And that made her incredibly alluring to him.

Warning himself to take it slow and easy, Shanaco turned back the covers, extended his hand and said softly, "Come into my arms, Maggie. Let me hold you."

Her heart now racing, Maggie got into the soft, warm bed with him. Shanaco quickly drew the covers up over her. She lay on her back, her hair fanned out on the pillow. Shanaco lay on his side against her, his weight supported on an elbow.

He gazed down at her face with his hypnotic eyes, and Maggie found herself lifting her head off the pillow, longing for him to kiss her, feeling as if she couldn't wait one more second to have his lips on hers again.

Shanaco laid the back of his hand on her cheek, let his knuckles slip slowly down to the side of her throat. He turned his hand over, curled lean fingers around the side of her neck and placed the tip of his thumb in the sensitive hollow of her throat. He slowly rubbed his thumb up to her chin and back down again. He continued to gently stroke her throat, her chin, her cheek as he told her how beautiful she was, how sweet, how much he wanted her, how much he wanted to please her.

And then at last he said, his voice barely above a whisper, "Kiss me, Maggie. Kiss me like you've never kissed any other man."

Before she could reply, his mouth came down on hers and he kissed her for a long, long time, each kiss growing hotter, longer, more stirring. As his tongue urgently searched the insides of her mouth, Shanaco slowly eased the covers down until they rested around Maggie's waist. She hardly realized that the covering sheet and blanket had moved.

His heated mouth so dazzled her, it was a minute or two before Maggie became aware that Shanaco's smooth, hard chest was now pressing down on her bare breasts as he kissed her. She emitted a little strangled cry of pleasure at the electrifying contact of skin on skin. Suddenly she felt as if her nipples were on fire. Anxiously she clasped Shanaco's biceps and rubbed her aching breasts against the muscled wall of his naked chest.

Maggie moaned her protest when Shanaco moved and the thrilling contact was lost. His heated lips left hers and he raised his head. She gave him a questioning look. Then her breath erupted in a rush when, gazing into her eyes, Shanaco put a warm hand on her right breast and cupped it gently. He rubbed the pad of his thumb back and forth over the nipple and watched the changing emotions march across her beautiful face.

She sighed heavily.

Shanaco whispered her name and plucked at the nipple with all five fingers, gently molding it into a temptingly rigid point of passion. Again he said her name, took his hand away, lowered his head and kissed the peaking nipple. Maggie gasped, closed her eyes, clutched at the mattress and held her breath as his tongue circled the nipple teasingly and then leisurely licked it as one might lick a delicious piece of hard candy.

"Shanaco, Shanaco," she breathed, squirming, sighing with rising pleasure.

Her eyes opened and widened when Shanaco began to suck on the sensitive nipple. She could feel his lips tugging forcefully, could see his jaws flexing. She was glad that his eyes were closed and that his long hair was tied back with one of her hair ribbons so she could see his handsome face bent to her. She liked watching him love her like this, liked seeing his mouth enclosing her nipple, liked watching the firm pull of his lips on her responsive flesh.

Hot and happy, Maggie lay there on her back watching the handsome Shanaco suckle her breasts. She sighed and stretched and found it curious and wonderful that she could feel the tugging of his lips not just on her nipples but in her lower belly and even between her tightly squeezed legs.

Immediately a forbidden vision flashed through her racing brain; the sight of Shanaco kissing her all over. Everywhere. Her hands. Her feet. Her knees. Her stomach. Her thighs. Even…even….

Shanaco raised his head.

"I want," he said, tangling his fingers in her long red hair, "to make love to you until you think I've loved you all I can." He smiled wickedly and added, "Then I'll love you just a little bit more."

She smiled her approval. Shanaco kissed her mouth, and while his lips moved on hers, Maggie felt his impressive erection throbbing insistently against her thigh in tempo with his thrusting tongue. She felt his fingers enclose her wrist and move her hand down to his hard, heavy flesh. He released her hand but continued to kiss her ardently. With an innate knowledge born of passion, Maggie gently enclosed the pulsing shaft and began to gently stroke him.

Shanaco's lips left hers. He again braced his weight on an elbow and lay on his side. Never releasing her hold on him, Maggie turned over onto her side so she faced him. Gripping him a trifle too firmly, she asked, "Is this the way? Does this feel good?"

"Loosen your hold a little, sweetheart," he gently instructed.

"Oh, sorry."

"It's all right. All right. Now, start at the very base and slide your fingers slowly up." She complied, watching his face to be sure she wasn't hurting him. "Now back down again," he said.

"Like this?" she asked, warming to the exercise.

"Yes," he praised, "exactly like that." Soon he was in danger of climaxing. He quickly moved her hand away.

He leaned to her and kissed her. While he kissed her he pressed her back down and fanned his hand across her flat belly. He felt her shiver at his touch. He kept his mouth on hers while he moved his hand steadily lower. Pausing for a second, Shanaco gently raked lean fingers through the fiery coils of her groin, then coaxed her legs apart.

When he touched the slick flesh between, Maggie tore her lips from his and looked at him, her mouth rounding into an O of surprised pleasure. Shanaco smiled. And he continued to caress her. He stroked her with a slow, encompassing touch, his forefinger circling that tiny button of pure sensation, then slipping farther down to the source of wetness to test her level of excitement.

He wanted her to be highly aroused, but he didn't want her to climax. Not just yet. He wanted their first orgasm to be a shared one that would never be forgotten by either of them. So he teased and toyed with her, thrilling her, readying her for the act of total lovemaking.

Judging the intensity of her arousal—she was almost ready but not quite—Shanaco took his hand from her, stretched out on his back and drew her over to lie atop him. For the next few minutes he allowed the sexually awakened and healthily curious Maggie to acquaint herself fully with his body.

She loved it.

Careful to avoid the worst of the many bruises and broken skin decorating his flesh, Maggie squirmed and trembled and rubbed herself against him while Shanaco held her in his arms and told her of all the forbidden sexual pleasures they were going to share.

Maggie hardly knew when they changed positions. But soon she found herself on her back with Shanaco atop her. His handsome chiseled face and wide sculpted shoulders loomed above, the dying firelight casting shadows on his high cheekbones and passion-hardened mouth.

Shanaco kissed her, and as he kissed her he gently nudged her legs wider apart with his knee. He moved his slim hips between her open thighs and carefully positioned himself so that the smooth tip of his erection was cradled in the red coils, lightly touching her slick, swollen female flesh.

Maggie closed her eyes in expectation of his penetration.

"Look at me," he said softly. "Open your eyes, Maggie."

Maggie wordlessly obeyed. She looked directly into his molten-silver eyes and shivered. While they gazed at each other, Shanaco again took her hand, drew it down between their bodies and wrapped it around his aching erection. He moved his hand up to her face and cupped her fever-hot cheek.

"Take me, Maggie. Make me yours. Love me, sweetheart."

"I will," she whispered, and while he obligingly slid down into position, she guided him up into her, ignoring the brief discomfort, longing to have him become a part of her.

His penetration was careful and leisurely, his only concern that he might hurt her. When he was fully inside her, Shanaco sighed with elation and kissed Maggie. For a time he lay perfectly still, not daring to move until her tensed body began to relax and more comfortably accept him. Only then did he cautiously begin the deep, rhythmic thrusting. Slow and easy until Maggie stopped grimacing, wrapped her arms around his neck and began to lift her pelvis, eagerly accepting him, loving the feel of him moving inside her.

Shanaco was so hot for this flamed-haired beauty

he could hardly keep from climaxing immediately. He closed his eyes so that he wouldn't be looking at her glowing face, her passion-clouded eyes.

But Maggie wouldn't allow it.

"Open your eyes, Shanaco," she said softly, repeating the request he had made to her only moments ago. "Look at me while you love me."

Shanaco opened his eyes. "Maggie, Maggie," he groaned, and realized that he didn't have to hold back any longer. Like him, she was on the verge of release. Shanaco's thrusts grew faster and deeper. Maggie moved with him, her body burning hot, her heart racing.

Maggie cried out his name and desperately clung to Shanaco as she felt herself losing control. She found herself being swept away on a rising tide of carnal pleasure that was threatening to drown her. The joy was too great; the feelings too intense.

She could no longer stand it!

All at once the spiraling sensation of ecstasy was so intense she bit Shanaco's shoulder viciously. And then that sweet explosion washed over her and she knew that Shanaco was climaxing with her. It was joyous, wonderful, total bliss. All she'd ever dreamed of and more. Her arms around his neck, her breath coming in quick, shallow pants, Maggie hugged Shanaco to her and kept her legs wrapped tightly around him.

"Don't move for a while," she whispered against his sweat-dampened jaw.

"I couldn't if I wanted to," he said truthfully.

Maggie smiled, nodded and finally let her weak arms and legs fall away. She sighed with contentment, feeling every muscle in her sated body slacken and relax.

At last Shanaco raised his head, smiled, kissed her, slid out of her and fell tiredly over onto his back. For a long, silent time they lay there on their backs, holding hands, allowing their breathing to return to normal, their heartbeats to slow.

It was Maggie who spoke first. Without moving, she said, "We've been unwise. You're badly hurt and we shouldn't have...we behaved foolishly."

"Could be," he said with a lazy grin.

"Undoubtedly."

"You're sure of that?"

"Absolutely."

"There's only one thing I'm sure of."

"What's that?"

"That we are going to behave foolishly again before this night is over."

Thirty-One

Maggie laughed and assured Shanaco that he was wrong. They would *not* behave foolishly again before the night was over.

But a couple of hours later she got back into the bed with him. During the time she'd been up she had allowed Pistol back inside to get warm. She had fed the hungry wolfhound, then fixed a meal of sorts for Shanaco and herself.

After the dishes were cleared away she had built up the fire, heated water atop the cookstove and announced that she was giving him a much-needed bath.

Shanaco didn't argue. Nor did he object when she tossed the covers to the foot of the bed and went to work in a no-nonsense manner, nurse to patient.

Fully clothed, Maggie began to carefully bathe Shanaco's lean body, taking care not to hurt him, frowning at the sight of the many bruises and abrasions marring his bronzed skin. Shanaco sighed and stretched and loved every minute of it. And inevitably, the bed bath became more of a sensual exercise in pleasure than a simple cleansing of the flesh.

Maggie gently stroked him with the damp cloth,

running it lightly over his wide shoulders, the hard planes of his chest, and down his flat belly. She felt her face grow warm when she maneuvered the cloth down the insides of his thighs, the back of her hand brushing against his groin. Causing it to stir.

"There," she said at last, "all done."

She dropped the cloth and hurriedly blotted the moisture from his body with a large, thirsty towel. Then she placed fresh bandages on the worst of his cuts and bruises.

"Think you can get up? Walk to the sofa if I help you?"

"I'll try."

Maggie helped him sit up and swing his long legs to the floor. She saw him grimace and wondered how on earth he had been able to make love to her. She shouldn't have let him. She draped a blanket around his shoulders and assisted him as he slowly crossed to the horsehide sofa.

When she was sure he was comfortable, she stripped the soiled linens from the bed and put on clean sheets and pillowcases. She fluffed up the pillows and smoothed the blanket taut. Then helped Shanaco back to the nice clean bed and, over his protest, quickly turned away.

Maggie heated more water, brought in the wooden tub from outside the back door, set it before the fire and filled it. She again let Pistol out, locked the door and began stripping off her clothes.

Watching from the bed, Shanaco swallowed hard

when, naked and beautiful, her glorious hair pinned up atop her head, she stepped into the tub. She took a long, leisurely bath that Shanaco enjoyed as much as she. Maggie hummed as she raised a wet washcloth to her throat and let it slide slowly down to her breasts. She knew Shanaco was watching, but she didn't mind. It was thrilling to feel his eyes resting on her, examining her, admiring her.

The bath finished, Maggie rose regally from the tub, her slender body gleaming wet. The flickering firelight licked at her pale thighs and high breasts and set her red hair ablaze. Diamond droplets of water clung to her pointed nipples and to the flaming curls of her groin.

Shanaco stared in awe, knowing instinctively that this vision of Maggie would be indelibly stamped on his brain for the rest of his life. Long after they had parted, he would remember exactly how she had looked on this cold snowy night.

He watched bewitched as she toweled herself dry, each move of her lithe body inherently provocative. He smiled as she slipped a long white nightgown over her head but did not fasten it up the front. The gown was undone to her waist. Finally she came to join him.

Maggie stood beside the bed and looked at Shanaco. He was propped against the pillows. The covers rested around his waist. His taut muscles gleamed in the shadowy firelight. His raven hair was tied back and his penetrating eyes smoldered with desire.

Just looking at him made her long to be in his arms. But it would be, Maggie knew, totally irresponsible for the two of them to make love again. Once had been foolhardy enough. She had to remember that Shanaco had been badly hurt. *Was* badly hurt. He was suffering the lasting effects of a vicious beating. His handsome face and exquisite body were covered with wounds and bruises. She was supposed to be caring for him, not allowing him to further injure himself.

"Come to bed, sweetheart," Shanaco said softly, his hand outstretched to her.

"I will," she said, "but only if you understand that we can't…"

The sentence was never finished. Shanaco reached out, caught hold her gown and reeled her closer. He released the gown, clasped her wrist and drew her hand up to his mouth.

He kissed the warm palm and said against it, "Maggie, if you'll get into bed with me, I swear you won't have to make love to me."

Skeptical, Maggie sank down onto the edge of the mattress facing him. She laid a warm hand on his smooth chest.

"You mean it?" she asked. Shanaco smiled and nodded. "Very well," she said. "We'll just talk awhile then go to sleep. Lord knows we both could use the rest."

Maggie rose to her feet, turned back the covers and got into bed. Her head had hardly touched the pillow before Shanaco's lean fingers were stroking her throat and sliding beneath the gown's fabric to caress a soft, warm breast.

"Shanaco," she said, beginning to scold him, but his mouth quickly claimed hers in a scorching kiss.

His lips taunted hers with kisses; gentle, teasing, then hotly demanding, his tongue ran along the inside of her bottom lip before plunging between her teeth to probe the sensitive insides of her mouth.

Maggie moaned and Shanaco's lips finally lifted to hover just above hers.

"You swore," she reminded him, already lost, wanting more of his kisses, more of him. "Remember?"

"I swore that you wouldn't have to make love to me," he said, his breath fanning her face. "And you won't. *I* will make love to *you.*" He lifted a hand, plucked the pins from her hair and watched it spill onto the pillow. He reached across her, laid the pins on the bureau.

"But you're not able to…to…aah," she breathed as his lips touched her throat.

Shanaco whispered words of love in a mixture of English and Comanche as he nudged the open nightgown apart with his hot face and his mouth moved down to capture a stiffening nipple. He teased and toyed with the nipple, rolling it on his tongue, nipping gently with his teeth. He sucked at it until it was achingly erect, then moved to the other nipple.

Her back arching, her heart pounding, Maggie could feel her thighs eagerly opening to him as Shanaco deftly moved between her legs, eased the gown up out of his way and pressed a kiss to her navel. When he probed the small indentation with the tip of his tongue, Maggie anxiously lifted her arms up over her head and wrapped her hands around the rungs of the iron bedstead.

Shanaco's tongue sensuously circled her navel, then slipped lower to lick at the baby-fine line of pale red hair leading down her belly. Maggie knew instinctively what he was going to do to her.

She was shocked.

She was powerless to stop him.

She no longer belonged to herself, but to him. She existed only for passion; was but a burning vessel of desire.

Maggie's fingers tightened on the iron rungs of the bedstead as Shanaco gripped her hips and his burning lips pressed soft kisses down her bare belly, moving steadily lower. Maggie moaned and her head tossed from side to side on the pillow when his mouth reached the springy coils between her thighs.

She gasped and her pelvis surged upward when his tongue parted the curls, then touched her where she burned the most. Maggie clung to the iron rungs and allowed Shanaco to lift her legs up over his shoulders. She grew dizzy and weak with pleasure as his mouth mastered her totally, his lips enclosing her, his tongue plunging, stroking, licking her with the heat of a thousand suns.

Wave after wave of unequaled pleasure washed

over Maggie until she was sure she would literally burst into flame. The ecstasy built and built as his torturing tongue slipped lower still and she felt it go inside her. She gasped and arched and pushed herself up against that fiery tongue, knowing that a helpless scream was forming in the back of her throat.

But just before the coming explosion, Shanaco abruptly took his mouth from her.

Maggie whimpered her protest and her hands left the rungs of the bedstead. Frantically she reached for him, tried to pull him back into place as his lips moved down the insides of her open thighs.

Then all at once he was above her, his handsome face inches from her own. She smelled herself on him, her scent mixing with his. He kissed her and she tasted herself on his mouth. But while he kissed her, Shanaco slowly—so that she would feel every hot inch of his throbbing erection—came into her, filling her, stretching her, conquering her.

His lips released hers. He raised his head. He stared down at her with those mesmerizing silver eyes. He began the slow, rhythmic thrusting, the surging of his lean hips. Maggie sighed with sexual joy and began to lift her pelvis to meet each dazzling thrust.

Her hands again moved up to grip the bedstead's iron rungs, and she whispered his name over and over as smoothly, unhurriedly Shanaco took her closer and closer to total bliss. He carefully kept his own rising passion in check to prolong her pleasure.

Consumed with raging desire, Maggie selfishly forgot that Shanaco's body was battered. Didn't care that the handsome face above her own was bruised. She wasn't worried that their actions might further injure him—nothing mattered except what he was doing to her at this moment in time.

She gloried in the luscious loving, bucking eagerly against him, squeezing him possessively with her thighs, wanting to have him stay buried deep inside her for all eternity.

Perfectly gauging the level of her building excitement, Shanaco continued, for a time, to languidly love her, setting a slow, sensual pace, gliding in and then almost out, making her hotter and hotter.

Until her hands left the bedstead, clutched at his shoulders and she began to beg him.

"Shanaco, Shanaco," she murmured, suddenly terrified that these wonderful sensations she was feeling would leave her. That *he* would leave her. That she would be left like this, suspended, yearning, hurting.

"I know, sweetheart," Shanaco soothed, and speeded his movements, thrusting faster, plunging deeper, driving into her with the full force of his unleashed passion. He knew the exact second that her climax started.

"Oh, oh yes, yes," she cried as the elation quickly spiraled out of control and she felt as if she could stand it no longer.

And then that wondrous explosion, that wrenching ecstasy, that total abandon. Her hands were back on the iron rungs and she held on for dear life. She screamed out as she was buffeted by a joy so intense it was almost painful. She looked at Shanaco's face, hardened now with passion as his own release came. She could feel him throbbing powerfully inside her, knew that his ecstasy matched her own.

The wayward thought came to her that his strong male body was like a fierce volcano, erupting now with pent-up heat, the hot lava of love shooting high up into her.

"Darling," she sighed when at last the storm had passed and they were both limp with satisfaction, their bodies still joined, hearts beating as one.

"My love," he murmured on an exhaling breath of contentment.

They lay as they were for a long, lovely time, holding each other, savoring the bliss, basking in the hazy afterglow and peace that comes from beautiful lovemaking. Maggie fondly stroked Shanaco's deeply clefted back and pressed kisses to his bruised jaw. Shanaco buried his face in her wild red hair and inhaled its clean scent. For both it was the sweetest of restful interludes and each was reluctant to move and break the spell.

Still, as they clung to each other, a troubling thought went through Maggie's mind. This serenity, this happiness was not to last. Just days from now Shanaco would be gone and they would never see each other again.

Shanaco slowly raised his head, looked at Maggie, and in his beautiful eyes she saw her own melancholy reflected there. She knew that he was thinking the same thing she was thinking.

He started to speak.

She stopped him.

"No, Shanaco," she whispered, "don't say it."

He nodded his understanding and replied, "Kiss me, sweetheart. Just kiss me."

Thirty-Two

Monday morning at ten minutes of eight Maggie hurried toward the schoolhouse.

She was nervous. Shanaco had assured her there was nothing to worry about. She hoped he was right.

Maggie steeled herself to maintain her composure when, at straight up eight o'clock, she entered the classroom. The children were unusually noisy and nervous. All were up out of their seats, huddled about in clusters, talking excitedly.

Maggie knew that the subject of their conversations was Shanaco.

Word of his alleged crime had quickly spread and had become the main topic of gossip in every dwelling both on and off the reservation. Everyone, even the children, had heard about the shocking events. The grown boys, those who were fifteen and sixteen, talked knowingly among themselves, discussing the rape of the white woman and of Shanaco's daring escape.

The girls, some red-faced, all shocked and disappointed by Chief Shanaco's behavior, whispered and shook their heads sadly. The little ones, like Bright

Feather, didn't understand what Shanaco had done. Bright Feather knew only that the tall Comanche chieftain who paid attention to him, and whom he liked so much, had been punished for something bad that he had done. He knew as well that Shanaco had escaped and that the troopers were searching everywhere for him.

Maggie raised her hands for silence. "Students, take your seats, please."

It took a few moments for everyone to settle down and stop talking. When finally everyone was in their seats and looking at her, Maggie felt it necessary to address the issue. She glanced at Old Coyote and saw the worried look in his eyes. She could not tell him or indicate in any way that Shanaco was safe. She could not give him a reassuring look, lest one of the students read her meaning. Old Coyote would have to wait.

"I want to say a few words regarding Chief Shanaco," she began in a soft but firm voice. She crossed her arms over her chest. Her chin lifted slightly. "Despite what you've been told, or may have heard, no one knows for certain what actually happened last Thursday night. As you know, Chief Shanaco is no longer here on the reservation. But let me remind you that his absence does not mean that he is guilty of anything." She looked from face to face and concluded, "All I am saying is that you should not judge Shanaco without knowing all the facts. None of us should. If you admired him before, and I know that many of you did, I would not let this awful allegation change the way you feel about him.'' She uncrossed her arms, smiled and said, ''Let us now turn our attention to today's lessons.''

For the next four hours Maggie patiently taught her students. She listened as, one by one, they stood and struggled to read aloud in halting English. Then she nodded and praised them when—a half dozen at a time—they went to the blackboard, picked up new pieces of chalk and wrote the latest English words they had learned to spell.

Maggie conducted herself as she always did. She behaved as if what was taking place in this classroom was the only thing on her mind. Nothing could have been further from the truth. Try as she might to keep her mind on the reading and spelling, her thoughts kept returning to Shanaco.

More than once she felt a delicious shiver skip up her spine at the vivid recollection of their lovemaking. She counted the minutes until she could return to him. Time had never dragged so slowly before. Maggie kept glancing at the big clock mounted above the blackboard, wondering if noon was ever going to come.

At last it did.

The children jumped up out of the seats and rushed from the room. Maggie fought the impulse to beat them to the door. She didn't move, but stayed right where she was, calmly waiting as the room emptied of all students save Old Coyote.

"He's safe," she then said without preamble. "At my cottage."

"He was badly hurt."

"He was, but Shanaco is a young, vigorous man. He is already better. Much better. He's going to be all right."

"How he get to your house?" Coyote asked.

Maggie knew he was eager to hear everything, and would appreciate the story as much as Shanaco had, so she told him exactly what had happened. Old Coyote's eyes twinkled and he smiled broadly and clapped his hands together as she related the snowy midnight rescue.

"Now," she concluded, "tell me what you have heard. What are they saying? What's going to happen?"

"Is said that Major Courteen back in hospital, very sick. Pneumonia. Hear nothing else. Nobody talking much, but mounted troopers have ridden all over reservation, stalking unannounced into every tepee and lodge. Tribes are infuriated." His old eyes again lighting slightly, he added, "Some of the young angry braves get away, leave reservation, not come back ever."

Maggie was not surprised, but she hated to hear it. Still, she fully understood their wrath.

"In a few days Shanaco must leave," Maggie stated. "You and I, Old Coyote, will help him escape."

"I do whatever you tell me."

"I know you will. Now, go and don't worry. Soon Shanaco will be able to travel."

"Where he go?"

"I don't know," she said honestly. "Have no idea. All I know is that he is innocent and you and I are not going to let him pay for something he did not do."

"I tell no one where he is," Coyote promised, then smiled and asked, "You take good care of Shanaco?"

"I will," Maggie said, and hoped she wasn't blushing guiltily.

Thirty-Three

Maggie threw on her heavy woolen cape, rushed out of the schoolhouse and hurried across the parade ground. Teeth chattering from the cold—and from rising anticipation—she rounded the corner of the bakery and dashed the last few steps to the teacher's quarters with Pistol racing ahead of her.

At the door she pointed a finger at Pistol and said to the wolfhound, "You stay right here on the porch and guard us with your life!"

She didn't wait for his response, but opened the door and burst inside on a blast of frigid air. She slammed the door in Pistol's face, locked it, turned about and leaned back against it.

She looked across the room and felt her breath grow short, her cheeks get warm. Shanaco was sitting up in bed, sheet resting at his waist, raven hair loose and touching his bare shoulders. He was smiling. A lazy, sensual smile that instantly burned away any traces of lingering cold.

Maggie shrugged out of her long cape, hung it on the coat tree and immediately started undressing. Too eager to bother with being her usual orderly self, she discarded the garments where she stood. In seconds she was as naked as Eve in the garden and the handsome man in bed was staring fixedly at her, a hot light burning in his eyes.

Knowing that he liked her hair down, Maggie took out the pins as she crossed to the bed. She shook her head about and allowed the long tresses to spill around her bare shoulders.

"Miss me?" she said, and put a knee on the mattress. Shanaco threw back the covers.

"What kept you?" he teased.

To which she smartly rejoined, "You going to talk all afternoon?" And she quickly got into the bed.

Shanaco laughed heartily, kissed her and drew her into his arms. Each was so hot for the other, they had no time for sweet preliminaries. At once Maggie was beneath Shanaco, sighing with pleasure as he swiftly came into her. They made ardent, anxious love, kicking off all the covers, rocking the bed, climaxing almost immediately. Quickly sated, they sagged limply into the softness of the mattress.

After only a few moments' rest, they made love again.

This time in a slow, dreamy fashion. It began with kisses. Soft kisses. Sweet kisses. Worshipful kisses. Slow, burning kisses. Long, drugging kisses. Hot, invasive kisses. Fierce, demanding kisses.

Throughout the ever-changing kisses, they kept switching positions. First Maggie's head rested on the pillow while Shanaco leaned over her, kissing her, his lips slanting across hers, his tongue tasting and teasing. Then they languidly rolled over and it was Shanaco's dark head on the pillow and Maggie leaning over him, kissing him, licking his lips, thrusting her tongue into his mouth.

Then they'd change again.

And yet again.

Until Shanaco, lying on his back, head resting on the pillow and Maggie pressing kisses to his lips said softly, "I don't think I can hold out much longer, sweetheart. I want to be inside you. Now."

"I want it, too," she whispered, and made a move to stretch out on her back.

"No," he said, gently gripping her arms, stopping her. "I'm lazy today, sweetheart. Let me lie here and you get on top." Maggie gave him a questioning look. He smiled. "Climb astride me, Maggie, and do the honors."

Eager to do any and everything with this handsome lover of her dreams, Maggie agilely rose up onto her knees, threw a leg over and sank down onto his pelvis. Her positioning was perfect. Just right. His awesome erection was snugly fitted between her open thighs, its heavy hardness reflexively surging up to seek her warmth.

Maggie exhaled heavily, clasped Shanaco's ribs, settled herself comfortably upon him and smiled down at him. "May I play for just a while?"

A muscle danced in his lean jaw. He raised his arms over his head and, as she had done the night before, wrapped long fingers around the rungs of the iron bedstead.

"I'm yours to do with as you please," he said. "Play. Experiment. Torture me. But don't make me wait *too* long."

Maggie nodded, slowly bent forward, flipped her hair down over her head so that it spilled forward into his face and across his shoulders and torso. She lowered her lips to his chest. While the silky ends of her hair tickled him pleasantly, she began brushing kisses to his naked flesh. She loved the way his body responded.

The muscles in his powerful chest and bulging biceps tautened and his abdomen tightened until it became concave.

Heady with feminine power, Maggie teased and tormented Shanaco, hearing him groan, feeling his body vibrate as if it were a fine instrument and she the talented artist.

She unhurriedly swished her hair back and forth against his chest. She kissed, licked and nipped at the smooth bronzed skin. She boldly bussed a circle around a flat brown nipple and heard him emit a strangled sound from deep in the back of his throat.

Placing an angel-soft kiss on that masculine nipple, Maggie raised her head. She sat up, raked her hair back off her face and gazed at Shanaco with a wicked gleam in her eyes. She rolled her hips provocatively and slid slowly up and down his throbbing erection, teasing him, toying with him.

She saw a vein on his forehead stand out and pulse, watched his jaw grow rigid with the fierce clenching of his teeth. She took pity and extended a hand to him.

Shanaco released his hold on the bedstead, let his left arm drop to his side and gave her his right hand. Maggie took that hand in both of her own and guided it down to where she sat atop him. She released him.

"Touch me, Shanaco," she whispered. "Touch me and tell me. Tell me if I am ready." She placed her hands on her spread thighs and waited.

Shanaco agilely rolled his shoulders up off the mattress and sat up. He wrapped one long arm around Maggie's waist, laid her back against that supporting arm and put his hand between her legs. Looking directly into her eyes, he dipped his fore and middle fingers into the silky wetness flowing freely from her. He caressed her while she squirmed and sighed and anxiously rubbed herself against his loving hand.

Shanaco toyed with her until his fingers were soaked with her liquid heat. Then he took his hand away and spread that moisture over the tip of his erection until it gleamed wetly.

"You are," he said huskily, "almost as hot as I."

He lay back down and folded an arm beneath his head, determined to have her make love to him. He swallowed hard when Maggie rose up onto her knees, wrapped her fingers around him and carefully guided the gleaming tip of his throbbing shaft up just inside her.

She then let go, gripped his ribs lightly and slowly, carefully lowered herself down onto him.

When he was fully inside her, she released her breath and began the slow, rhythmic rolling of her hips.

"How's that?" she whispered, squeezing him artfully, thrusting her pelvis forward, her breasts swaying seductively with her movements.

"Ah, Maggie, promise you'll stay right where you are all afternoon," he murmured, his eyes glazed with passion, his hands again wrapped around the rungs of the bedstead.

"I promise," she said, and meant it.

But too soon incredible heat and joy washed over them both. They moved together as if they were one body; she rocking and rotating her hips, he surging and thrusting his pelvis. She breathlessly lunging. He zealously plunging. She setting the pace. He patiently following. Loving each other, thrilling each other. Pleasing each other until finally the splendor was too great. The pleasure too intense.

"Shanaco…I…I…can't…wait…" Maggie gasped, her burning body no longer under her control.

"Let go, sweetheart," he murmured, huskily, taking his hands from the bedstead to hold her hips. "I can't wait, either. Let it come, baby, let it come."

Then he groaned in his own shuddering release as Maggie cried out his name in ecstasy.

Thirty-Four

"All that we see or seem
Is but a dream within a dream."

Maggie smiled dreamily as she murmured those words. She then raised her head and gazed fondly at Shanaco.

They lay stretched out on the bed, talking quietly, touching, kissing as the hour grew late. Both sleepy. Both hating to say good-night.

"I must admit to being quite impressed that afternoon at the poetry picnic when you recited those lines from Poe," she said, touching Shanaco's smooth bare chest with her fingertips and feeling it all the way down to her toes.

Shanaco covered her hand with his own. "Had I chosen to do so, teacher, I could have quoted the entire poem."

"I don't doubt it," she replied, freeing her hand to again lightly stroke the granite muscles of his chest.

"From the time I was a small child," he said, "my

mother taught me to appreciate poetry and literature. She had no books, but she had memorized favorite poems and stories and recited them to me. Then when I went to live in the white man's world, I bought books, books and more books."

Maggie listened, entranced, as he spoke of the genteel woman who had raised him and was responsible for his being much more than a fierce warrior like his Comanche father.

When Shanaco finally fell silent, Maggie asked softly, "Was your mother content to live among the Comanches? Didn't she want to go home?"

"She was home."

"You know what I mean."

"She was given the opportunity and turned it down." He lifted a thick lock of Maggie's heavy hair and fanned his fingers through it. "One morning she was with several women at Lagunas Sabinas. They were getting water from the creek when a trio of Texas Rangers came upon them. The Rangers immediately saw that my mother was white. They offered to take her back to her family. She refused to go."

"Were you there with her that morning?"

"No. Miles away with my father on a buffalo hunt."

"That's why she wouldn't go with the Rangers," Maggie reasoned aloud. "She couldn't bear leaving you."

"That was not the only reason, Maggie. She loved my father very much. She was his only wife and they were devoted. They even died within hours of each other."

"Were they...?"

"Killed by the whites? Yes, they were. A surprise attack in the Red River campaign."

"How awful. I'm so sorry, Shanaco."

"At least they died together."

Continuing to stroke his chest, she ventured, "And since their deaths, you've lived in the white man's world."

"Off and on since I turned sixteen."

"Have you ever looked up your mother's people? They're your blood kin so surely you..."

Shanaco's eyes darkened to the color of smoke and he interrupted her. "I did visit them once, when I was eighteen. I learned from the Bureau of Indian Affairs where they lived. I rode down to see them that summer."

Maggie waited breathlessly.

Shanaco said no more.

Curious, she prompted, "And? Your grandparents? Aunts or uncles? Were they there? Did they...?"

"The entire Cooper family was there," he said in a low monotone. "My mother's father and mother, her two brothers and their wives and children. All living on the Cooper farm six miles from the settlement of Decatur." Shanaco paused, toyed with a strand of Maggie's hair and smiled sardonically. "I was not welcome. I introduced myself, but the family wanted nothing to do with me." He laughed and added, "They strongly requested that I leave and never return. My maternal grandfather backed up that request with a loaded rifle.''

Maggie made a face of horror. She felt her heart squeeze as she envisioned the young Shanaco being turned away by his own family. ''How cruel!''

He shrugged bare shoulders. ''No matter. I had a loving father and mother and the greatest grandfather a boy could ever have.''

''Tell me about Gray Wolf,'' she said, but her eyelids were growing heavy and she couldn't stifle a yawn.

''I've kept you up too late. You're sleepy.''

Maggie laid her head on his shoulder and snuggled close.

''A little,'' she murmured, then closed her eyes, sighed and fell asleep.

He didn't.

Shanaco stayed awake for a long time.

He held Maggie in his arms and gazed at her while she slept. For a time he smiled, captivated by the sight of her beautiful face in repose. He had never felt this way before. Had never loved a woman the way he loved this one. Would never love another. Would always love her.

His smile fled and his eyes clouded with despair. His jaw hardened. In a couple of days he would have to leave her.

Never to see her again.

It would be the hardest thing he had ever done in his life.

* * *

The fort and the reservation continued to gossip about all that had happened. The troopers were angry that Shanaco had managed to escape them. The Indians were glad he had gotten away.

The colonel's distraught daughter had not left her quarters, refused to get out of bed. Except for mysterious nocturnal visits from the regimental surgeon and provost marshall, no one had called on her.

The worried Margaret Tullison was looking after Lois, attempting to calm the near hysterical young woman. And getting the sharp edge of Lois's tongue for her efforts. Weeping almost constantly, Lois was angry that Daniel Wilde had not bothered to visit, had not even stopped by to check on her.

Whispered rumors of an early Saturday morning meeting with Major Courteen in attendance had begun circulating through the fort by midweek. But no one, not even the troopers, put much credence to the story. If it were true they would have heard what had taken place in such a meeting.

Besides, the major was in the regimental hospital, gravely ill. It was said that he had been in and out of consciousness and had now slipped into a deep coma.

For Maggie and Shanaco the days and nights went flying by—precious hours too quickly slipping away like the sands pouring through an hourglass.

Maggie knew that Shanaco must soon leave. She knew as well that it would break her heart to see him go. If she lived to be an old woman, she would never forget him. And she would never feel about another man the way she felt about him.

Never had she been as happy as she hàd these past few days, shut away from the world with this magnificent man, unknowing and uncaring what was going on outside.

Maggie was sure that Shanaco had been happy here, too.

She couldn't help but feel a deep sense of pride in realizing that she had, in less than one unforgettable week, done what no one else—white or Comanche—had managed. She had tamed the mighty Shanaco. The silent, sullen warrior who had ridden onto the fort that sunny October morning now talked and laughed with ease. This once fierce war chief was, with her, the gentlest of men.

Dazzled by each other, they made love often.

Shanaco patiently taught the eager Maggie all he knew about sensual pleasure. It was, for them both, undiluted joy to make love the minute Maggie returned from her morning classes. And then again after the evening meal as a cold winter dusk fell outside. And especially in the silence of midnight while the rest of the fort was sleeping.

After the loving, Maggie relished lying in Shanaco's strong arms to sleep. Yet there were times she didn't sleep, couldn't. She lay awake against him, dreading the nights ahead when he would no longer be here. Times when she would fall asleep only to wake up in the middle of night, gaze at him, and feel tears filling her eyes.

* * *

On a cold Wednesday evening—Shanaco's sixth night at Maggie's cottage—the two of them sat before the fire at bedtime. There was no light in the room save the dancing flames in the grate.

Shanaco, bare-chested but with a large white towel wrapped around his waist, sat in the armless rocker. Maggie, in her long white nightgown, sat on the floor between his knees.

Shanaco had told Maggie that from that first night he had come to her cottage with Double Jimmy and had seen her hairbrush lying on the bureau, he had yearned to brush her hair.

"Oh, please do," she had said, and kissed him.

So now she sat hugging her knees while Shanaco carefully drew the gold-handled brush through her long, luxurious locks again and again.

"You have," he said in a low, soft voice, "the most beautiful hair I have ever seen."

Maggie smiled, pleased. "I'll snip a lock for you to take with you when you go." The brush abruptly paused. Maggie waited for him to speak. He said nothing. She drew a slow breath and said, "You're just about fully recovered, aren't you?"

"Yes, thanks to you."

Maggie turned halfway about, laid her head back against his knee and looked up at him. "Shanaco, you must go. And soon. If you stay here they will find you and punish you even more than they already have."

For a long moment he said nothing. At last he shook his head. "I can't go."

"You can't...? What are you talking about? You have to go!"

Shanaco laid the hairbrush aside. He reached down and cupped Maggie's cheeks. "I cannot leave you, sweetheart."

She clasped his wrists. "But you must. You have to. You can't stay here."

Shanaco moved his hands from her face, leaned down and lifted her up onto his lap. He wrapped his arms loosely around her hips.

Looking into her eyes, he said, "No. I've made up my mind. I'm not leaving. I'll turn myself in and—"

"No, you will not! I won't let you," she interrupted, her eyes snapping. "Don't talk like that. You have to leave! You know you do. No one would believe you over the colonel's daughter. You haven't a chance if you stay here. Please, please, Shanaco, you simply *must* leave."

"How can I? I love you, Maggie," he said. "I'll stay here and take my chances. I cannot leave you. I won't."

"You don't have to leave me. I'll go with you." She was quick to come up with a solution. "I love you, darling. Take me with you. We can leave right away."

"No, Maggie. That wouldn't be fair to you. You're happy here teaching the children and—"

"That was before you, before us," she said. "I won't be happy without you. I'll be miserable. I love you, Shanaco. I'm wildly in love with you. Take me with you."

"Maggie, Maggie," he said, tucking a loose lock of hair behind her ear, "I can list a hundred reasons why you shouldn't come with me. The main one being that I am not accepted in the white world and never will be. If you come with me, you won't be accepted, either."

"I don't give a fig! It makes no difference."

"Yes, it does. You've told me about your aristocratic family and how much you love them. Do you really suppose they would approve of their beautiful young daughter marrying a half-breed?"

"I can't answer that," she told him truthfully. "From the time I was a child I was raised and taught to question everything." She paused, then said, "I believe that once my mother and father meet you and see how much I love you, they will love you, too. Let me worry about my family."

Shanaco exhaled. "Sweetheart, you will have no friends. You'll be lonely."

"I will have you. I won't be lonely. I truly love you, Shanaco. If you love me, then take me with you."

"You sure you wouldn't live to regret it?"

"Never!" she said, with such conviction Shanaco finally began to smile. Her eyes flashing, she asked, "Where will you go? I'll go anywhere with you!"

Shanaco laughed with delight and tightened his arms around her. "I have a little place up in the high country of northern New Mexico. It's beautiful but very remote. I was living there before I came to the fort.'' Maggie looked surprised. He said, ''It's mine legally, Maggie. I bought some unclaimed federal land and built a house and corral on it. I plan on stocking the ranch next summer. The house isn't much. I built it by myself and—''

''I'll love any house you built,'' she said, hugging him.

''You can fix it up any way you like,'' he told her. ''When we stop in Santa Fe to get married, we'll get a wagon and pick up some things before we head on up to the ranch.''

''I can't wait,'' she said, her face aglow. Then immediately she sobered and asked, worried, ''Does the command know about the ranch?''

''No.'' Shanaco looked thoughtful for a minute. ''I mentioned it to Double Jimmy in passing, told him approximately where the ranch is located. But no one else. I doubt he even remembers it.''

''Even if he does, Double Jimmy would never betray us.''

''Then it's settled?''

''It is,'' she said happily. ''When shall we leave?''

''Can we be ready to go in forty-eight hours?''

''Yes. Absolutely.''

''Good, but remember, you can't say goodbye to anyone.''

She nodded. ''Only to Old Coyote. He knows you're here with me. He's kept quiet, he can be trusted.''

''One more thing,'' Shanaco said with a smile,

"much as I enjoy being naked with you, I'm going to need something to wear, so I'll have to—"

"That presents no real problem," she said decisively. "I'll simply send Old Coyote out to your cabin for some of your clothes. Whatever you need."

Shanaco laughed and shook his head. "Sweetheart, Old Coyote can't even remember where he lives half the time, so how—"

Interrupting, she said, "I believe there's a very good reason he's so forgetful. Bless his old heart, he was once, not so long ago, a respected and mighty war chief. An entire tribe depended on him, looked up to him, came to him for advice. Now he lives here on a reservation and has nothing to do. No one needs him. No one pays much attention to him."

"That's true," Shanaco admitted.

"If we give him something to do, something he knows is really important, he will not let us down. He will not forget. I'd stake my life on it."

Admonished, Shanaco said, "No wonder I love you so much, Maggie Bankhead. Not only are you the most beautiful woman I've ever known, you're also the wisest and the kindest."

"So we enlist Old Coyote's help. I will send him to your cottage for some clothes tomorrow night."

"Indeed. And while he's at it, there is a great deal of greenback money hidden in the cabin." Shanaco lowered his voice conspiratorially. "It's in a leather pouch hidden behind a loose stone at the south base of the fireplace. We'll need cash for our journey."

"What about horses?"

"I suppose he could take care of that as well. My black's now stabled out there in the remuda with the Comanches' other horses. But it will have to be late at night, way past his bedtime. No, that's too much to ask. Tell him not to worry about the horses. You and I can slip out to the stables at midnight Friday. I can easily cut the black out of the herd, choose a gentle mare for you, and a packhorse to carry whatever you want to take along."

"Pistol," she said. "We have to take him."

"We can take the wolfhound, but he can't bark until we're well away from the fort."

"Pistol is well trained," she said. "Still, I'm curious, what is it about you? Right from the beginning, you could silence him with a look."

Shanaco just shrugged bare shoulders.

"It's awfully late, we better go to bed." She laughed then and said, "Not that it'll do much good. I'm so excited I'll never fall asleep."

Shanaco grinned and hugged her close. "Let me rock you to sleep, baby."

Thirty-Five

''Sounds like a great idea.'' Maggie sighed contentedly. She laid her head on Shanaco's shoulder and relaxed against him. Shanaco set the rocker in motion. Slowly he rocked, back and forth, back and forth.

''When are you going to...?'' she began, but he silenced her.

''Don't talk, Maggie. Just rest here quietly in my arms.''

''If you insist,'' she said, and yawned sleepily.

''I do insist,'' he said, his voice low and soothing. ''However, before you fall asleep, please give me one little good-night kiss.''

''With pleasure.''

At once Shanaco's mouth was on Maggie's in the gentlest of kisses. But as he kissed her, Maggie moved her warm hand down along his right arm and over to his chest. She felt him tremble when her hand touched the hollow beneath his ribs. Shanaco instantly deepened the kiss, his lips persuasive, demanding.

Maggie thrilled to the hot touch of his drum-tight belly. Still, she had no intention of this going any further. He was right, she was sleepy. She needed to get some rest. So did he.

Shanaco's lips finally left hers but hovered just above. He looked into Maggie's eyes, raised a hand and tugged at the fasteners of her nightgown. The gown parted and her breasts burned against his naked chest.

He rocked the chair back and forth, back and forth.

"Shanaco, we really do need to get some sleep," Maggie reminded him, then drew a shallow breath when Shanaco's handsome face lowered to the swell of her bosom.

"I know we do," he murmured.

Then, purposely making her wait so that she would grow steadily more aroused, Shanaco kissed the side of her throat, her collarbone, the sensitive spot behind her ear and the delicate hollow of her throat. When his lips began their agonizingly slow descent, Maggie squirmed and tensed in sweet anticipation.

She was no longer sleepy. She was wide-awake. She could not wait one more second to have his searing mouth at her breasts. Shanaco continued to tease her, kissing the softly rounded sides of her breasts and blowing his fever-hot breath on her nipples, knowing that by now those rigid nipples were stinging and longing for his kisses.

"Kiss me, Shanaco," Maggie finally beseeched him.

Deviling her, he lifted his head and kissed her mouth. Maggie abruptly tore her lips from his, clutched a handful of his thick raven hair and said, "That's not exactly what I meant."

"No?" His silver eyes flashed in the firelight.

"That's not where I most want to be kissed."

"Then you'll have to tell me or show me, sweetheart."

She did.

Her hands clasping his hair, Maggie anxiously guided his face down to her breast, positioning his mouth directly over her left nipple. Then she sighed with pleasure when his lips warmly enclosed it.

"Yes," she murmured approvingly. "Oh, yes, Shanaco."

Shanaco gave her what she wanted. He kissed, licked and sucked at her nipples until she was gasping and clutching his shoulders and arching her back to press her breasts ever closer to his hot face.

Finally she began whispering, "Darling, darling, let's get into bed."

With one last plucking kiss, Shanaco released a pebble-hard nipple and raised his head. Her pulse pounding, Maggie immediately got up off his lap and rose to stand on shaky legs. Shanaco quickly came to his feet directly behind her, dropped his covering towel and slipped his arms around her waist.

Maggie felt his nakedness against her. She felt the animal heat of him pressing against her. Her eyes closed as she felt her long nightgown slowly sliding up her legs, past her hips and over her stomach and breasts. She shivered and raised her arms to help.

Shanaco lifted her gown up over her head and dropped it to the floor.

She was naked against him.

She swayed slightly, not sure her weak legs would support her. His strong arms came around her again. She leaned back against him. She could feel his smooth chest beneath her shoulders, his heavy erection pressing against the cleft of her buttocks.

She became aware that his beautiful, artistic hands were on her. All over her. His right hand was at her breasts, caressing, lifting, plucking at the kiss-moistened nipples. His left was on her quivering stomach, his lean forefinger tracing the line of baby-fine hair going down her belly.

Maggie turned her face inward, sighed, and wondered when he was going to carry her to the bed. She murmured his name when his hand came to rest on the triangle of red curls between her thighs. Kissing the side of her throat and possessively cupping her groin, Shanaco said huskily into her ear, "Sweetheart, tell me this is mine, say it belongs to me. Say you belong to me."

"It's yours, my love," she told him. "No one but you has ever touched me, will ever touch me. I belong to you."

"Ah, baby," he murmured, then raked gently through the springy red coils and began caressing that tiny button of flesh that caused Maggie to shudder with building ecstasy.

Maggie could feel his hard, hot erection throb

against her. Her temperature immediately rose. Were they standing too close to the fire? Feeling feverish and breathless, she lifted her head from Shanaco's supporting shoulder and guiltily looked down to watch as he caressed her.

It was incredibly erotic to see his bronzed forearm lying against her pale white belly, his long, lean fingers between her legs, intimately stroking her burning flesh.

She felt her face flush with guilt and quickly closed her eyes when, his firm jaw coming to rest against her temple, Shanaco said in soft, low tones, "I, too, find it incredibly thrilling to watch us like this, my hand loving you this way." When she gave no reply, he said, "Maggie, you need never be embarrassed with me. Open your eyes, sweetheart, and we'll enjoy this together."

Maggie opened her eyes. And she said, "I admit it excites me to see your hand between my legs, touching me, caressing me."

Shanaco smiled and continued to gently massage her until finally, squirming and tingling, she said, "Please, darling, let's go to bed now."

Shanaco took his hand away, swiftly turned her about to face him and said, "Maggie, remember when I said that since I first saw your brush on the bureau I wanted to brush your hair?"

"You've already done that," she said with rising impatience.

"I know. But there's something else. The armless rocker."

Maggie glanced over her shoulder at the rocker. Empty, it continued to rock slowly back and forth, back and forth.

"What about it? I don't understand."

"Since I first saw the rocker, I've wanted to make love to you sitting in it," he said, and took her hand in his. "I've envisioned it many times. The two of us naked, making love, rocking back and forth before the fire."

Shanaco didn't wait for her response. He sat down in the rocker and drew her to stand between his spread legs. His hands resting lightly on her hips, he leaned forward, brushed a kiss to her belly and teased, "Let me *really* rock you to sleep, Maggie."

He felt his heart leap with joy when she replied, "I can think of nothing I'd like better."

With that she came down astride him and laid her hands atop his shoulders. They kissed hotly, passionately and while they kissed, Shanaco urged Maggie to rise up a little. Her bare bottom lifted a few inches off his hard thighs. Shanaco put a hand between them, gripped himself and placed the tip of his pulsing erection inside her.

And he rocked the chair back and forth, back and forth.

While they rocked Maggie carefully lowered herself onto him, taking her time, inching slowly down, making an exciting exercise of it. And all the while

Shanaco continued to rock the chair back and forth, back and forth.

When he was fully inside her, Shanaco placed his hands on her hips and planted his bare feet firmly on the floor. Maggie gripped the twin newels of the chair's tall back and pressed her toes to the floor.

And then the rocking really began.

Slow and easy at first. Rhythmically rocking back and forth, back and forth, the lovers looked steadily into each other's eyes. The rocking of the chair added a new dimension to their lovemaking. It was seductive. It was sensual. It was sex at its thrilling best.

Maggie loved every minute of this unique coupling. Shanaco filled his hands with the twin cheeks of her bottom and made slow, exquisite love to her. With his knees spread and his feet on the floor, he kept the chair in motion.

Slow motion.

Maggie was astride his lap, her legs draped over his hard thighs. He felt her soft buttocks moving stirringly against his hard cock and had to use every ounce of his self-control to keep from exploding inside her. She pressed her pelvis down on his and moved so sweetly, so hotly, he felt himself throb inside her.

She felt it, too.

Maggie was as hot and as aroused as Shanaco. With each backward rock of the chair, she surged against Shanaco, thrusting her pelvis forward, impaling herself more fully upon him. With each forward rock of the chair she felt Shanaco driving more deeply into her, giving her all he had, taking her to the very brink of release.

But not quite all the way to paradise.

Both wanting to prolong the incredible pleasure, they rocked seductively slowly, back and forth, back and forth. They gazed continuously into each other's eyes, each daring the other to hold out, to not let go, not just yet.

Shanaco carefully controlled the cadence of the rocking chair to match the leisurely tempo of their movements. Until finally each time the chair rocked backward, Maggie became more feverish and more aggressive, digging her toes into the floor, bucking and thrusting her pelvis against him. Then as the chair rocked forward, Shanaco drove more forcefully into her, plunging deeply.

Give and take, back and forth, until finally the chair was rocking rapidly. Shanaco had purposely accelerated the motion of the rocker and at the same time speeded the thrusting of his pelvis to perfectly match the brisk movement of the chair. It became a wild and exhilarating ride. The chair—and their damp, sliding bodies—moving back and forth, back and forth so fast they became light-headed.

"Oh, Shanaco," Maggie murmured, moving with him, as if they had become one body, her hands gripping his biceps so tightly her nails cut into his flesh.

Frantically they rocked the chair, back and forth, back and forth.

Until at last that great explosion of heat, their bodies burning, melting together, their hearts beating double time. Maggie cried out in her shuddering orgasm. Shanaco held her tight, buried his face in her breasts and groaned in his own blinding release.

Several minutes passed with the spent lovers staying just as they were, Maggie draped astride Shanaco, her arms tightly hugging his dark head to her breasts.

And the chair rocking back and forth, back and forth.

Clinging to each other, gasping for breath, they murmured breathless words of adoration and amazement at the incredible sexual joy they had shared. Finally the limp, sated Maggie loosened her arms, allowing Shanaco to raise his head and look at her. They smiled at each other, happy to be alive, happy to be in love.

And Maggie threw back her head and laughed heartily when Shanaco said, "Know something, darlin'? When we get to Santa Fe, the first thing we have to buy is an armless rocker."

Thirty-Six

The snow had melted.

Only a few small patches of dirty drifts remained in the constantly shaded areas like porch overhangs, leeward sides of buildings and beneath scattered cedar trees.

A bright sun shone down from a cloudless blue sky. The biting cold had passed with the storm. The temperature had climbed to a pleasant fifty degrees.

Maggie skirted the muddy parade ground on her way to Thursday morning classes. Bleary-eyed and tired from the late nights, she was nonetheless glowing. Happy and excited. She was not plagued with small twinges of doubt or apprehension regarding her decision to go away with Shanaco. She loved him. She wanted to spend the rest of her life with him. She looked forward to the challenges ahead with eagerness and optimism. And, she promised herself that she would never look back or question her decision.

In the classroom Maggie acted as if there was nothing more on her mind than the day's reading and spelling lessons. If she glanced fondly at Bright

Feather more often than usual, she did it so covertly no one noticed, not even him.

Once classes had ended and the children had gone, Maggie turned to Old Coyote and announced without preamble, "The time has come."

"Shanaco healthy? Ready to leave reservation?"

"He is. He will leave shortly after midnight tomorrow."

"What I do? How I help?" The old chief's slumping shoulders lifted slightly. He was keenly interested in what she had to say.

Maggie sat down in the kneehole desk next to him. "Shanaco needs warm clothes for traveling. I know it is asking a great deal of you, but could you—without alerting anyone—slip down to Shanaco's cabin tonight and gather up some things for him? It would have to be late, after everyone's asleep."

"Not care. I happy to stay up, go in middle of night. Make sure nobody see me. I get Shanaco whatever he needs."

"I've made a list," she said, and withdrew a piece of small folded note paper from a pocket of her dress.

She watched the old man's eyes shine with excitement as she handed it to him. While he studied it, she covered the items on the list, clicking them off one by one, using her fingers.

"Buckskin leggings and matching shirt. Moccasins. Boots and woolen socks. Sheepskin jacket and..."

Maggie continued naming the articles Coyote was to pick up and the old man was nodding as she spoke.

"One last thing," Maggie said, "the most important item of all. And it's not on the list."

"Why not on list? What if I forget?"

"You won't forget, Old Coyote," she said with conviction, and he beamed with pride. "There is a small leather pouch filled with money. The pouch is hidden behind a loose stone at the base—on the left side—of the fireplace in Shanaco's cottage. You must get it. He will need the money." She smiled then, blushed, and said, "*We* will need the money. I'm going with him."

Old Coyote's eyes widened and for a long moment he was speechless. "What you mean, you go with him?"

Maggie reached over and placed her hand atop his where it rested on the desktop. "Shanaco and I have fallen in love. We are going to be married."

Coyote stared at her in disbelief, then a wide smile came to his heavily wrinkled face. Eyes twinkling, he said, "Happen mighty fast if you ask me."

Maggie laughed musically. "Yes, indeed it did happen mighty fast. But he's a wonderful man and I'm absolutely certain he's the one I have waited for all my life."

Nodding, Old Coyote said, "Is good. Very good. Shanaco fine man. Hope you be very happy, Miss Maggie."

"I will be. Now, Old Coyote, as you know you

must keep all this our secret," she said, patting his hand. "Once we're gone, everyone will likely suspect what has happened, but it will make no difference then."

"No one know but me?"

"No one but you."

"I never tell."

She smiled. "No one but Double Jimmy. You may tell him so that he won't worry. Once Double Jimmy gets back to the reservation, catch him alone and tell him what I've told you this morning."

"I will tell Double Jimmy. Tell no one else."

"That's right." She moved her hand from his and laced her fingers together atop the scarred desk. "Be sure to tell Double Jimmy that I went of my own free will. Tell him Shanaco and I are getting married and that I will send my family a telegram just as soon as we are settled."

Maggie waited for him to ask where she and Shanaco were going. When he didn't she was relieved.

He said, "You will need horses. I get horses for you when—"

"No, you don't have to worry about the horses. Shanaco said his stallion is stabled with the other Comanche ponies. He's sure he can quietly cut the black out of the herd. Then he'll choose a mare for me. Perhaps even a packhorse from the remuda."

"When he do that?"

"Tomorrow after midnight. Once the fort and the reservation are sleeping, we'll slip out of my cottage, go out to the stables, get the horses and ride away.'' Maggie got to her feet. ''Now, I better be going. I've a lot yet to do before we leave tomorrow night.''

Coyote slowly got out of his chair. He put the list she had given him inside his breast pocket, patted it and said, ''Tonight I slip out to Shanaco's cabin.'' He grinned. ''Be as quiet as an Indian.''

Maggie laughed with him.

Old Coyote quickly sobered and looked around as if someone might be eavesdropping. Lowering his voice to a whisper, he said, ''I get pouch of money from behind stone at base of fireplace.'' Maggie nodded. He asked, ''How I get things to you?''

''I thought about that,'' she said. ''Wrap the clothes in one of your colorful blankets and bring the filled blanket to class tomorrow morning. Come early and put it under my desk. After classes are dismissed, I'll take the bundle with me. I don't think anyone will suspect anything. After all, they believe Shanaco has already gone.''

''Nobody notice what I do,'' he reasoned. ''Nobody suspect you of anything.''

She smiled. ''Then it's settled. Tonight you will get the clothes and the money and bring them here in the morning. Oh, and one last thing, look around, see if you can find one of the thin leather cords Shanaco uses to hold his hair back.''

The old Indian nodded, then said with a sly smile, ''You worry I not remember how to get to Shanaco's cabin?''

''No. Not for a minute, Chief Coyote.''

* * *

Twenty-four hours later Maggie stood before her class for the very last time. Looking out over the sea of bright young faces, she longed to bid them good-bye and tell them how much she had enjoyed being their teacher. How much she would miss them all. But she couldn't. She had to pretend that she would see them, as usual, bright and early Monday morning.

When the noon bell rang, the children jumped up out of their seats, anxious to go out and play in the unseasonably mild weather. Smiling, Maggie watched them hurriedly file out. But when she turned her attention to Bright Feather, she felt her heart miss a beat. She watched as the adorable little boy limped slowly toward the door.

She had every intention of staying where she was, as she was. But she couldn't do it.

"Wait a moment, Bright Feather," she anxiously called to him.

The child stopped a few feet from the door, turned back and gave her a questioning look. "Yes, Miss Maggie?"

She quickly crossed to him, went down on her heels before him, smiled and said, "Would you give your teacher a little hug?"

Bright Feather laughed, threw his short arms around Maggie's neck, clasped his wrists behind her head and hugged her. Her eyes closing, Maggie wrapped her arms around his tiny waist and kissed his smooth coppery cheek.

She squeezed the child so tightly he began to struggle and said, ''Miss Maggie, I can't breathe.''

''I'm sorry, sweetheart,'' she said, then released him, set him back and struggled to hold back the unshed tears that had sprung to her eyes.

Bright Feather tilted his head to one side and stared at her, puzzled. He reached out and awkwardly patted her cheek, as if to console her. ''Are you sad?'' he asked.

Maggie swallowed with difficulty. ''No, dear. I'm not sad. I'm very happy.''

Bright Feather bobbed his head and turned to leave. He limped to the door, looked back, flashed Maggie the dazzling smile that always melted her heart and said, ''See you Monday, Miss Maggie.''

Thirty-Seven

Friday, half-past midnight.

Fort Sill was dark and silent.

The troopers were in their barracks, the officers in their quarters. Everyone at the fort was asleep save a sentry patrolling the parade ground and another posted at the front gates.

And Maggie and Shanaco.

They were not sleeping. They were wide-awake and warmly dressed for a long, cold journey ahead. Maggie wore a gabardine riding suit: long split skirt, short bolero jacket, knitted sweater and tall boots. Kid gloves and fur-lined woolen cape—to be donned before leaving—completed the outfit.

Shanaco, his hair held back with a leather cord, wore fringed buckskin pants and matching shirt, sheepskin jacket and cowboy boots.

"Ready to leave, Maggie?" Shanaco asked.

"Ready," she said.

"Wait thirty minutes after I've gone before you step foot outside. By then I'll hopefully have the horses cut out of the remuda and saddled. As soon as you get there, we mount up and ride away."

"Why can't we go together?" she asked.

"We've been over this a dozen times. I am trying to protect you. If something goes wrong, if I'm spotted, you will never be implicated as my accomplice. They won't know that I've been here with you all along. That you've been harboring a criminal."

"I know, but—"

"And you are not to tell them. No matter what happens to me. Now, promise you'll keep quiet."

"I promise," she said reluctantly.

"Should you be seen, say that you couldn't sleep so you took Pistol out for a walk. Will you do that?"

"I will," she said, "but you better not leave without me." Shanaco smiled and shook his head. "Never, Maggie. Now, remember, once you're out behind Suds Row, turn and walk away from the fort in a southerly direction. Head for the trees and go straight through them and on out toward that empty corral at the north edge of the Comanche reservation. Keep walking until you've gone no less than two hundred steps. If you do that you should bump squarely into me."

Maggie nodded her understanding. Shanaco glanced at the huge bundle resting on the floor. A well-tied blanket filled with the things she had so meticulously packed to take on the trip.

"This is everything you'll need until we get to Santa Fe?"

"I hope so."

Shanaco swung the heavy pack up onto his right

shoulder. He leaned to Maggie, gave her a quick kiss and said, "I'll meet you in a half hour two hundred steps from the laundresses' quarters on Suds Row."

"I'll be there," she said, and opened the front door for him. Shanaco slipped out into the darkness. Keeping the door cracked for a second, Maggie watched with held breath, praying he wouldn't be seen. He disappeared into the shadows and she quietly closed the door. She leaned back against it and began a thirty-minute wait that seemed more like three hours.

Maggie pushed away from the door and, absently touching objects she wished she could take, sauntered around the room one last time. The room where she had spent the happiest days—and nights—of her life. She smiled as she stood beside the neatly made bed. She ran a hand over the mattress and touched a pillow where Shanaco's dark head had lain a few hours ago.

She turned and moved to the armless rocker. She shivered, smiled foolishly, reached out and set the chair in motion.

The chair rocked back and forth, back and forth.

Finally Maggie gathered herself, checked to be sure the fire in the grate had gone completely out. Then she rolled down the wick, blew out the last lamp and returned to the door. At last it was time to leave.

She swirled the fur-lined cape around her shoulders, lifted the hood up over her hair and drew on the kid-leather gloves. She then cautioned Pistol, warning him not to make a sound. She drew a deep breath and opened the door. The wolfhound went out and Maggie followed.

Silently they slipped around to the back of the cottage. There they paused, looked both ways and saw no one. Swiftly they moved along behind the line of darkened barracks, Maggie crouching low so she wouldn't be seen from the windows.

When she crossed the narrow alley toward Suds Row, she felt her heart thump in her chest. A lamp burned in one of the quarters housing the laundresses. Perhaps there was an illness. Someone was awake inside. Someone who might have seen Shanaco.

The lamp went out as Maggie approached. She hurried around to the back of the buildings, turned immediately and walked southward toward the corral she could not see but knew was there in a small meadow just past a stand of trees bordering the fort. As agreed, she set out to walk exactly two hundred steps.

But after a hundred and fifty, Maggie stopped short and blinked, her heart starting to hammer again. She saw the distinct outline of a man directly ahead, but he was not alone. Someone was with him. All she could think of was that Shanaco had been caught. One of the laundresses had seen him slipping past their quarters and had alerted a trooper. Dear Lord, he would be thrown in prison again!

Maggie hurried forward.

And had to clamp her hand over her mouth to keep from shouting with joy when she recognized Old

Coyote standing in the darkness beside Shanaco. Shanaco wrapped an arm around Maggie's waist and guided her farther away from the fort. Coyote fell into step beside them. All remained silent.

But when they were a safe distance away from Suds Row, Shanaco said softly, "Maggie, we owe Chief Coyote a great debt of gratitude. When I got here he already had the horses saddled and ready for us. My black, a roan mare for you and a sturdy pack-horse to carry our gear."

Maggie was amazed. To Old Coyote, she said, "You got up in the middle of the night and—"

"No, not get up. Never go to sleep," said Old Coyote, smiling. "Mounts tethered to log fence. See?" He pointed to the corral just ahead.

"I sure do," she said as the three of them walked on out to the corral. The black nickered, eager to be gone. Shanaco snapped his fingers and the stallion fell silent. He untied the roan mare's reins, drew them up over its head and wound them around the saddle horn.

"We better go," he said to Maggie.

"Yes." But she didn't move.

Shanaco turned to Old Coyote, clasped the old man's hand and shook it firmly. "Our sincere thanks, Chief Coyote. We couldn't have done this without you."

"No such thing," protested a modest but pleased Old Coyote.

"It's true," Maggie praised. "You've bravely risked your life to help and that help has been invaluable. We will never forget what you've done for us."

"I happy to help, happy somebody need me," he said with heartbreaking honesty.

Maggie felt a lump forming in her throat. She stepped forward, put her arms around Old Coyote's neck and hugged him. "We have to go now, Chief."

"Wish I was going, too," the old man said, and when Maggie pulled back, she saw bright tears shining in his eyes. She started to speak, but before she could say a word, Old Coyote had turned and slowly walked away.

"Shanaco, he..." she began.

"I know, sweetheart." Shanaco put his hands to Maggie's waist and lifted her up on the roan mare. He tied the packhorse's long leather reins to the black's rear-rigging saddle ring and swung up onto the stallion's back. Turning, he looked at Maggie and said, "It's not too late."

"Not too late?"

"To change your mind about going with me."

"Well, it's darned sure too late for you to change *your* mind. You've promised to make an honest woman of me and I'm holding you to it!"

Shanaco laughed softly and they cantered away with Pistol darting out ahead. At the edge of the clearing, Maggie turned in the saddle and looked back. She caught a glimpse of Old Coyote making his slow way home to his tepee. She lifted her hand and waved, but he never saw her.

Maggie exhaled slowly.

"Remember this, Maggie" came Shanaco's low voice, and she turned to look at him. "Thanks to you, the old Kiowa chief's enjoyed himself more in the last couple of days than he has in years."

They rode at a fast gallop for the first few miles, skirting the southern edge of the Wichita Mountains, heading due west. When Shanaco was confident they had made a safe escape, he drew rein and Maggie pulled up on the roan.

Shanaco dismounted, dropping the black's reins to the ground. He stepped up to Maggie, laid a hand on her thigh and said, "We'll slow the pace now that we're away from the fort. If we take it easy, do you think you can ride until dawn?"

"My dear, I'm no hothouse flower," she quickly pointed out. "I can ride as fast and as far as you can."

Shanaco laughed and affectionately squeezed her knee. Then it was Maggie's turn to laugh.

She watched Shanaco walk over to the panting Pistol, pat the wolfhound's head and ask, "How about you, boy? You want to ride for a while?"

Pistol barked his enthusiasm and, wagging his tail, followed Shanaco to the packhorse. Shanaco rearranged the huge bundle on the horse's back, making room for a canine passenger. He lifted Pistol up onto the mount's back, loosely tied the dog in place against the bundle and said, "Doze while you can, my friend, we've got a long way to go." Pistol barked and tried to lick Shanaco's face. Shanaco ducked back out of the way. "You're welcome."

And so their week-long journey had begun.

A week of hardships.

Long, arduous hours in the saddle and cold, unappetizing meals and washing in ice-crusted streams and hurrying to take cover from rain and windstorms.

A week of happiness.

Long, lazy nights in sheltering caves with freshly caught trout sizzling over campfires and bathing together in those hard-to-find hot springs bubbling up out of the rocks.

Shanaco knew the land like the back of his hand. He had roamed every mile of it from the time he was a boy. He knew the minute they left the Oklahoma Territory and rode onto the high plains of north Texas. He told Maggie that this great tableland was the Llano Estacado or Staked Plains.

While the wind came hard and chilling from the north, they skirted that huge, deep chasm in the earth, the Palo Duro Canyon. Pulling up on the reins and cautioning her to do the same, Shanaco pointed out the awesome abyss to Maggie.

He told her that he had been born in the Palo Duro. The canyon pleased the Comanche; it had made the ideal homeland. Palo Duro Canyon provided good water, wood and a safe haven from the high plains' brutal winters.

"And," he added, "it was a hiding place that could not be easily seen from afar."

Awed by the vast chasm before them, Maggie asked, ''Did all Comanches live in the canyon?''

''No. Most of the People moved farther south. But not the Kwahadi. They had found a home in the canyon and considered it their own personal domain. My family is buried here.''

''Oh, Shanaco. Can we ride down into Palo Duro?''

''Not this trip. It takes a great deal of time to get down to the canyon floor and you never know when a snowstorm might sweep across these plains and trap us inside. But we'll come back some summer, ride down into the canyon and camp out along the Red River.''

''I'd like that,'' she said, and smiled at him.

On they rode.

Just when Maggie thought they would never get out of the forbidding Texas Panhandle, Shanaco told her they had crossed into New Mexico. It was a bright sunny day and so warm Maggie shed her cape. She laughed when Shanaco stripped off his sheepskin jacket and buckskin shirt, leaving his chest bare save for the scarlet bandanna knotted loosely at his throat.

By the next day the weather had changed dramatically. Frigid air swept down from southern Colorado, sending the temperature plunging. It was back on with their heavy wraps and still they were shivering from the cold.

And when, a couple of days later they began their

slow ascent up into the Sangre de Cristo Mountains of New Mexico, snow had begun to fall.

A full week after leaving Fort Sill they reached a low mesa on the outskirts above the city of Santa Fe, the lights of New Mexico's finest jewel glittering in the gathering dusk.

Snowflakes clinging to his shoulders and eyelashes, Shanaco turned in the saddle and said, "There she is, Maggie. Santa Fe. If you can ride for one more hour, tonight you will soak in a tub of hot, sudsy water, dine on steak and champagne and sleep in a soft feather bed."

Thirty-Eight

Two tired travelers stood at the registration desk of Santa Fe's La Fonda hotel. The clerk behind the marble counter recognized Shanaco, despite the week's growth of black beard and casual attire.

"Welcome to La Fonda, sir," said the hotel employee, far too discreet to mention, in front of the woman who was apparently the latest in a long line of Shanaco's female companions, the warrior's frequent stays at the plaza-fronting establishment.

"Thank you," said a smiling Shanaco. "We need a suite for a few days. Make it a corner suite on the top floor overlooking the plaza. There are three horses outside. Please send someone out to see that they are stabled and fed. Also, we have a canine friend with us." Shanaco pointed to the silver wolfhound standing obediently still at Maggie's side and pulled out some bills. He slid the bills across the counter. "The dog needs to be fed and housed here in the hotel. I'm sure you have facilities for pets. If not, he can stay in the suite with us."

"We have a nice, large, well-heated hall in the

basement with spacious pens and comfortable berths for our guests' household pets,'' said the clerk.

Shanaco looked at Maggie. She nodded but said, ''We can take him out for walks anytime?''

''Certainly, miss,'' said the clerk.

''We need a hot bath drawn immediately,'' Shanaco continued.

The clerk snapped his fingers at a uniformed maid who was busy polishing furniture in the opulent lobby. ''Run a hot bath in suite 418,'' he said, and the woman hurried away.

''In an hour, we'll dine in our suite. We'd like thick steaks with all the trimmings and your finest bottle of champagne. Make that two bottles.'' Shanaco turned to Maggie. ''You like chocolate cake, sweetheart?''

''It's my favorite,'' she said.

Shanaco turned back to the hotel clerk. ''Chocolate cake with plenty of icing.'' He scratched his whiskered chin. ''And fresh-cut flowers sent up to the suite in an hour. Delivered along with our meal.''

''The florist next door is closed, but...''

Shanaco slid more bills across the counter. ''See if the proprietor will open up.''

''I'm sure he will,'' said the hotel employee, nodding.

''A final favor,'' said Shanaco, signing the registration book and handing the pen back across the desk. ''In the morning, could you see that the justice of the peace is alerted. Tell him we'd like him to perform a short wedding ceremony in his office at straight up noon."

"I may never get out of this tub," Maggie said with a sigh.

"I'm staying as long as you stay," Shanaco said.

In the big white bathroom lit only by a tall white candle in a silver candelabra, the lovers luxuriated in a tub of hot, sudsy water. Shanaco reclined against the tub's tall back, his head resting on the padded headrest. Maggie sat between his legs, her head on his shoulder.

On the floor beside the tub were their hastily discarded clothes. Beneath the clothes, a large downy bath mat covered most of the white marble floor. Two matching white robes were draped over a stool in the corner of the room. In shelves at the foot of the tub, several fluffy white bath towels were neatly stacked.

Directly across from the tub a silver-framed, free-standing mirror reflected the room, the tub and the two people in it. Overhead in this top-floor suite, a glass-paned skylight, stretching the length of the long tub, brought the outside in. Snowflakes fluttered down to hit the warm panes and melt. Silvery moonlight shone through the streaked glass.

"Have you ever been this happy in your life?" Maggie asked.

"Not even half this happy, sweetheart," Shanaco said and then he leaned down and kissed her slippery shoulder. He raised his head and, his eyes clouding slightly, added, "I hope you'll still be happy up at the ranch."

"Why wouldn't I be?" she asked, running her hands over the wet, muscular forearms wrapped securely around her.

"Maggie, you'll have no one but me," he said. "You'll miss your friends and your students."

Maggie loosened Shanaco's arms, sat up and half turned to face him. "I won't deny that I'll miss my students, but not nearly as much as I would miss you if I'd stayed behind at the fort. I love you, Shanaco. More than you'll ever know. I'll be happy wherever you are, darling."

Shanaco lifted a hand, tangled his fingers in her hair. "I hope so. I'll do everything in my power to keep you happy." He leaned down, brushed a quick kiss to her mouth.

He reached for a clean washcloth and a bar of soap and held them up. Maggie nodded her consent. Then she sighed and squirmed as Shanaco gave her a thorough bath. When not one single spot on her body had been neglected and she was tingling from head to toe, Maggie said breathlessly, "Now it's my turn." And she reached for another clean washcloth.

Her eyes aglow, she dipped the cloth into the water, lathered it on the bar of soap, turned about, got up onto her knees between Shanaco's legs and began washing his broad chest and long arms. In a playful mood, she sank down onto her heels, moved back away from him and ordered, ''Lean up toward me and scoot down this way, please.''

Shanaco did as he was told. Maggie giggled and, catching him off guard, stood up in the tub and, holding onto his shoulder, stepped around behind him. There she sank back down into the water, her knees apart and resting on either side of him.

And she began scrubbing his back. Shanaco groaned his approval and closed his eyes. But when Maggie finished with his broad shoulders and deeply clefted back, she slyly slipped her arms under his and around his waist. She then lowered the soapy washcloth to his groin.

''Well, what have we here?'' she teased when he instantly stirred to her touch.

''Keep that up, my wicked enchantress, and you'll find out.''

Provocatively rubbing her breasts against his back, Maggie murmured, ''That is my intent.''

She withdrew her arms from around him, dropped the cloth and stood up behind Shanaco. She filled her hands with his loose raven hair, urged his head back against her supportive thighs and looked down at him. ''Is there time to make love before our dinner arrives?''

''We'll make the time,'' he said. He lifted his head, got to his feet and turned to face her, ''But I figured you'd want me to shave first.''

Maggie smiled, ran a hand over his beard-stubbled

jaw and said, "Perhaps you're right. Why don't you kiss me and I'll make up my mind."

Shanaco put his hands on her hips, drew her to him, bent his head and kissed her. At once his mouth was hot and demanding, his tongue thrusting, his heavy beard pleasantly ticklish to her cheeks. Water sluicing down their bodies, arms around each other, they stood there knee-deep in the water kissing, growing more and more aroused.

When at last Shanaco's lips lifted from hers, they looked at each other and knew they couldn't wait.

Still, Shanaco asked, "So what's the verdict? Think you can tolerate my beard?"

"Try me," she said, her eyes flashing fire. "And then I'll decide."

Shanaco stepped out of the tub, turned and plucked her from the water. He kicked their soiled clothes out of the way, and grabbing a couple of the large white towels from the shelf, he hurriedly spread them atop the soft fleecy bath mat, directly in front of the free-standing mirror. Maggie nodded and sank down onto her knees atop the towels. Shanaco, standing above, cupped her upturned face in his hands, bent and kissed her.

"I want," he said against her mouth, "to love you tonight in every way a man can love a woman."

"I want that, too," she whispered.

"Do you, sweetheart?"

Before she could reply, Shanaco stepped around to kneel behind her, his knees inside hers. He put his hands to Maggie's bare shoulders and gently drew her back against him. He gazed at her in the mirror, then pressed his face into her flaming hair. She sighed, reached back and laid nervous hands on his hard thighs.

She said, "Love me, Shanaco. Love me any way you want and you'll find that I want it, too."

Then her eyes closed when Shanaco's hand, wet and warm, slid down over her bare belly to the triangle of damp red curls between her legs. For a long moment, he did nothing more than cup her possessively, pressing her back onto the throbbing erection stirring against her bottom.

Maggie waited, tensed. Then drew a shallow breath when his long, lean fingers gently combed through the wet, blazing curls and he began caressing her with just the right touch, in just the way he knew she liked.

Shanaco had, the first time they'd made love, quickly found the key that had unlocked all her carefully leashed passions. And now, as he tenderly touched and caressed that incredibly sensitive spot, he found her already swollen and wet with desire.

"Move your knees just a little farther apart, sweetheart," he said, and she did.

Together they knelt there in the warm, candle-lit room before the mirror, their bodies wet and slippery, their breaths shallow and quick, their naked reflections adding to their excitement. Maggie sighed with pleasure when Shanaco lowered his head and pressed kisses to the curve of her neck and shoulder. He murmured endearments in English and Comanche and she felt the blood singe through her veins.

Through lowered lashes she continued to gaze steadily into the mirror—she thrilled to the sight of her lover's skillful hand spreading fire from where he touched her to every part of her body. Her fingertips tingled and her toes curled and her nipples tightened and her belly contracted and her thighs twitched.

She felt her slick flesh throb against his circling middle finger and knew at that moment she wanted to do everything they'd ever done and all the things they had never done.

"Shanaco, Shanaco," she breathed, her dreamy gaze locking with his in the mirror.

"Maggie, my own, my sweet love," he murmured, and gently urged her over onto all fours.

Unquestioning, Maggie placed her spread palms on the floor and moved her knees wider apart. Knowing instinctively what he intended, she found it to be the most natural thing in the world. An exciting new way to love and be loved by him.

His heart now hammering in his chest, Shanaco placed a gentle hand on the curve of Maggie's hip, wrapped wet fingers around himself and slid the smooth, hot tip of his swollen member into her.

Carefully, cautiously he sank slowly into her and both exhaled with pleasure. Shanaco then withdrew, almost completely, before thrusting into her again. Deliberately taking it slow and easy, he didn't give her all of himself. Prudent, fearful of hurting her, he thrust only a portion of his rigid length into her.

Just enough to make her want more.

Maggie knew he had more to give and she wanted it, wanted it now, wanted all of him. She rolled her hips. She sighed and moaned. She arched her back. Her breasts swayed back and forth and her damp hair spilled down over her face.

Watching the two of them in the mirror, Shanaco felt his passion blaze out of control. He clasped the twin cheeks of Maggie's pale bottom, spread them and drove a little more deeply into her. The fire in Maggie's blood immediately boiled hotter.

She murmured his name as they began to languidly move together. But just when Maggie had found his slow, sensual rhythm, a loud knock came on the door of the suite's sitting room.

Maggie instantly tensed. A little sob escaped her lips at the prospect of being left in this state of suspension.

"It's all right, sweetheart." Shanaco knew just how to handle the situation. He kept his voice low, soothing. "The door is locked. No one can come in. We've all the time in the world." A vein on his head throbbing, he couldn't have stopped if the entire world had wanted into the suite.

He continued the rhythmic, unhurried thrusting. Inch by inch he sunk more fully into her, increasing the length of his strokes, filling her completely. Driving all doubts and logical thought from her head. "I've got you, baby. Feel me, love me."

"Yes, Shanaco, oh yes," she breathed, choking with sexual excitement, the intrusion forgotten in the frenzy of the desire. Nobody else existed. There was just the two of them, their wet, heated bodies slipping and sliding together so perfectly.

"There's just you and me," Shanaco assured her, "nobody else. Just us."

Maggie responded to his low, soft-spoken assurances. She began rolling her hips and bucking back against her lover. Her palms, knees and toes on the towels, her hair spilling into her eyes, Maggie was so hot she behaved like an untamed creature. She made love with total abandon, her wildness thrilling her lover more than she could ever have imagined.

Inflamed by her total abandon, Shanaco couldn't get enough of his beautiful lover, nor could he give her enough. He longed to increase her pleasure, to take her to new heights of ecstasy. He leaned forward, clasped Maggie's shoulders and drew her up into a kneeling position back against him.

They knelt there before the mirror with him still fully inside her. "That feels good, doesn't it, sweetheart?" he asked, his lips against her feverish temple.

"You know it does," she managed breathlessly.

Taking her with him, Shanaco sat back on his heels and spread his knees wide. He positioned Maggie's soft bottom on his hard thighs, placed a gentle hand on her throat and urged her head back against his shoulder.

His voice low and husky, he said, "Maggie, Maggie, I so want to please you. I want to give you pleasure and..."

"Darling, I don't believe I can possibly experience any greater pleasure than you've already given me."

"Yes, you can" was his whispered reply.

Maggie found out that she could.

While Shanaco's fingers stroked the sensitive hollow of her throat, he placed a hand on her stomach. He kissed her temple and began stroking the line of fine red hair going down her belly. And all the while he continued to rhythmically thrust his pelvis against her buttocks, plunging his hard, throbbing flesh high up in her.

Maggie sighed and squirmed and thrilled to the fiery fingers stroking her throat, her breasts, her belly while Shanaco continued to drive into her. The sight of them in the mirror, making love in this unique manner, added to the potent carnal pleasure. A pleasure that became so intense any lingering inhibitions on Maggie's part swiftly melted in the scalding heat.

Emboldened, shamelessly pursuing even greater elation, Maggie murmured, "You really want to give me even more pleasure, darling?"

"You know I do," he said, his voice hoarse with passion.

"I believe you know what I want you to do."

"Yes, but I want to hear you say it. Ask me for it, Maggie. Anything you want, I'll do it."

Maggie was so hot, she did just that. Saying words she'd never before spoken, she asked him to do what she most wanted. Hearing her lovely, cultured southern voice speak those words aloud thoroughly excited Shanaco.

Their eyes meeting in the mirror, Maggie sighed with bliss when Shanaco gave her what she had wanted so badly. He put his hand between her parted thighs, found that tiny nubbin of sensitive female flesh and began to expertly caress her while he continued to thrust into her.

"Shanaco, Shanaco." Maggie thanked him, her head falling back on his shoulder, her eyes closing.

"Yes, sweetheart, I know, I know."

For the next several minutes Shanaco sat back on his heels on the towel-covered floor and made love to Maggie, shamelessly watching in the mirror, lifting and lowering his pelvis, thrusting into her. At the same time his fingers were stroking, coaxing, circling. And his deep voice was encouraging, caressing, praising.

Maggie's eyes opened, then closed. Then opened again. She, too, watched as they made exquisite love, secure in the knowledge that this man she loved so much would never be shocked by anything she said or did during their heated lovemaking. Nor would he ever leave her suspended, wanting more, unsatisfied.

Maggie was right in that assumption.

But she had no idea that Shanaco was now in sexual agony, his need to climax so powerful he had to bite the inside of his jaw to keep from coming.

Shanaco fought off his approaching orgasm, but it wasn't easy. Maggie's wild red hair was whipping about in his face. Her beautiful, feverish body was slipping and sliding so gloriously on his. In the mirror he could glimpse the slick female flesh he was caressing. And Maggie was saying his name over and over in a litany of love.

Shanaco knew he couldn't hold back much longer. The effortless control that he had always prided himself on was missing with this woman he loved so much.

Now Maggie's body was gripping him madly and she was breathing rapidly through her mouth and gasping, "No, no-o-o…I…I…"

"Yes, baby," Shanaco eagerly urged, feeling the deep contractions squeezing him. "Let it come, darling. Let go. Come with me."

Maggie, hotter than she'd ever been, was seized with a joy so potent it was frightening. She screamed out Shanaco's name in her building ecstasy. Shanaco gave what she begged for, pumping forcefully into her, taking her all the way to total rapture. And when he was sure that her climax was all she needed and more, he let himself go.

His orgasm explosive, he shuddered violently.

His deep groans of satisfaction mixed with Maggie's cries of fulfillment. Until at last, together they tumbled over onto the floor, murmuring "I love you, I love you," breathing hard, completely spent.

Finally they fell silent.

There was a loud knocking on the suite's door. They looked at each other and smiled.

"What do you bet our dinner's cold," Shanaco said, struggling to his feet to don a robe.

Maggie laughed and stayed right where she was.

Thirty-Nine

Shanaco and Maggie blithely ignored the disapproving looks from the justice of the peace, J. Martin Weeks. Holding the marriage license issued to Shan Cooper—Shanaco used his white mother's family name—and Maggie Bankhead, the justice peered at Shanaco over his wire-rimmed glasses and frowned. He shifted his gaze to Maggie and shook his head.

But he performed the brief ceremony, and at ten minutes past noon, Mr. and Mrs. Shan Cooper exited Weeks's office smiling. The pair spent most of the snowy afternoon shopping. Shanaco told Maggie she could choose anything she wanted or needed to take up to the ranch.

"How will we transport our treasures?" Maggie asked as hand in hand they walked into a cavernous dry goods store.

"We'll buy a wagon to haul everything," Shanaco replied.

"In that case..." Maggie said as she dropped his hand and moved toward a table of glassware.

When they left the store hours later, Maggie had made many purchases for the new home she was to share with Shanaco. Each item she had picked up, he'd said, "You want it, get it." Assuring the proprietor they would be back for their purchases in a couple of days, they left.

"Back to the hotel now?" Maggie asked.

"Not just yet," Shanaco said. "I want to take my beautiful bride down to dinner this evening."

"Yes!" Maggie was enthusiastic. "I'd like that."

"Then we'll need something elegant to wear."

Maggie smiled. "You are *so* handsome in evening clothes. When you walked into the officers' ball I almost swooned."

Shanaco remembered the ball as well. "When I saw you in that lilac velvet gown with your hair falling around your shoulders, I wanted to come right over, grab you and kiss you senseless in front of all those officers and their haughty wives."

"Really? I had no idea," Maggie said, pleased.

"Yes, you did," he accused, and stopped directly before a ladies' boutique. "They say this is the finest shop in Santa Fe. Think you can find something suitable in an hour?"

"Watch me!"

"No. I'm not coming in with you, Maggie," he told her. "I'll be just down the street at a men's store."

"You'll come back for me?"

Shanaco kissed her forehead, then winked at her. "What do you think?"

"I love you," she said.

"You better."

* * *

It was nearing four-thirty in the afternoon when they hurried back toward the hotel. The snow had continued to fall throughout the day, and now as evening approached, it was heavier, the flakes bigger and wetter. There was no longer any horizon; it was a total whiteout. And it was cold, bitter cold.

The newlyweds laughed as they rushed into La Fonda's opulent lobby. Inside a half-dozen guests were seated around the huge fireplace, talking and drinking coffee. They immediately fell silent. They turned and stared and it was easy to discern what they were thinking.

Shanaco's jaw tightened and his silver eyes blazed. He took Maggie's arm and forcefully ushered her to the grand staircase. Halfway up, he stopped, turned to her and said, "This is how it is going to be for you, Maggie. People staring and whispering."

Maggie shrugged slender shoulders. "Let them stare and whisper. I couldn't care less, darling. I need no one's approval but yours." She went on up the stairs. Exhaling, Shanaco followed. In the suite, she said, "Give me my dress. I don't want you to see it until I'm wearing it."

"Fair enough," Shanaco said, and handed her the package. "We'll dine at eight if that suits you." She nodded. "Which means we have time to relax." He started to grin. "Or to do anything else we can think of to do."

Maggie smiled, tossed the wrapped package onto a beige brocade sofa, threw off her cape and said, "Bet I can get undressed quicker that you."

"You have yourself a wager," he said. Dropping the package containing his newly purchased evening clothes, he shrugged out of his jacket and then peeled his buckskin shirt up over his head and off in one swift, fluid movement.

"I win," he said within seconds when all his clothes lay on the floor and he stood before the blazing fire, totally naked.

"Yes? Well guess what the prize is," Maggie said saucily, shedding the last of her garments and taking a step toward him.

Shanaco laughed, swept her up into his arms and carried her to the bedroom. While she clung to his neck and giggled and kicked her bare feet, Shanaco managed to turn back the counterpane, tossing the heavy spread to the foot of the bed. He yanked the covering blanket and top sheet down out of the way and shoved the half-dozen satin-and-lace-cased pillows up against the tall mahogany headboard.

Then he carefully placed Maggie in the middle of the bed against the stacked pillows. She sighed happily when Shanaco joined her. But she gave him a puzzled look when, instead of taking her in his arms, he stretched out on his back beside her and folded his hands beneath his head.

"Let's play a game," he said, his eyes flashing

with mischief. "Let's see just how long we can keep from making love."

Maggie laughed with delight, turned onto her side facing him, rose up onto an elbow and laid a warm hand on his belly. "By the looks of things," she teased, pointedly focusing on his rapidly forming erection, "it'll be about five minutes."

"Five minutes? Why, darlin', I can't possibly wait *that* long."

At eight that evening the handsomely dressed newlyweds walked into the hotel's crowded dining room. Again people turned to stare, but Shanaco and Maggie hardly noticed. Relaxed and happy, the pair had just spent a couple of incredibly pleasurable hours in bed and were so in love they had eyes only for each other.

At the far end of the marble-columned room, discreetly hidden behind lush potted palms, a six-piece orchestra in evening attire played dinner music while white-jacketed waiters deftly weaved their way between tables with loaded trays balanced on upraised palms.

The meal was sumptuous and the lovers were famished. They ate with gusto. At last the smartly uniformed waiter brought the coffee and dessert.

Maggie took one look at the perfectly molded blancmange, patted her straining midriff through the lush turquoise velvet of her new gown and leaned across the table to whisper, "I can't possibly take one more bite lest I pop right out of this dress."

"Push the dessert away then, sweetheart," he said. "I'll have a little treat sent up to the suite later." He arched dark eyebrows in a devilish leer and added, "You can get out of that dress and really enjoy your dessert."

"You are so thoughtful," she said. "I'll become a spoiled woman."

"You'll become *my* spoiled woman," he said, then turned and almost imperceptibly waved his hand in the air.

At once the six-piece orchestra began playing the sweetly sentimental love song, "When You and I Were Young, Maggie."

Her eyes round with surprise, Maggie stared at Shanaco. "You? You had them play…?"

"I did," Shanaco said, reaching for her hand across the table. "And when we celebrate our golden wedding anniversary, I'll have them play it again."

Tears sprang to Maggie's eyes as she gazed at the perfectly groomed, strikingly handsome man who was her adored husband. When she could speak past the tightness in her throat, she said, "Shanaco, can I ask you to do something?"

He gently squeezed her soft hand and said, "Ask me to do anything but stop loving you."

At that, the tears spilled over and slipped down Maggie's cheeks. Shanaco tossed his napkin on the table, pushed his chair back, came around, helped her to her feet and escorted her out of the dining room.

Once they were on the stairs and alone, he stopped,

took a clean white handkerchief from the inside breast pocket of his dark evening jacket and offered it to her.

"What is it, darling?" he asked. "Tell me and I'll fix it."

Maggie dabbed at her eyes with the handkerchief, laughed at herself, then sniffed, "I'm sorry, I... Nothing's wrong. I'm behaving foolishly, I know. It's just...just...you're so good to me and I love you so much and I...I..."

"You're just happy," he supplied the words.

"Y-yes."

"So am I, sweetheart, so am I."

Forty

The snowstorm finally passed.

After four days of the wind-driven blizzard roaring through the Sangre de Cristos, a bright warming sun finally rose on the city of Santa Fe. As the sun climbed higher, light streamed in through the tall windows of the La Fonda hotel suite where two honeymooners slept.

The sunshine awakened Shanaco. He blinked, tossed back the covers and went to the windows. He stood for a long minute looking out, checking the condition of the streets, peering up over the buildings to the mountain peaks beyond.

"Could that strange new light actually be the sun?" a sleepy Maggie asked from the bed.

Shanaco turned and smiled at her. "Hard to believe, but it is. So get up, lazybones and get dressed." He came to the bed, yanked the covers off her and said, "Let's go home, sweetheart."

"If you're waiting on me, you're wasting time," Maggie told him and bounded out of bed.

By 8:00 a.m. the warmly dressed pair were ready to depart. Shanaco's black stallion and the roan mare were hitched to a heavily loaded wagon. The pack-horse—also weighed down—was tied to the wagon's rear. Stashed beneath the wagon's high front seat was a loaded pearl-handled revolver. Maggie was already sitting on the bench seat, and directly behind her, balanced on a crate, Pistol barked his growing excitement.

Shanaco stood in the street. He carefully checked the bridles and riggings yoking the horses to the wagon. Finally satisfied, he walked slowly around the wagon, examining, yanking on taut ropes and leather straps securing the cargo. He didn't want to start up a steep, snow-covered grade and lose everything due to careless packing.

"Will we get there by nightfall?" Maggie asked when Shanaco climbed up onto the seat beside her and unwrapped the long leather reins from around the brake.

"With any luck," he said, and flicked the reins over the horses' backs. "I calculate we'll reach the house with at least an hour or more of daylight left."

"Good," Maggie said with a smile. "I can't wait. I'm almost as excited as Pistol."

The pair headed out of Santa Fe with their purchases. Atop the many valises and boxes and crates and barrels, sat a brand-new cane-bottom armless rocker. They had laughed when they bought the rocking chair until the clerk had looked at them piteously and shaken his head. Now they laughed again on seeing the rocker riding high atop the load.

On the outskirts of the city, Shanaco pointed to the soaring, cloud-shrouded summit of Elk Mountain in the range to the east.

"That where we're headed?" Maggie asked.

"It is. A wide pass threads through those mountains," he said. "The ranch is there in a high, lush valley. Just to the south of Glorieta Pass."

"Glorieta Pass. A beautiful name."

"A beautiful place."

The journey was pleasant. The day grew warmer as the alpine sun climbed steadily higher. While the groaning wagon bumped along over a winding, slippery trail, Shanaco and Maggie talked and laughed and sang and enjoyed the outing. They were still in great high spirits when, at midafternoon, the heavy wagon became too much of a burden for the tired, winded horses.

"We need to lighten the load to get over that next ridge," Shanaco said. "Think you can walk for a mile or two?"

"Certainly," Maggie said with a smile. "I need to stretch my legs anyhow."

She laughed merrily as Shanaco plucked her off the high seat, gave her a quick kiss and set her on her feet. Pistol had already shot down off the wagon and raced ahead, tail wagging.

Shanaco took hold of the horses' bridles and coaxed them up to the next plateau. They walked for an hour, taking it slow and easy, then climbed back onto the wagon. It was not the last time the couple had to get off and walk, but they didn't mind.

When the sun that had shone brightly all day began to sink slowly toward the western mountain peaks, they reached the ranch. Rounding a corner in a high, wide valley, Shanaco pulled up on the reins and brought the wagon to a standstill.

And Maggie got her first glimpse of the ranch house. Set against a tumbled wall of rock that soared directly behind it, the small frame house was barely visible through the stands of cedar and juniper and pines.

Maggie was craning to get a better look when she became aware of a muted roar. She turned and gave Shanaco a questioning look. He laughed and inclined his head, directing her attention to the rush of gleaming water spilling down the rocky hillside and into a wide clear pool not a hundred yards from the house.

Even now in the dead of winter this remote high-meadow ranch was awesomely beautiful. Maggie looked forward to the cold, snowy nights inside before a blazing fire. And she could well imagine the lush green valley in the summertime when the two of them could swim in the crystalline pool.

"Shanaco, this place is breathtaking," she said. "You never told me. I had no idea." Her face aglow, she started to jump down and hurry to the house.

Shanaco, suddenly frowning, put a hand on her arm and stopped her.

"Wait, Maggie," he said sharply.

"Why? What is it?"

"You stay here," he said, and swung down from the wagon seat.

"No, I'm coming with you," she said, grabbing his shirtsleeve.

"Very well," he said, lifting her to the ground, "but stay behind me."

She nodded. Shanaco reached beneath the seat for his loaded revolver, then pointed a finger at Pistol, signaling the wolfhound to keep silent. As they quietly approached the house, Maggie saw that the front door was open.

"Is somebody...?"

"Shhh," Shanaco warned.

They reached the porch and climbed the front steps. Gun raised, Shanaco again warned Maggie to stay outside. She obeyed. He went inside. After a long minute Maggie heard him curse. She hurried in, looked around and her hand went to her mouth.

The house had been vandalized. All the furniture was overturned and smashed. The mattress had been dragged out of the bedroom, dumped before the fireplace and slashed. Feathers covered the floor. Pottery was broken and scattered about. Books had been pulled from bookcases, the pages torn out. The windows were shattered.

And those responsible for the destruction had left their calling card.

"Stay away, Injun!" was scrawled on the walls in black paint.

Shanaco laid the revolver on the nearby mantel and exhaled heavily. ''I should never have brought you here,'' he said through thinned lips, his face taut with anger.

Maggie saw the hurt in his eyes and her heart ached for him. She stepped forward and put her arms around him.

''Darling, don't say that.''

''It's the truth, Maggie. You don't belong here. I should have had better sense than to bring you here.''

''Shanaco, this is where I want to be. Right here with you. We'll get this mess cleaned up in no time,'' she said as if the destruction was nothing more than a trivial irritation. ''We'll start over with the things we bought in Santa Fe. After all, we have the rocking chair. What else do we really need?'' She teased, attempting to lighten his mood.

It didn't work.

His handsome face was a mask of controlled fury and she could feel the coiled tension in his lean body as she stood against him.

''Please, don't let this upset you,'' she said. ''It doesn't matter, darling. I love you and I don't need anyone else. *We* don't need anyone else, just each other.''

She paused and held her breath, waiting for him to speak. He said nothing. Nor did his arms lift and reassuringly come around her. Desperate, she pressed her cheek against his chest and felt the fierce hammering of his heart.

She said softly, "Darling, together we'll make our home here."

"It's no good, Maggie." Shanaco finally spoke and he sounded tired, defeated. "I've been selfish and irresponsible and I'm sorry. You deserve more than a lonely life of being shunned because you are a half-breed's wife. I'm taking you back to—"

Interrupting, Maggie said heatedly, "You're taking me nowhere! Have you so little faith in me? Do you really suppose that this minor incident could scare me away? Don't you know me better than that? Shame on you for doubting me! Why, I'm the woman who knocked a big armed trooper unconscious with a baseball bat and then dragged you to my place, remember?"

"I've forgotten nothing, Maggie. And I've never questioned your courage or determination. But this—"he made a sweeping gesture of the wrecked room and the telltale message written on the wall "—is what you're in for if you stay with me. It's too much to ask. I can't put you through this and—"

Interrupting again, Maggie said, "Remember the evening back in Santa Fe when we got all dressed up and went to dinner downstairs at La Fonda?" Shanaco nodded. "That night you said to me, 'Ask me to do anything but stop loving you.' I feel the same way, Shanaco. So don't ask me to live without you. I could no more stop loving you than I could stop breathing. I don't want to stop loving you and you can't make me. So there!" Her eyes flashed with the exclamation and she saw the corners of Shanaco's tight lips begin to lift ever so slightly.

So she laughed and was tremendously relieved when he laughed with her.

"Yes, ma'am," he said, and finally put his arms around her.

"Now, that's settled and we'll not speak of it again. So why don't you go on out and tend the horses while I start cleaning up."

"On my way." He released her and crossed to the door. He stopped there, turned back, looked at her with all his love and admiration shining in his eyes. He shook his head and said, "Baby, how did I ever get so lucky?"

"Luck had nothing to do with it," Maggie said with a mischievous smile.

"No?"

"No. I decided—that first time you kissed me—that you were going to be *mine.*"

Forty-One

Colonel Norman S. Harkins was furious.

The portly commandant, having returned from the inspection tour with General Sherman, had been back at Fort Sill for only an hour.

But it had been the longest hour of his life.

He wished that he had never returned. Wished he was still out on the frontier, blissfully ignorant of what had happened here in his absence. Wished that he could go to sleep and wake up to find it had all been a bad dream.

Alone now in his office, the colonel gritted his teeth until his fleshy jaws ached. His weeping daughter's shocking disclosure kept ringing in his ears no matter how much he tried to silence it. He shook his head sorrowfully. It was his fault—he was responsible. He should never have allowed his young, beautiful daughter to visit him at this frontier fort. He had to have been out of his mind to suppose that Lois would be safe with wild Indians living within a stone's throw of their quarters.

Colonel Harkins leaned up to the desk and put his face in his hands. Again and again he had relived those first few horrible moments when he'd arrived back at the fort. Tired and dusty from the trail, he had gone directly to his residence. There he'd been met at the door by Margaret Tullison, the trooper's wife who had promised to look after Lois. Mrs. Tullison had, upon seeing him, burst into tears, put her hand over her mouth and frantically gestured in the direction of Lois's bedroom.

His heart had started to pound painfully when he found Lois, looking pale and wan, still in bed although it was midafternoon. On seeing him, she too had immediately burst into tears. When she'd calmed a little, Lois told him—the words coming out in a rush—that the half-breed Shanaco had brutally raped her.

Then, sobbing and coughing as he put comforting arms around her, Lois related the appalling facts of the brutal assault in vivid detail. She had painted a picture he could not put from his mind. He kept envisioning the dirty, drunken Comanche half-breed forcing the terrified Lois to do unspeakable things, threatening her life if she refused.

Now, alone here in his office, the colonel swore, "I'll kill him. I'll have him hunted down and shot like the mad dog he is, Indian chief or no! I'll have his head on a platter, by God! I'll see to it that the red bastard never harms another helpless female! I'll..."

A knock on the door startled him. Colonel Harkins

looked up as the sergeant major said, ''Sir, the company clerk requests permission to see you.''

''What the hell does he want?'' a scowling Harkins replied.

''Says it's confidential, sir.''

Harkins exhaled heavily. ''Send him in.''

The company clerk marched into the office. ''Colonel Harkins, I have the sad duty to report the death of Major Miles Courteen.''

''No! Miles dead?'' Harkins repeated in stunned disbelief. ''Jesus God, what next? Miles can't be dead, he...he...'' His words trailed away and his flushed face turned ashen at this latest blow.

''Sadly it is true, sir. The major died of pernicious pneumonia minutes ago,'' said the company clerk. ''I was at his side when the end came.'' He leaned across the desk and handed Harkins a sheaf of papers stuck inside a maroon file folder. ''Major Courteen's dying orders were to 'deliver this file to Colonel Harkins and to no one else.'''

Harkins nodded and dismissed him. The company clerk turned and left. Colonel Harkins placed the file on his desk, wondering what sensitive information could be in the file that it was to be delivered to the commanding officer and no one else.

He tugged at the string binding and had the folder open, but closed it without reading a word when the sergeant major announced Double Jimmy's presence.

''Colonel, I just returned and thought I'd stop by

to..." Double Jimmy began, and was immediately waved to silence by a grim-faced Harkins.

"Sit down!" the colonel barked, and Double Jimmy dropped down into a chair.

As Harkins pounded his desk to punctuate every sentence, his voice cracked as he related Shanaco's vicious attack on Lois and of the half-breed's subsequent escape. Double Jimmy's eyes widened with shock. He listened respectfully as the livid colonel exploded, swearing loudly. But Double Jimmy didn't believe for a minute that Shanaco had harmed Lois Harkins.

Harkins ranted and raved, his face growing redder by the minute. Finally concluding, he said, "By God, I hope you're satisfied now! You and all your Indian-loving bureau employees, always taking up for the savages, always preaching that they are human beings, too, and should be treated with respect! Attempting to civilize them, for God's sake! See what you get for your misplaced trust! I'll tell you what you get, a beautiful young girl's life ruined! My sweet, innocent daughter violated by that animal!"

"Colonel, I am terribly sorry to hear that—"

"I don't want your sympathy, Double Jimmy! I want action! You're the Indian agent and responsible for those red-skinned devils! Go on, ride out of here right now. Find that Comanche and bring him to me."

"Colonel, be reasonable. I told you, I just got back a half hour ago and—"

"I don't give a damn!" thundered Harkins. "You

know his haunts. Go after that half-breed and don't come back until you've caught him.''

Double Jimmy stared at the fuming Harkins. There was no reasoning with him. The colonel was far too upset to listen. And the last thing Harkins would want to hear was that there was little chance of apprehending Shanaco. Even less of bringing him back to the fort to face punishment.

''Why are you continuing to sit there?'' boomed Harkins. ''There's daylight left and you're wasting it. I want that Comanche beast delivered to me, do you hear?''

Double Jimmy didn't argue. He rose to his feet and left the office with the angry Harkins shouting after him.

Colonel Harkins finally fell silent, sighed wearily and leaned back in his chair. He sat there quietly for several long minutes. Then finally the maroon file folder caught his attention. He had little interest in what it contained, but it was something Major Courteen thought important enough for his eyes only.

Harkins began to read.

His eyes widened and his jaw went slack. He read the entire file, then read it again. He closed the folder. Jaw now clamped down tight, the colonel sat in stunned silence for a long moment.

He pinched the bridge of his nose, pushed his chair back and rose to his feet. He turned to the bookcase behind his desk. A number of legal reference books were shelved there. Harkins glanced through the volumes and took down one of the books. A heavy, blood-red, leather-bound book: Steven V. Benet's *Military Law and Courts-Martial.*

He placed the leather-bound book on his desk but did not open it.

His hand lying atop the book's smooth leather, he summoned the sergeant major into his office and with a sad face said, "Send the company clerk for Double Jimmy."

Forty-Two

The first night Shanaco and Maggie spent at the ranch was a happy one. Since dusk was rapidly descending, they decided to wait until morning to start putting the wreckage right. They had all that was necessary. Fire for warmth, food for supper and bedding to sleep on.

Shanaco gathered wood and built a fire in the grate. The vandals had helped themselves to the stacks of cord wood he had laboriously cut last summer. He collected loose limbs and kindling while Maggie covered the broken windows with strips of the ruined sheets and blankets.

Once the windows were covered and a bright fire blazed in the stone fireplace, they went out to the loaded wagon. Shivering, Maggie pointed out the valises and packages containing items they would most need for the night. Everything else could stay on the wagon and be unpacked later.

"That about do it, sweetheart?" Shanaco asked when he was loaded down, his arms full.

"Mmm. Just one last thing," Maggie said as she plucked another package from the wagon and placed it atop those he held. "It's fragile, so be careful," she warned.

By nine that night all of the boxes had been opened, the needed articles unpacked and their chores finished.

Time to relax.

They sat cross-legged on a new, soft downy counterpane spread out on the floor in front of the fire. They laughed and talked as they dined on food that had been packed in a large picnic hamper by La Fonda's hotel kitchen staff. Salted nuts and cheddar cheese and smoked ham and deviled eggs and French bread and fresh fruit and chocolate cake. To wash it all down, they drank chilled wine from the delicate long-stemmed glasses that Maggie had carefully unwrapped.

Enjoying the feast, they talked about their immediate plans for restoring the house. Shanaco assured Maggie he was a pretty fair carpenter. He could repair at least some of the broken furniture and then in a couple of weeks they could go back to Santa Fe and buy a whole houseful of new things.

Soon Maggie was half-tipsy from the wine. She sighed contentedly as she listened to Shanaco speak of his long-term plans to stock the ranch with purebred cattle and blooded horses. He promised that once they got the ranch operating, they would build a fine home, big enough for a growing family.

They talked and planned and dreamed. And finally when all the chocolate cake was gone and the wineglasses were empty and they were warm and mellow and half-sleepy, they smiled at each other and started moving dishes out of the way. Shanaco built up the fire while Maggie began undressing.

When both were bare, they knelt together before the blazing fire, kissing and vowing their undying love. Soon they stretched out on the feathery counterpane and continued to kiss. Lazy but oh so in love, they made sweet, languid love in the firelight.

Shanaco awakened with the sun.

He opened his eyes, slowly turned his head and gazed at the beautiful flame-haired woman asleep in his arms. He felt his heart constrict in his bare chest. He loved her more than life, but he had done her a terrible injustice by marrying her and bringing her here. She would have no friends. She would be shunned. She would be lonely and unhappy. She would come to hate him for what he'd done to her.

His brow furrowed and his eyes clouded with concern. She would stop loving him. She would leave him one day and break his heart. And he couldn't blame her if she did.

Shanaco shuddered when Maggie snuggled closer, pressing her bare, soft body against his. And then his heart swelled with happiness when, without even opening her eyes, Maggie murmured sleepily, "Love me even half as much as I love you?"

"Twice as much, sweetheart," he said, and kissed her.

* * *

Working side by side they began slowly restoring the homestead. Maggie made it a point to be energetic and cheerful. She teased Shanaco, poked fun at herself for her ineptness at cooking and stopped often in midtask to impulsively throw her arms around him and demand to be kissed.

Sensitive to his feelings, she knew Shanaco was worried that she might be lonely and unhappy. She did everything she could to put his mind at ease. She assured him that she had no regrets. She loved him. She needed no one else. She wanted only to spend the rest of her life with him.

But Maggie didn't delude herself. She realized that they would have only each other, never any friends. They would not be accepted by their neighbors. Would never have visitors stop by to say hello. It made no difference to her. Her one and only regret had been leaving Bright Feather. She missed him. There were times at day's end when, gazing at the sun setting behind the highest mountain peaks, Maggie missed the sweet little boy so much she had to blink back unshed tears.

The wind whipped across the Oklahoma plains and cut through his heavy greatcoat like an icy knife. Colonel Harkins shivered and hunched his shoulders. Even with his collar turned up, his ears felt like they might freeze and fall off.

Alone in the fort cemetery on that early frigid

morning, the troubled colonel stood at the newly dug grave of Major Miles Courteen. Campaign hat in his gloved hands, eyes downcast, Harkins addressed the dutiful career soldier resting there, "Old friend, forgive me, please forgive me. It was a terrible burden that fell on your shoulders and, sick as you were, you discharged your unpleasant duty without question or complaint. Your willingness to meet this awful obligation hastened your demise and for that I shall be eternally sorry." Tears sprang to the colonel's eyes and he choked when he added, "I will set these matters right, old friend. I will do what has to be done, no matter how hard, just as you did."

Colonel Harkins put on his campaign hat, squared it on his head, drew himself up and smartly snapped off a military salute to his fallen comrade.

Pivoting about, he walked away as the sun rose over the awakening fort. He went directly to the administration building. There in his private office, he closed the door and took off his campaign hat, heavy coat and gloves.

He circled the desk. He unlocked the bottom drawer and took out the maroon file folder. The file that Major Courteen had ordered delivered upon his death.

Colonel Harkins placed the folder on his desk.

No need to read it again. If he tried, he could never forget what was in it. Every damning word was etched on his memory where it would stay forever.

Colonel Harkins sat down in his chair, leaned back

and closed his eyes. He felt old and uncommonly tired. His chest hurt. He suffered palpitations of the heart. He clutched the chair arms tightly and again choked back tears as he recalled that terrible moment when he had first opened the file and read every shocking word.

There it was in black and white. In his absence, Major Courteen had conducted a secret hearing regarding the events surrounding Lois's alleged rape and Shanaco's subsequent punishment at the hands of Captain Daniel Wilde and four subordinates.

Major Courteen had, immediately after the hearing, sent regimental surgeon Ledette to the colonel's residence to examine Lois. Over her fierce objections, the surgeon had carried out his orders. Doctor Ledette reported in writing that "upon my thorough examination of Miss Lois Harkins, I found no evidence of forced penetration. Furthermore, it is my firm belief, based on years of experience and observation, that the superficial bruises to Miss Harkins's body were self-inflicted."

Then came the sworn deposition of C. C. Sweeney, the proprietor of the general mercantile store. Sweeney testified that on the evening in question, Thursday, November 18th, Miss Lois Harkins did not—at any time—come to his store to purchase a tin of pain tablets or anything else.

Sitting alone now in his office, the heartsick colonel blamed himself for everything. It was all his fault.

He should never have allowed Lois to come out to the frontier. He loved his daughter, but in his heart, he had known what she was all along. A lovely, deceitful temptress. Just like her mother. Just like the beautiful woman who had broken his heart so many years ago.

Blood had told. They were two of a kind, mother and daughter. Selfish, spoiled, determined. Desirable, wily, dangerous.

It was not easy to admit, but Lois was a heartless liar. A spoiled, vengeful young woman who thought nothing of wrongly accusing an innocent man of rape. All because the man in question couldn't be easily conquered by her feminine charms as most men were.

As Captain Daniel Wilde had been.

Wilde would have to pay.

Loathe Shanaco though he might, the half-breed was innocent.

Colonel Harkins pushed back his chair, rose and turned to the bookshelves. Once again he took down that blood-red leather-bound book, *Military Law and Courts-Martial.*

Forty-Three

Maggie and Shanaco had been at the mountain ranch for only a couple of weeks when, at supper time one evening, they heard the sound of drumming hoofbeats. Someone on horseback was rapidly approaching. Pistol, dozing before the fire, jumped up and started barking.

Shanaco rose from the table and snapped his fingers to silence Pistol. Maggie stayed where she was but laid her fork down and folded her hands in her lap. Shanaco went for his revolver and crossed to the door.

They heard heavy footsteps on the porch, then a loud knock. Shanaco glanced back at Maggie. Gun cocked and raised, he opened the door.

And there stood a broadly smiling Double Jimmy. "Don't shoot, Chief. I come in peace."

Shanaco laughed, lowered the gun and shook the Indian agent's hand. Maggie was already up from the table and hurrying to greet her old friend. "What on earth brings you here?" she asked when he caught her up in a bear hug.

"I missed you," he said as he squeezed her waist and then released her.

"You're just in time for supper," she said, smiling, glad to see him. "Down, Pistol," she scolded the happy wolfhound who was jumping up on the white-haired man he recognized as a friend.

Pleasantries were exchanged. Maggie happily informed Double Jimmy that she and Shanaco were married. Double Jimmy offered heartfelt congratulations. Finally the three of them sat down to supper.

That's when Double Jimmy said, "I have some things to say." He paused, looking at them purposefully. "And I want you both to hear me out before you protest or interrupt. Will you do that, please?"

Shanaco and Maggie looked at each other. She nodded. Shanaco said, "We will listen."

"Good. First, I want you to know that I'm truly sorry for what happened to you, Shanaco. You'll be pleased to hear that Lieutenant Daniel Wilde was confined to quarters for having you beaten. He faces certain court-martial and discharge.

"As for the colonel's daughter, Lois has been sent back East to her mother." Double Jimmy paused and shook his head. "Poor Colonel Harkins, when he returned to the fort, Lois wept and told him she had been brutally raped by you and he believed her. But the late Major Miles Courteen—bless him, he died of influenza just days after your beating—had held a confidential hearing in the colonel's absence. Lois was proved a liar and so—"

"How?" Maggie asked.

"Major Courteen insisted she be examined by the

regimental surgeon and..." Double Jimmy shrugged, cleared his throat and looked down at his plate. When he looked up he said, "C. C. Sweeney testified to the provost marshal that Lois had never been to the general mercantile on the evening of November 18 as she had claimed. All sub-rosa.

"Finally, after the colonel had read the damning files Major Courteen had ordered delivered to Harkins upon his death, the colonel confronted Lois and she broke down and admitted that she had fabricated the story of the rape."

"Makes little difference now," Shanaco said.

"But it does," said Double Jimmy. He reached inside his buckskin shirt and withdrew a legal document. "Read it, Shanaco. You've been given full amnesty. A 'safe passage' order signed by Colonel Harkins."

Shanaco carefully studied the document. Then handed it to Maggie. She read it, looked up, smiled and leaned across the table to kiss her husband.

They both listened as Double Jimmy spent the remainder of the meal telling them how the unfortunate incident had brought chaos and unrest to the reservation.

"Many of the young men have fled, swearing they'll never return," Double Jimmy said.

"That's a shame," said Shanaco, lifting his coffee cup.

"They must return to the reservation. They'll starve if they don't." Double Jimmy paused, glanced at Maggie and said, "Come back to the fort, Shanaco. Your People need you. Who better than you to show them the white man's road? And you, Maggie, the children miss you and need you. You've said it yourself, if they don't learn to speak English, what chance do they have in life? Those children love you, Maggie. Little Bright Feather was brokenhearted when he learned you had gone."

A persuasive man, Double Jimmy talked and talked, ready with an answer for every objection Shanaco raised. You won't be a prisoner at the fort; you can come and go as you please. You want to be a rancher? You can be a successful rancher at the reservation. And you can teach young braves to be ranchers. You want a big house? You can build a big house on the banks of the Red River right there at the edge of the reservation.

Double Jimmy wisely appealed to Shanaco's sense of duty and honor. "Now, son, I'll admit," he said, "that your returning would mean dedicating yourself to helping your People adjust and accept their new way of life. It wouldn't be easy." He took a long swig of coffee and said, "News of your return would quickly spread and that would draw the angry rebels back to the safety of the reservation."

Maggie looked at her husband and reached for his hand. Softly she said, "Who better to teach the People to live in peace than the last Comanche war chief?"

Christmas Eve, 1875
Fort Sill, Oklahoma

The Christmas Eve wagon train was a yuletide tradition at posts all across the frontier. Fort Sill was no exception.

Everyone—whites and Indians alike—were gathered along the road leading into the fort. Excitement ran high as the noon hour approached. Children laughed and darted out into the road, anxiously looking for the first signs of the wagon train.

It was a high spot for the children and they all crowded up so they could be close to the arriving wagons.

"There it is!" someone shouted at straight up noon, and a loud roar went up from the crowd.

The lead wagon was driven by the jolly, red-clad Old Santa Claus himself, and beside him on the seat was the smiling, waving Mrs. Claus. When the wagon came through the fort's front gates, the children rushed toward it, shouting, "Santa! Santa!"

The coppery-skinned Santa and the pale Mrs. Claus smiled and waved. Pistol, a white-tasseled red Santa's cap on his great head, guarded the Christmas Eve wagon. Maggie and Shanaco reached into the bag resting behind the seat and began throwing hard candy to the crowd.

The happy children laughed and squealed and scrambled to catch the tossed candy. Maggie looked anxiously around. She saw Old Coyote, happy tears shining in his eyes, wave. Then he pointed just ahead. Maggie turned, looked and spotted the adorable little boy.

"Look, Santa." She tugged on Shanaco's red sleeve.

Then beamed with joy when Shanaco nodded,

abruptly pulled up on the reins, swung down from the wagon, scooped up Bright Feather with one strong arm and deposited the child on the seat beside Maggie.

His eyes big, Bright Feather gazed at Mrs. Claus in wonder and said, "Miss Maggie?"

"Yes, darlin'," she said and hugged him.

"Are you...are you married to Santa Claus?" He turned to stare at Santa.

"Ho! Ho! Ho!" said Santa, and winked at the boy.

Bright Feather laughed happily.

NAN RYAN

66893	THE SCANDALOUS MISS HOWARD	___ $6.50 U.S.	___ $7.99 CAN.
66814	THE SEDUCTION OF ELLEN	___ $6.50 U.S.	___ $7.99 CAN.
66676	NAUGHTY MARIETTA	___ $6.50 U.S.	___ $7.99 CAN.
66591	THE COUNTESS MISBEHAVES	___ $6.50 U.S.	___ $7.99 CAN.
66521	WANTING YOU	___ $5.99 U.S.	___ $6.99 CAN.

(*limited quantities available*)

TOTAL AMOUNT $__________
POSTAGE & HANDLING $__________
($1.00 for one book; 50¢ for each additional)
APPLICABLE TAXES* $__________
TOTAL PAYABLE $__________
(check or money order—please do not send cash)

To order, complete this form and send it, along with a check or money order for the total above, payable to MIRA Books, to: **In the U.S.:** 3010 Walden Avenue, P.O. Box 9077, Buffalo, NY 14269-9077; **In Canada:** P.O. Box 636, Fort Erie, Ontario, L2A 5X3.

Name:______________________________
Address:__________________ City:__________________
State/Prov.:__________________ Zip/Postal Code:__________
Account Number (if applicable):__________________
075 CSAS

*New York residents remit applicable sales taxes.
Canadian residents remit applicable
GST and provincial taxes.

Visit us at www.mirabooks.com MNR0204BL

Nan Ryan is the author of more than twenty sizzling historical romances. Readers love her trademark style—American historical stories brimming with fiery passion and fast-paced action.

When not writing, Nan can usually be found at the local library, researching her next novel.

She and her husband, Joe, currently live at the edge of Arizona's ruggedly beautiful Sonoran desert.

MNRBIO99